WHAT REMAINS AT THE END

To Otto and Betty Fischer

And to all the named and nameless who have been
forgotten by the world's terrible histories.

WHAT REMAINS AT THE END

A NOVEL BY

ALEXANDRA FORD

SEREN

Seren is the book imprint of
Poetry Wales Press Ltd,
57 Nolton Street, Bridgend, Wales, CF31 3AE

www.serenbooks.com
facebook.com/SerenBooks
Twitter: @SerenBooks

This is a work of fiction. All of the characters, organisations, and events
portrayed in this novel are either products of the author's imagination or
are used ficticiously.

ISBN: 9781781725559
Ebook: 9781781725566

A CIP record for this title is available from the British Library.

The publisher acknowledges the financial assistance
of the Welsh Books Council.

Printed by Severn, Gloucester

CONTENTS

Before the war an apple tree had stood behind the church.
It was an apple tree that ate its own apples.

Herta Müller, *The Passport*

MARIE KOHLER:
GREAT EGG HARBOR BAY,
NEW JERSEY: 1998

A GIRL WENT TO THE BEACH with her grandparents when she was twelve. They rented a house past where the boardwalk ends in Ocean City, New Jersey. Oma spent the whole week inside the house, sitting at the kitchen table with her feet on the cold tile floor. She polished spoons and watched a portable television with a screen the size of a toaster, and Opa sat diagonally across from her. He did crossword puzzles. The girl woke up extra early in the mornings to listen for the sound of his pencil on soft paper. There were half-finished crossword magazines everywhere with no earmarks in the covers or the pages—only occasional paperclips marking where he'd left off. The girl liked to fill sloppy letters in the empty boxes when he wasn't looking. She loved putting letters in tiny homes.

A few hours each day, Opa came outside to stand with the girl on the sand. His legs and arms and face and chest were slathered in so much sunscreen his skin was the color of whole milk—so white it made his teeth look yellow. The girl ran around the surf without any sunscreen. Her hair turned blonde while Opa wore an oversized safari hat to keep his from falling out. He watched his granddaughter carefully while she plucked sand fleas out of the wash and dropped them in buckets. He would line her seashells out to dry on towels. And when they went back to the house in the afternoon, Oma was waiting to scrub the shells clean with soap. She picked out the bits of sea glass and threw them away, and shrieked when her granddaughter showed off the captive fleas.

"They tickle your hands," the girl said. "See."

She opened her palm to show how the tiny crustacean burrowed its way into her skin.

"Out!" Oma said, and the girl sped barefoot through the kitchen with her bucket sloshing sandy water on the tiles. She opened the sliding glass door and climbed over the wooden patio fence, scrambled over hot dunes, and collapsed laughing in the surf. She named the sand fleas, one by one, let them tickle her palms one last time, and released them, watched as they burrowed backwards into the wet sand like little moles before the tiny waves broke over their noses.

In the evenings, the girl walked with her grandfather to the Great Egg Harbor Bay and listened to bullfrogs and stories from fishermen about sharks being born in the bay water with full sets of teeth. Local boys picked up bead-skinned toads from the marsh with their bare fingers, and she rescued them with handfuls of grass because someone once told her that human fingers burn amphibian skin. She played ankle-deep in the too-soft sand until Opa called from the shore in his house shoes, a robe hanging open over swim trunks that never touched the water. Together, they walked back where Oma had citronella candles, bug spray, and mugs of mint chocolate chip ice cream waiting on the patio.

One morning Opa looked at the sun on the water and squinted. He told his granddaughter about the Danube. He told happy stories —one about bathing in secret in Hungary, another about visiting a village called Apatin to fish in the river with his cousin when he was eight. And then he grabbed the girl by the armpits and lifted her up, humming Johann Strauss. He propped her bare feet on top of his, put one hand on her waist, and held her right hand with the other. His pinky fingernail was longer than the rest, and the tops of his feet were soft and cold beneath her calloused soles. As he waltzed across the wet sand, the girl could feel the tendons working from his toes to his ankles. Whenever he came to the part of the waltz that sounded like rocks skipping over water, Opa tightened his grip on her waist and spun the girl in a circle so fast her feet left his.

PHILADELPHIA: JANUARY 2012

SID OFFERED TO DRIVE ME to Philadelphia International. We sat in the car for thirty-five minutes and didn't speak. The sun had turned the sky the color of Pepto Bismol. It made me want to throw up. But it was also beautiful, driving across the Platt Bridge, the way the clouds and sun were framed in steel trusses. I didn't understand how Sid was capable of driving me to the airport. He was my husband, and my eight o'clock flight would take me to Vienna.

To Sid, Vienna wasn't a city. It was a man named David.

When Sid parked the car outside departures, I said thank you. I wanted to say I'm sorry. I wanted to say he shouldn't have taken me. I wanted him to put up a fight. He pulled my luggage out of his trunk and stood on the sidewalk without talking. He looked at me, and his eyes said, "I don't like it when you leave." Usually his eyes were the color of a sunny ocean—a clear one, not the muddy one in New Jersey. But standing there outside the ticket hall, they were the gray-blue color of dusk.

"I love you," he said. I wanted to say I loved him too. Instead, I kissed his cheek and left him standing by the trunk of his car. I looked back at him before wheeling my luggage through the automatic door, and his eyes looked like the end.

"I'm sorry," I said under my breath, but it was too late.

In the check-in line, the man in front of me spoke loudly on his cell phone about his gig doing visual effects for Star Trek. When he hung up, he leaned on the handle of his suitcase and smiled.

"Hi," he said. "I'm Robert."

"Hi, Robert," I said. Robert talked a lot about his job, as if he knew it sounded impressive to strangers. I told him my husband was a rocket scientist.

It felt like lying, saying husband. I hadn't used that word in months.

Robert said, "Cool," then didn't speak for the rest of our wait.

All I could think was how much I wanted to tell Sid I'd met a guy who worked on Star Trek. I wanted to tell Sid like I told Sid everything. I always told him everything—I told him for years that we were broken. I told him so often the word broken felt empty. His mind was always in orbit, somewhere between me and the International Space Station. Maybe he took the word to space with his thoughts and left it there. Maybe he left all his memories of how we used to be up there, too. Memories of making love in the afternoon, of kisses that made us feel like teenagers. Maybe he stored them inside the docking bay of his new spaceship.

Seven months had passed since Sid was asked to build space vehicles in Washington DC. When he told me he got the job, he was like a little boy going to space camp. I was excited for him, but I told him maybe it was best if I stayed in Philadelphia. He said okay. He always said okay. So he moved out in June. We used the word separated, but it was more complicated than that.

Sid called me on his way to work every morning, and I called him before bed—out of fear or habit or some other kind of love. When he visited our East Falls apartment on weekends, we acted like nothing was different. We laughed and went for walks along the Schuylkill River and listened to the passenger trains pulling into 30th Street Station, and to the screeching brakes of freight trains riding the bank. I drank wine and he drank beer and we talked about work and the weather and other peoples' problems.

Just after Thanksgiving, I told him I'd met someone. I remembered watching snow blur the early Christmas lights outside the window when I said it, when I told him that in all our seven years I'd never been attracted to anyone else until David. I remember the draft in the living room as Sid's shoulders sagged.

I didn't tell him the rest until the next day.

"He's taking me to Europe."

"How long?"

"Two weeks. In January."

"Did you sleep with him?" he asked.

"No," I said. And then, "Yes."

I was nervous before takeoff—nervous something would go wrong, nervous we'd crash. I felt like maybe karma would have something to say and send me nose-first into the Atlantic Ocean. Maybe that volcano in Iceland would erupt mid-flight and the engines would stall from the ash. Maybe the engine blades would catch a really fat goose and we'd blow up before we even made it to three thousand feet. Maybe we'd hit a hot air pocket and drop straight down to earth. "Adulteress on board!" a flight attendant would shout over the PA. "She doesn't deserve two good men loving her, we're taking her down." I imagined the faces around me. The man from Virginia Beach in the seat beside me, so wide he took up part of my seat. His face turned into a tomato. The woman three rows ahead turned blotchy and called me a tramp. A baby cried from all the way in the back of coach. The passengers from first class elected to throw me overboard.

Both David and Sid, if they had been there, would have told me I was being silly. They would have explained exactly why none of my crash scenarios were possible. Or at least probable.

I heard Sid in my head, *You see, hot air has less density than cold air, so when a 200-ton 767 flies into hot air, it falls until it reaches air dense enough to hold it up.* I was angry with myself for thinking of him, for missing his reassuring science. Sid would have known exactly how the air moved through the plane, how old breaths got the spit sucked out of them and cycled back through the air conditioning. He'd have known how the air was kept at the right pressure, and how much air, down to a handful of ounces, was trapped inside the cabin with all the dried-out people. He'd have known exactly what path of tubes the excrement flushed in the bathroom would have traveled, and how long it would have taken to get to waste storage. I had always thought there was a little trap door at the bottom of airplanes where human waste was ejected.

But what if the hot air pocket goes all the way to the ground? I asked my absent husband. *It's possible, but very unlikely, he replied. Most likely the pocket was just another plane's jet stream. Don't worry. That wasn't a brush with death you just experienced.*

"My little angel," Opa used to say, and Oma beside him with her rosary dangling beneath her sweater and a crucifix above it. Opa didn't wear a cross around his neck; he wore a thin gold chain with a pendant on it that said, "Number 1 Lover." And he had a trucker hat made of black polyester with magenta script that read, "Crazy Nude Girls." I stole the hat once, off the credenza in the foyer of our house. I put it on and there were mirrors everywhere. The wall across from the credenza was a mirror, the closet doors were a mirror, and the longest wall in the living room—the one with the record player in front of it—was a mirror. I used to like to hide between the potted rubber tree and the old Zenith. I'd crouch under the broad shiny leaves and put my palms against my reflection, smearing fingerprints over the surface until Oma came running in with a bottle of Windex and a paper towel, shouting, "Lass mich dich nicht mit dem Holzlöffel jagen!"

She'd usually threaten the wooden spoon in English, but only ever tap my bottom with her open palm as I ran for the sofa. Then she'd call me her little angel and bring me raspberry linzer cookies on a plate with blue flowers painted around the edge.

The time I stole Opa's stripper hat was an exception. She'd brought me extra cookies and an Andes mint to make up for the wince I made from her spoon when I sat on her overstuffed cushions.

My grandparents rarely ever talked about Yugoslavia. About either of their lives before coming to America. Until I was nineteen, I didn't even know what Danube Swabian meant, that they were a Southern German people who resettled the naked farmland of the Pannonian Plains in the eighteenth century, while it still belonged to the Habsburg Empire. That five hundred thousand lived in what became northern Yugoslavia after World War I. That though they made up a small minority of the kingdom, there were nearly as many Swabians as Serbs in the region called Vojvodina.

At the end of the Second World War, Josip Broz Tito, a working-class revolutionary buoyed by the Allied Forces, took back control of the Kingdom of Yugoslavia from Hungary and Germany. As many as sixty thousand civilian Swabians were exterminated by Tito's Partisans—either by death camps or forced labor in Siberian mines. Twenty-six thousand Swabian soldiers died fighting for whichever army they were drafted into—many fought as citizens of Yugoslavia against the Wehrmacht, though there were many, too, who fought for the Reich. I read an account once about Swabians getting drafted into the Yugoslav army and then killed in the army depot by Serbian draftees, even though the Swabians were prepared to fight for their country and not their mother tongue.

And then there were the quarter of a million Swabians who escaped the genocide with little more than their lives. They fled in freight trains and wagons and on foot through the woods in the dead of night.

How did I not know this history existed, when all my life I knew my grandparents fled to Austria before they immigrated to the United States? I knew they had been refugees. But the story ended there. The only details of their past life that were shared in our home on Anita Drive, the home I was raised in, by them, were fond memories of childhood before the war. On the rare occasions they spoke of their flight, I thought what they spoke of was the nature of war. They never said they were survivors of genocide.

I closed my eyes and imagined Opa in the Danube, up to his thighs in the river with a fishing pole made of wood and yarn from his grandmother's basket. There was a strip of pork gristle tied to the end and flecks of pig beneath his fingernails. He cast the rod and the bait landed in the middle of his reflection, scattering his body across the surface.

I wanted to say that I was a Danube Swabian too, a Donauschwaben. But I didn't know how I could be something that I had never even heard of. I didn't know how many generations it took in America to lose your ethnicity.

David was a walking testament to his culture, a handsome incarnation of Winston Churchill. When he smiled, he looked like an old man. He left space on one side of his mouth for a fat cigar. I loved his face in profile, the way his nose curved to a point and sloped down into his upper lip. It was a British rock star nose. A Mickey Finn nose, David Bowie's Thin White Duke. And the way his lips were like a ripe plum—I just wanted to kiss them until only the pit was left.

I thought of David waiting in arrivals in Vienna, tapping his leather oxfords on the linoleum, checking his watch, adjusting the shoulders of his tailored suit coat. Waiting to gather me in his arms and take me to my family's beginning.

I thought of Sid, of how his sweat always smelled the same as my grandfather's and felt like home. Home. I didn't know if home was the failed marriage I spent the last seven years building, if it was David, if home could even exist in a person. If home was somewhere in Yugoslavia, or East Falls, or my grandparents' house in Northeast Philadelphia.

I wished I could have gone back in time, buried my head under the pillows of their sofa, and hidden until I could accept that I would always be a coward.

ANJA THOMPSON:
MILFORD, NEW JERSEY: 2011

ANJA THOMPSON POURS HERSELF a glass of wine the color of the stains on her fingertips. When she swallows, acid bites her throat. She coughs and catches a glimpse of herself in the bowl of her glass.

"What can you do?" she says to the living room. The W comes out sounding like a V.

Anja Thompson extinguishes her cigarette in a butter dish and pours herself more wine. She leans back in her armchair and looks at the empty recliner beside her. There's an end table between the two chairs, a 1950's geometric piece with veneer overlay displaying a faded photograph of children posed in Easter clothes. The eldest, her son, is due to be a grandfather soon. Thank God, Anja says to herself, he is not like his father. Anja's first husband ran away to Florida. There hadn't even been another woman as far as Anja knew—just the promise of palm trees and freedom and endless tumblers of vodka with pineapples and paper umbrellas on the rim. Her second husband's name was Albert. Albert died in a plane crash on his way home from Baltimore. It had been a small plane, a twelve-seater prop full of businessmen. Only two passengers survived. Some suggest it was a bad engine that pitched the plane into a cornfield, but others speculate it was the pilot's error. Albert had been the pilot.

Anja is four-foot-eight inches tall. Because I lived my childhood on potatoes and broth, she told the neighbors back in Fishtown and the ladies from church. Anja's mother used to say that too, only when she said it, there was anger in her eyes.

Her mother died young of a botched hysterectomy. The doctors said a blood clot had formed and travelled to her lungs. Afterward, Anja's father slipped nose-first down the neck of a whiskey bottle. Between his wife's death and everything he'd seen in the old country that he refused to speak of, there was no getting out. Only his nightmares betrayed him. Anja can't remember the last time she saw her father look as if he'd had a full night's sleep, aside from the morning she found him beside the bathtub in an ocean of bile and shit. His collection of empty Jim Beam bottles twinkled on every windowsill. A few had dead flowers in them that he'd stolen from the neighbor's garden and left to mold and shrivel in the glass.

Anja eats too much. Mushroom soup and pumpernickel, Piroulines, Chips Ahoy. Almost-expired strawberry wafers. She crunches through bags of cough drops—lemon Robitussin with liquid honey centers. She over-salts her chuck roast. Tomato sandwiches. Pigs feet. She even salts her chocolate mousse. But she never eats potatoes. They taste like a drafty wooden room in an old army barrack and the straw cot that poked her rib bones while she slept.

She turns on a polka record while she sips another glass of wine. A photograph of her sister sits caddy corner to the picture of her children, in a smaller plastic frame. Her sister is all she has left of her family, aside from her children. Which reminds her, Edie's granddaughter left a message on the answering machine the other day saying she wanted to ask Anja some questions. She'd called the other week, too. "Please, Aunt Anja," she'd said. The voice on the machine sounded just like Edie without her Swabian accent. She half expected her grandniece to start scolding her the way Edie had always done.

Anja borrowed Edie's best Sunday dress from their shared trunk at the refugee camp—a white cotton wrap dress with hundreds of tiny birds printed on the fabric. Anja put it on with a pair of heavy tights while Edie was babysitting one of the farmer's children. She meant to wear it for a walk into town so that a handsome man might notice her. But she ran into Friedrich coming back from fetching his mother's cigarettes, and they ended up climbing a tree together to watch the neighbors: mostly camp residents walking home from the fields. Though they did see crazy Mrs. Deutschle, who lost her husband and children in Bloody October. She was throwing pebbles at a chicken.

Anja tore the hem of her sister's dress as she shimmied down the trunk. It caught on a branch and she didn't notice until she heard the tearing sound.

"Scheisse," she remembers saying. She also remembers the look on Friedrich's face.

"Edie's going to be mad," he said.

Anja hurried home and tucked the dress back inside the trunk.

When Edie found the dress on Sunday, with the tear and a leaf somehow folded into the dirty skirt, she threw a nasty look at Anja. Even when she was angry, Edie was beautiful. Pinched waist and delicate knees, a pert little nose and full curving eyebrows that furrowed at the center with a single wrinkle. Even her scowl was delicate.

"You ugly little thief," she said.

"It wasn't me," Anja replied.

It's been two years since Anja has seen her sister, since Edie last recounted to Anja all the dresses she'd ruined and stockings she'd torn. They'd met for dinner in one of the Balkan restaurants on Bustleton Avenue for Anja's seventy-sixth birthday. The owners' voices had made both sisters feel like children again. When the bulky waiter asked in his heavy voice if Edie would like beef or cheese burek, Anja heard, "It doesn't matter where you run, we'll find you."

"No wonder I spent so much time in trees," Anja whispered to Edie over a bowl of stuffed cabbage, staring at the waiter. "That's a colossus, not a man."

"Everybody is a colossus to you."

Dessert came with no candle to blow out. Instead, they laughed about Friedrich's pimples over slices of anthill cake. "If only his specks were as tiny as poppy seeds," Edie said. "Then maybe you wouldn't have stopped him trying to kiss you in those bushes." They laughed with open lips and full mouths.

Anja has been meaning to visit Edie since she moved into the nursing home. But every time she packs her purse with bus tokens, tissues, and hard candies, she realizes she's forgotten something or strains a muscle when she bends to tie her shoes and decides it's not the right day to see Edie. She says, I'll go tomorrow, and plucks a Robitussin drop from her purse, unwraps it, and pops it in her mouth. And then another. And another. Until the medicinal lemon numbs her tongue.

Ah well, she thinks, it's not like Edie would know I'm there anyway.

And she'd probably smell like piss.

A nurse told her once that the demented appear so lost because their minds cross over before their bodies.

Anja lifts her Bakelite telephone to her ear and twists the dial.

"You called?"

"Hi, Aunt Anja."

"How's your grandmother?" Anja asks with a slight slur in her voice.

"She won't let the nurses put her false teeth in. But she seems to smile a lot."

"She smells like piss," her grandniece adds. "I went in yesterday and there was a puddle beneath her wheelchair. The nurses told me it was just water, but I could smell it."

"All of us old farts smell," Anja says. "Our nooks and crannies are harder to reach than they used to be. Don't even get me started on cleaning under these pancakes," she says, flipping her breast with her free hand.

"She asks why her husband doesn't come to see her," the young woman continues. "I don't know how to tell her Opa's been dead for nearly five years."

Albert has been dead for nearly twenty, and sometimes Anja still wakes up thinking she can feel the weight of his body on the mattress beside her.

Edie has always been the lucky one. Even now. She doesn't have the memory to grieve.

"I know why you called," Anja says. "But I was only ten when they came for us. I'm seventy-eight now," she says. "How's an old woman supposed to remember things from so long ago?"

"But what about—

"You should have asked your grandmother," Anja says, picturing Edie watching her from the other side of the ether. "She could have told you so much."

Edie could have recounted the exact hue of the wheat grass in the autumn of 1944. While I slept under blankets in a covered wagon, she stayed awake and peered through a rip in the cover and watched the fields rush backwards. She could have told you the exact angle of sunlight at the moment we were told we had a place on a ship to America. She could have told you how many fingernails were missing off the dead hand in the middle of the road in Gašinci. She could have told you about the cow the Croatians stole from our backyard when we left.

Anja, silent, hangs up.

Young people only ever call when they want something. They have no shame. From her worn armchair in her tobacco-brown living room, Anja picks at the skin around her fingernails until they bleed.

She watches the blood make rivers around her nails. It stains the white tips dark. Dark like the mud she dug with her hands to steal potatoes on her way home to the barracks from school. She saw such terrible things before they fled. Edie talked about it, but not Anja. She didn't even tell Albert about most of it.

The phone rings.

Anja Thompson looks at the empty glass in her hand and lets the rotary bell chime, trembling under the cradle.

PHILADELPHIA: 2011

WHEN I SAT DOWN AT NINETEEN to interview my grandparents for a family history project, Opa told me he was kidnapped and forced into the Nazi Youth under someone else's name. He made me promise not to tell anyone until he died, in case a mysterious 'they' found out and shipped him back to Yugoslavia. What I was allowed to put in my school project: he was only allowed to leave his home in Batschki-Brestowatz with a single suitcase, and he cried because he had to leave his dog behind. He called it his "doggie" but he didn't tell me its name. He also didn't tell me what they were fleeing. Just that he listened to his dog bark until he couldn't hear it anymore. Miles later, in the wagon, he thought he heard it following them and peeked through the cloth wall at an empty road.

He talked about the shed attached to the back of his house that he would sneak into to sit on piles of imported fruit and eat oranges. "It was a place unlike anywhere else," he said. His eyes filled with nostalgia when he told me about the town crier and the outhouses and the baths he took in water heated on the stove.

When I sat down with Oma and asked the same questions, she cried and spoke of finding body parts in a ditch one morning in Gašinci. She talked about her Aunt who used to beat her, said she hoped the Croats' farm animals had moved into her Aunt's empty house. She hoped her Aunt was dead.

She talked about a bomb on Easter morning, the Easter after they fled for Austria. The siren went off as refugee workers were halfway between a bomb shelter and their camp. Half the refugees ran for the shelter, half ran back to the barracks. Oma and her mother went to the shelter. Walking home, her mother counted the bodies in the road under her breath.

I was disgusted with myself when I replayed the tape—with my "mmhmms" and "oh wows" and attempts to put words in their mouths when their age or their language or their memory made it difficult for them to finish the sentences they were looking for.

I thought it was the horror of war. That it was some kind of European norm in the forties.

I didn't understand.

Opa gave me a small stack of books the day I interviewed him, written in German. He pointed at the word Donauschwaben like it was a secret, a key that would unlock everything. But that word meant nothing surrounded by other words I couldn't pronounce.

"This is us," he said, running his finger over the 'D' and the 'u' and the 'e'. He ran it down the Danube River on a glossy map, from the Black Forest through Vienna and Budapest and all the way to Novi Sad.

After Sid moved to DC, I started cleaning out the apartment. I found Opa's books stacked in a canvas grocery bag in the back of my closet and felt a massive pang of guilt for forgetting them. Four years had passed since Opa died. Five had passed since he'd given me the books. I hadn't opened them once. Sid wasn't home, so I sat in one of his worn-out college t-shirts on our hardwood floor and flipped through the pages. There were photographs of Opa at school in Brestowatz, photographs of his class playing soccer, of the Catholic Church, the German community center brimming with Donauschwaben in festival garb: dark trachts with bell skirts and aprons, black silver-buttoned vests, floral hair wreaths. There were ear-leafed pages and underlined phrases I couldn't read. So many times the word Donauschwaben was underlined, as if Opa needed to underscore the letters to remind himself of a life that no longer existed. Or maybe he knew I'd take so long to look, that I'd need the encouragement of his pencil marks on the page to keep reading.

Like the pencil marks in his crossword puzzles that helped me along, the phonetic notes in the margins of the first books he read in English, the doodles on notepaper that he left on the kitchen table: eyes and suns and hearts and birds and coffee mugs with lines of steam arranged beside phone numbers and to-do lists like coded messages.

The next day I went to the Philadelphia Free Library and searched the catalog. Danube Swabian came up with nothing. Donauschwaben, nothing. I tried Yugoslavia and Tito, but all I got were books and articles on the civil war in the nineties. I typed in Yugoslavia German and the first book on the list was *Genocide of the Ethnic Germans of Yugoslavia, 1944-1948*. The words made my skin ripple.

Copper sat heavy on my tongue. That title was impossible. They would have told me. If something that big had happened, I would have known.

I wrote the catalog number on my palm. I'd always found the smell of dust, paper, and metal shelving in libraries comforting. That day it smelled like stagnancy and decay.

I touched the spine of *Genocide of the Ethnic Germans of Yugoslavia*, a bruised burgundy hardcover, and pulled at it until it unstuck from its neighbors. I wondered how long it had been since someone removed it from the shelves. I wondered how many people had ever even touched it. When I opened the cover, the pages inside shifted like stiff joints. They settled on a page with a phrase underlined: *one German girl was hung with wire slings in a doorframe and split in half with a butcher hatchet.*

My stomach turned to gelatin—not sweet, light orange-flavored Jell-O, but the clear salt jelly in Oma's refrigerator that suspended pigs' feet. And my knees, the bones in them felt out of whack. The muscles and tendons holding them together had disappeared. I sat on the floor, flipping pages, staring at the words and numbers without absorbing them.

All I could think of was the butcher hatchet, Oma's Easter bombing, Opa's singular suitcase, and the few words I'd managed to pull off the pages in front of me: mass graves, machine guns, liquidation camps, torture.

Why didn't they tell me? Had they even known?

Another indigestible phrase, about a camp commander: *his specialty was to electrify naked women's breasts and genitals.*

The saline jelly in my stomach rose again and again, burning the back of my throat, but I couldn't make it come out. I wanted to cry. I wanted to vomit. I wanted to hurt more. The shock of the words took away everything I should have felt. Except the guilt. Opa died knowing I hadn't opened his books, hadn't taken the time to find the stories hiding under the surface. His face leapt out of the pages, and the words came in his voice: *barbed wire, flee, starvation*, town names written in German with Serbian spellings beside them—*Neusatz/Novi Sad, Batschki-Brestowatz/Bački-Brestovac, Rudolfsgnad/Knićanin.*

Oma's face never mingled with the text. She was tucked safely inside the sallow walls of Bayside Nursing Home, eating food processed chicken tenders and smashed peas, forgetting what to do with the open carton of milk in her hand. Instead of drinking it, she poured it over her cube of yellow cake until it overflowed the plate and flooded her lunch tray. She was safe in her inability to remember exactly who I was, who she was, what she had survived.

Oma had always been naïve and childlike, big-hearted and easily hurt. As a wife and grandmother, she had given everything she thought she should give, the perfect game of house: cooking, sweeping, ironing, baking, foot-bathing, toe-nail clipping, birthing, raising, dusting. She was playing house in Bayside, too, only her role in the game had changed. She received baths and nail-clippings; she slept, ate, and fiddled with costume jewelry, dolls, and picture books.

She was twelve when her family fled Yugoslavia. She was nineteen by the time she got to America. Her schooling stopped and never resumed. Her whole life paused. It took me a long time to understand that she didn't pick up where she left off. Oma stopped growing up the day she saw her friend's father in pieces in a ditch. Instead, she cooked foods from the old country and chewed with her eyes closed, as if each bite of her fasnachts, spaetzle, goulasch, and krautsalat could transport her backwards, to a time when she was full of potential, even though she was just a farmer's daughter.

Not all of the Donauschwaben were innocent. Many of them weren't. The Prinz Eugen Division of the SS was made up of ethnic German men from Croatia's Slavonia, the Serbian Banat, and the province of Vojvodina. My grandfather's uncle was one of them. He moved to Germany after the war and never spoke to anyone about what happened, except to insist that he didn't know what the German army was doing when he joined. But his division was not unlike the men who strung up Swabian children from barns. They burned a church full of civilians alive, massacred whole villages, and followed their revenge policy to a tee: for every ethnic German killed by Tito's Partisans—soldier or civilian—they vowed to kill one hundred Slavic men, women, and children.

So many revenges and counter-revenges.

My history books didn't teach this history, but it didn't go unnoticed.

At the Potsdam Conference, the Allied Forces reacted to the unrest between ethnic Germans and other civilians throughout Eastern Europe:

The [United Kingdom, United States, and Soviet Union] having considered the question in all its aspects, recognize that the transfer [...] of German populations [...] will have to be undertaken [...] and should be [affected] in an orderly and humane manner.

As if such a thing were possible.

EDIE KÖNIG:
NEAR LINZ, AUSTRIA: 1945

ONE BEEF BONE. A POUND OF HAM. One onion. A head of cabbage. Sour cream. A pound of potatoes. Leeks if they have them, and dill, nutmeg, bay leaves. Beef, ham, onion, cabbage, sour cream, potatoes, leeks, dill, nutmeg, bay.

Today is Easter and we're having soup. We spent weeks saving up for it—soup with real ham, and a bone. And Mother sent me to the shop to pick it up, not Anja. Because Anja messes everything up. Like the dresses I made out of leftover fabric I collected from the other women in the refugee camp. You know she steals them and covers them in grass stains?

All the boys tell me I'm the pretty one. Mr. Herbert actually asked me to marry him. He even asked Mother and Father if I could marry him. I think I would have said yes, but Mother and Father said no. Mr. Herbert is almost as old as my father. He'd had a wife once, and a kid, but now he's alone. I think, if my parents had said yes, I wouldn't have to work in the fields anymore. Mr. Herbert told me I'm delicate. That I shouldn't have to bury my pretty fingers in the dirt.

I haven't always been a field hand. For a while I babysat one of the farmers' children. But they were bad kids. The oldest chased me around his backyard with a wooden spoon once, shouting that I wasn't his mother. His mother is dead. When I came home with a spoon-shaped bruise on my arm, Mother told me I was to stop babysitting and go to work in the fields with her. At least you won't come home with welts, she'd said.

Anja doesn't have to work. Father says she's too young. Which I don't think is fair because she's only two years younger than me.

What's the difference between eleven and thirteen except I'm a few inches taller? And I get to do the shopping. It feels wonderful to have coins in my pocket. I love the way they make my hands smell. And the noise they make when I shake them in my palm.

One beef bone. A pound of ham. One onion. Sour cream. A pound of potatoes. Leeks if they have them—and dill, nutmeg, bay leaves. I'm forgetting something. Cabbage. And they don't have leeks. I'll get garlic instead.

I have to give the shopkeeper cigarettes to get waited on because I'm not Austrian—Father gave me some for emergencies and told me not to tell Mother.

I get two reichspfennigs change, and the lady hands it to me in two coins instead of one. I'm going to ask Mother if I can keep one. Just to look at, not to spend. So I can keep it in my pocket and roll it between my thumb and forefinger until it leaves a crease in my skin. And one day when we leave Austria for America, since Father says we can't go home anymore and that his American cousins will take us in, I'll have lots of coins in my pocket, American ones. I wonder if they'll smell different than pfennigs. If they'll be smooth around the edges like a dinar or rough like my pfennig.

I wish we could play Epper for Easter this year. I always win. I mean, I'm sure Father lets me win, and maybe Mother loses on purpose too, but I beat Anja hands down. The best time was when Father went out first and already had his egg peeled and shoved into his mouth, and Mother, she was rolling her egg on the countertop so that it crackled like gossamer, slick from the water between the flesh and the shell. And then there was Anja, shoulders all hunched in preparation, her stubby fingers gripping the backside of her egg, pointing the skinny tip at my egg, which I balanced like china on my fingertips. One. Two. Three, Father said. And Anja jammed her egg so hard at my egg that she missed it altogether. She didn't just miss it. You should have been there. She chucked it right on the floor. It made the best crunching sound.

This year, instead of playing Epper, we have to work. I have to walk to the fields with my mother and spend the day seeding. The farmer says people don't stop to eat just because it's Easter. But I know that. And you know that too. Before we left home, when we had a proper kitchen, Mother made the best doughnuts on Shrove Tuesday. She spent all morning kneading the dough, and the smell of lard sizzling in the pan just as she dropped the first fasnacht in—as the sugar and butter hit the fresh lard—it smelled under ripe, yeasty and clean. As more doughnuts sank into the pot, the smell changed to burning and caramel and smoke. We ate them all, though Anja ate more than everyone else. Even Father. And then Ash Wednesday came and we got dirty smudges on our foreheads. I remember seeing you with your ash smudge once, walking down the road with your parents and their ash smudges. I bet your mother made nice fasnachts too.

We also burned a doll made out of straw. I named the doll Mamsell every year, and Anja shielded her eyes from the fire as the little golden face turned black and the doll's arms curled in.

But then we didn't eat anything nice at all. All the way until Easter Sunday, we ate bland food. Mother got skinny and Anja's elbows got lumpier, and Father lost the bit of fat under his chin. Easter mornings I ate so much eggs and potatoes and cabbage and peppers and bread and cakes and wurst and cheese and apricot palatschinke that my stomach hurt and I had strange nightmares about the food coming alive—wurst into greasy lips, lumpy potato noses, cabbage hair, and cracked eggs for runny eyes.

So I know people don't stop eating just because it's Easter. They start eating because it's Easter. And I guess if some other family somewhere gets to have wurst and palatschinke for Easter, then it's good I'm working on growing more food for next year. Only I also don't really get it—it's springtime, and we're just planting seeds, so what difference would it make if we got to stay home and eat our hambone soup? It's not like anyone depends on us to pick carrots today for their Easter feast.

I'm not complaining. At least I'm trying not to. We're not in Gašinci anymore and this morning I get to be the grocery-shopper. Even though later I still have to be the seed-planter. We don't even get horses to help us. There are so many of us in the fields that we just get little garden spades and an apron full of seeds. I don't know what the seeds are, but I don't like the shape of them. They're skinny and pointy at the ends. Sometimes when I stick my hands in my pockets they poke my fingers and make me bleed. Not a lot, just a pinprick. But still, it hurts, and then the dirt gets in the little hole and I get afraid it won't wash out and I'll be left with dirty freckles forever.

Everyone here is always worried about getting sick, so I worry that the pinpricks will get infected and turn my fingers green. If anybody gets sick, they lose their job and lose their chance at going home or moving to America or the Motherland. The Motherland is a funny place because I don't think I'm supposed to like it. I don't know why—Mother is supposed to be a good thing and our refugee camp is just dirty rooms: my feet are always black on the bottom, and it makes me think of Mamsell's doll feet right before she caught fire.

We don't even have a yard. I hate coming home and seeing the gray-brown street and the dead beige grass and the plain brown walls. I wish I didn't call it that, home. It doesn't feel like a home, except that it's got Mother and Father and Anja in it. It doesn't have Grandmother or Grandfather in it, or our mean Aunt. Oh, she was so mean. I bet she's still stuck in the village, in her house, kept prisoner like some of the other children say happened to the Aunts in their towns. Either that or she's dead. I know that's awful to say. But she used to hit me when I didn't fetch her water fast enough. And one time, when I went to the well, I got curious and looked into the hole to see if anything was in there except darkness, and the bucket slipped and hit the back of my head and my chin cracked off the stone. I ran back to her house with my hands over my head, and she laughed at the bump and the blood and told me I was stupid. Then she smacked my bottom for not bringing her water like I was supposed to.

I hope there are goats and pigs living in her house now.

Mother says I'm petty, and Father tells her, in his stern voice, "She's been through a lot, it's a coping mechanism." Well, I don't think I'm petty, and I don't know what a coping mechanism is.

"Hello, Mother. Yes, there was change—just a pfennig."

I know, I know, but I couldn't bear my pocket to hold only air again, especially when I went through so much trouble to warm the metal in my palm.

"Can I help you chop the carrots?"

See, I'm not petty. I'm grown up.

It's an hour walk to the field. I've had the same shoes since we moved here from Yugoslavia. For a while my feet hurt from how worn out they got. And not just hurt, I couldn't feel my toes. I couldn't feel my soles except for a too-hotness. And the stabbing pains in my foot bones that felt like shin splints. Except I've never had shin splints, so I can only imagine that's what they felt like. Whenever I ran in the yard at school, before we left the village, my chest would get all tight and my breaths would be too short and the teacher would tell me to sit down. He told my parents that I was a special child, too delicate for physical activity. He said I should focus on my book learning.

But my shoes. After a while of the stabbing and hotness, it all stopped. I grew funny bumps and rough patches on my feet, and my toes got crooked. Mother taught me a trick that another refugee taught her—if I wrap my feet in corn husks before I put them in my shoes, it helps keep them dry. It felt funny at first. The seam running down the middle of the husks and all the edges folded over each other felt like bunched up socks. But it's a lot better than wet feet and a cold that could turn into something worse.

There are almost thirty of us on the road to the fields. I don't know why we have to work in fields so far away from town. I know we need the money so we can move to America, and that I should be grateful for any job at all, but we walk past so many fields that use horses. Couldn't they use us instead? We'd probably be cheaper.

When we get out of here, I'm going to find a handsome man who makes enough money that I don't have to stand on my feet all day. I'm going to lay on a chaise longue in his library with those little ladders on the walls and big latticework windows like in my illustrated copy of Hans Christian Anderson. And he'll come to me and sit on the edge of the chaise and take my tiny hands in his big ones and say, "Look at those delicate fingertips, they're like carved ivory." He'll kiss my even fingernails and there won't be a speck of dirt underneath them, or in the pinprick holes that collect mud when I work.

Maybe if I wash my hands enough times, the soap will wash all signs of labor out. If I let them rest in cooking oil, maybe the rough spots will turn soft. I should try that on my feet.

Oh no, the siren's started. I hate that sound. It makes my teeth hurt. It must do the same thing to all the other people in the road because we all stop walking. I hold my breath and I don't know why.

The sky is perfect—blue like forget-me-nots with cottony splashes of cloud. It's one of those skies that screams spring. I want someone to pick me a bouquet of wildflowers and call me things like liebling, prinzessin, or knudel.

But the noise screams of something else. I gripped the pfennig in my pocket so tight I bet if I took my thumb and held it toward the sun, the imprint of a falcon would shine red and shadowy.

You know who they say flies the planes that make these sirens go off? They say it's the Americans. I don't believe them, because otherwise we wouldn't be working so hard to get there. I mean, that would be stupid, wouldn't it, if we got there and they just blew us up?

Maybe from up high we look like an army. I don't know how. We have no weapons and most of us are ladies wearing headscarves to shield our faces from the sun. But maybe it's hard to tell all that from an airplane. I bet we look like a bunch of fleas. Maybe we look like fleas with guns.

Half the people in the road run back toward the camp barracks, half run toward work. There's a bomb shelter near our farmer's land. There isn't one at the barracks, but camp isn't really a target. I mean, blowing it up wouldn't do much damage—it's just rotting wood and creaky doors and drafty windows. I hope they blow our awful door right off its hinges. It's a horrible thing. Rodents get in through the gap in the bottom—and not just mice. Rats the size of pine martens. I don't know what makes them so fat. Certainly not food from our kitchen since there is none.

Mother pulls me toward the shelter.

We run so fast the corn husks around my feet shift—pointy yellow tips poke out the top of my shoes. I don't know why we're in such a hurry. The sirens go off all the time and nothing happens.

And besides, what kind of monster would blow up Easter?

"What about Father?"

Mother says nothing. I know he has to be safe. He went to work early in the morning in a different set of fields.

"And Anja?"

She doesn't stay at home while we're at work, she gets to go to school. It's not fair that Anja gets to sit in a strange house that actually has real wood floors and an oven instead of dirt and a tiny stove. I bet the tutor makes them all sorts of terrible food—spaetzle with real butter and knockwurst and sugary palatschinke. But I guess if he did, she wouldn't be so skinny. She's so thin she's paler around her ribs and elbows because you can see through to her bones.

Could you squeeze Mother's hand just a little bit? I know she won't feel it, and that she doesn't see you, but maybe it'll stop her crying. I don't know why she's crying. Even if a bomb falls, we'll be at the shelter before anything happens. I can see it from here. A man is holding the door so we can all get in.

He's handsome, don't you think? Oh, just imagine him gathering me into his arms and carrying me off to someplace safe and peaceful and lazy. Somewhere with a library. Hello, dear heart, I would say from my chaise, with a book propped open between my thumb and my pinky. You must have had such a long day. Let me take off your shoes.

I'd slide off the chaise and onto my knees, but maybe I wouldn't take his shoes off. His feet would probably smell as bad as this shelter. It's sweaty in here. And people are making such awful noises. Maybe I'd make him dinner instead. Fasnachts for dessert.

Mother is gripping my arm so tight she could snap my bones. Her knuckles are white and the skin under her fingernails looks like porridge. It feels like too many breaths in one room in here— like when you cover your head with your blankets and breathe against the sheet until your face gets sticky.

❖

It's been quiet a while.

The handsome man still guards the door. It looks like he's counting to himself. Maybe it makes him feel better, counting in his head all the way until the second siren sounds. But who's to say the planes aren't up there hiding behind the trees, waiting for us to come out? They could get us twenty-three minutes from now. Or an hour. How would the siren-blower know?

The man's cheeks are red and puffy, like he's been holding his breath while he counts the seconds. Now that I look around, a lot of peoples' faces look like that.

Most of the other girls my age are crying. I know I'm more grown up because I have no tears. But even my mother, who's been grown up for a very long time, even she's crying. Mother cries without making a sound. She doesn't tremble or cover her face. You can only tell she's crying because her face is wet and her eyes shine.

Oh, thank goodness, the second siren. He's opening the door. The air feels so good and crisp. That man is such a gentleman. He's much handsomer than Mr. Herbert—thin and cleaner shaven, with teeth that look like polished quartz. And younger—his eyes don't have the shadows Mr. Herbert's have.

"Thank you, sir."

Did you see the way he looked at me when I smiled and curtseyed? Don't look at me like that. If he finds me back at camp, maybe he'll marry me and take me away. At least, if he marries me, even if he's a refugee too, he can do the work for both of us like Mr. Herbert would have done. And I know the ways a woman is supposed to behave for a man. I heard Heidi Müller talking about it before we left the village—saying things about lying on beds and making strange noises, about kissing parts of men that smell like salt. I can be a good wife.

Do you smell the burning? I see smoke—one of the pillars looks like it's coming from camp—but the sky is so blue and the sun is so beautiful. How can it smell so bad when the wheat still gleams?

I'm afraid to walk down the road back to camp. I'm afraid the road will look like the road in Gašinci the morning after the Partisans came. When we went looking for your father.

I'll never get it out of my head. I don't know if maybe you can't remember because you're dead, and so maybe I shouldn't say anything. But I'll never forget. I can't close my eyes without seeing it, the way his insides were outside, his arms on one side of the road and his legs on the other. I knew they were your father's arms because they looked the same as they had when I came to visit you after school, with the hair on the backs of his hands and fingers. They looked like normal attached arms, except they weren't.

And you were next to me, crying. I wanted to cry, too. I couldn't even be sick in the road like you were. And when you fell on your hands and knees in the street, I stayed standing.

Even when I found you in the garden behind your house the next day, with your skirt above your waist and blood on your belly. Your arms splayed out and staked into the dirt.

A man came up, a Serb from down the street. He looked at you and said something about what kind of a monster someone had to be to do something like that. And then I said it was the Partisans. He looked back at me and said, "The Partisans wouldn't do this. Only Russians and Nazi scum are capable of such things." I looked back at him and said nothing.

"I'd watch what I say, if I were you," he said, putting his hands in his pockets and dragging his feet over your ankles as he walked away.

I don't have to look to know that there are severed limbs in the road. I can hear the shouting before I'm close enough to see. But I also know the feeling in the air, the stillness that falls after something so awful.

The stillness makes everything look beautiful, like postcard photographs. The sun shines just right on the yellow-green shoots and the rows of mounded dirt, on the walnut branches and the unripe cherry blossoms. Even the gravel under my feet reflects the sun as if it were made of gold.

My mother can't keep her eyes off the ditches. I hear her count the bodies under her breath. I hear her rosary rattle against the pendant my father gave her. My own hand is in my coat pocket, fingering my reichspfennig.

You know the last time I remember crying? It's when Anja stole my favorite dress, muddied it up, tore it on a tree branch, and stuffed it back inside our trunk. I cried when I found it, when I held it up and looked at its reflection in my window.

Now my eyes are as dry as smoke, dry as burning.

Dry as the empty pot of soup we spent weeks saving for—one beef bone, a pound of ham, leeks if they have them, and dill, nutmeg, bay. It was so little compared with what we used to have: in our real house with rabbits and cows and pigs, with Mother's fasnachts and our well of fresh water that didn't have to be boiled and my clean hands and lovely dresses. With eggs and wurst and palatschinke. Mamsell made of straw. And you.

Our beautiful pot of soup full of carrots and potatoes and cabbage and onions, that had blown up with the rest of camp or fallen off the stove and spilled out so there was nothing left but emptiness and burning—like all the ruined people.

All the ruined people and the burning barracks and beds and doors that don't keep the rats out.

What happened to my tears? No one else lost theirs. Not Anja who cries over nothing. Or my father who cries over our mean Aunt. Over his parents. Over what it's like to be a father here.

I reach out for my mother's hand. It's dry, but her face is streaming.

VIENNA, AUSTRIA: JANUARY 2012

BEFORE THE LANDING GEAR met the tarmac at Vienna Airport, my heart crept into my throat. It stayed there through immigration, baggage claim, and customs. As I stepped into the arrivals hall and saw David, my heart leapt from my throat to my tongue. When we kissed, I had to catch my breath to stop my heart from lunging into his mouth.

He held my hand as we walked toward the train, squeezed my palm so tight my fingers tingled. We were anonymous here.

Smoke saturated the airport, the platform where we waited for the R train into the city center, the train car itself, and the brisk streets when we stepped out into the night. It was a fainter smoke smell that hung in the air around Vienna than at the airport. Both were fainter still than the heavy stink from all the smokers in the restaurant he took me to.

"I can see through your teeth," David said after we'd eaten and shared two glasses of red wine.

"Does that mean we're finished?" I asked, smiling so all my grey teeth were visible. The table was small and the restaurant was sweltering. My big toes rested on his big toes, and when we put our arms on the table to hold hands, we ended up holding just below our elbows. I could almost feel the sweat on his kneecaps through his trousers.

"Of course not," he said, ordering another round of Zweigelt and the bill.

He undid the top button of his shirt and fanned at the exposed triangle of chest.

It was the shirt he wore the day we met.

It was late June, Sid's company picnic. Sid's things were half-

packed in boxes in our apartment, nowhere near ready for his
move to Washington at the end of the week. His coworkers didn't
have hard feelings about his leaving. He stood with a group of
them, all wearing Phillies t-shirts, no doubt talking about how
much less fun it would be to watch baseball games from Nationals
Park.

I stood alone by the food table, shooing flies off a bowl of
potato salad.

"Hi," said a man I didn't recognize, scooping coleslaw onto a
paper plate. "I'm David."

"Hi," I said, lost for a moment in how out of place he seemed.

I don't remember what we talked about except that he was a
client in town from London. But I remember my heart racing at
the sound of his voice. And I remember that his dress shirt
matched the plastic gingham tablecloth under the coleslaw.

Sid's boss lit the fuse of a four-foot model rocket. Everyone
whooped as the rocket hissed and shot into the air. It left a smoke
spiral behind it and rose into the clouds.

While we waited for the rocket to fall back to earth, David gave
me his business card. I typed his number into my phone and then
"hello," which I erased, replaced with "hi :)," and sent.

"Reentry!" someone shouted. The rocket landed with a whomp
in the middle of a wheat field, the parachute a white flag in the
grass.

When David held the door open to Vienna Row and I stepped
onto the sidewalk, I was glad to be outside again, away from the
smell of tar and fried veal. But even in the night air I couldn't get
a deep enough breath. My heels wobbled on the uneven slabs of
concrete in the Naschmarkt.

All the stalls were closed and covered with graffitied metal and
shipping palates, except for a cheese monger still packing up for
the night. There were a few unauthorized vendors selling sou-
venirs from wooden carts. One said something in German that I
couldn't understand. I shook my head and smiled. "Danke," I said.

A month after the picnic, David returned to Philadelphia. We
walked through the city's summer breath until the heat overwhelmed us.

"Do you want to come back to my place?" I asked, scraping sweat-damp hair off my shoulders.

"That would be brilliant," he said.

We didn't talk as we walked down the hall, as I unlocked the door, as he stepped inside. He looked at Sid's empty desk in the corner and turned to flip through a pile of old photographs on the coffee table. In one, Oma wore a belted wool coat with faux fur at the collar, black peep toes. Opa wore his US Army uniform, hat slightly askew. He was supposed to be deployed to Korea the day the photo was taken, to draw maps from the air. Oma had come to see him off. But a cook's position had opened and he took it. There was relief in his face as Oma leaned against an old Buick, crossing her ankles and tilting her chin upward in a smile so perfect, it was as if she'd forgotten where she came from.

"You look like them," David said.

In the photograph, they didn't look like immigrants.

He moved his gaze to a stack of books and picked one up. It was one of Opa's, mostly in German.

"You read German?"

"No," I said. "It was my grandfather's."

I told him everything. It spilled out of my mouth. The Swabian migrations to Yugoslavia, the expulsion, the genocide, forced labor camps in Russia, being raised by my grandparents, never knowing they were survivors of something so terrible. I trailed off.

David put his hands in his pockets and looked at me. He was silent. And then, "I have to be in Paris next week, but let me take you."

"To Paris?"

"To Yugoslavia."

He took his hands out of his pockets.

"To—" I said and stopped. I saw red flags, stop signs, brake lights, blood pumping fast through arteries. Lip red. Apple red. "Really?"

"Yes," he said.

Then I kissed him.

Red and white Christmas bulbs ran like clotheslines between the buildings on Vienna's main streets as we walked to the holiday apartment David had rented. The lights turned the sidewalks red and reflected off unlit windowpanes like tiny rockets suspended in space.

The rain turned to sleet. He tightened his grip on my elbow each time I wobbled on the slick ground. When we slipped inside our room, lights off and feeling for furniture with our hands, I could still see the glow from our window. We hung our wet coats over the desk chair. I kicked my shoes off and pushed them under the desk. David was close behind me: I felt his breath on my neck as he tugged at the hem of my shirt.

"We've been too far apart all night." His lips were soft on my shoulder.

We made love in a room full of men. There was a clock in the sitting area made of porcelain, with a man in a loincloth flanked by two tigers, and he held up the clock face like Atlas holding the world. There was a storyboard of the death of a matador framed on the wall, with a thin sheet draped over his body, showing off the athletic build he'd had in life. Men were carved into the wardrobe doors with their phalluses dangling between their legs. A painting of an old man hung above the desk: the old man looked toward the edge of the frame, smoking a cigarette while another man stood behind him, staring out at the room, at me. At David. At the larger than life-size plaster statue of a naked Roman beside the bed. At the men carved into the four cherry bed posts and contorted into such impossible positions it was difficult to tell whether they were bent backward in erotic pleasure or pain.

Quiet and surrounded, I hugged my knees and leaned against the headboard. David lay beside me, warm knees grazing my cold ankles. Sid's knees were always cold, and I used to warm them with the soft skin behind my own.

"You okay?" David asked, pressing his lips against my shoulder.

I stayed silent a while longer. I thought maybe David knew I was thinking of Sid because I felt his nerves reaching for a string to hang onto, to pull me back to him like a little red balloon.

He reached for his iPad on the nightstand.

"I've got those satellite images saved," he said.

We curled up, wearing only skin and sweat, to compare notes and researched photographs to birds-eye-views of Austria and the former Yugoslavia. I felt exposed and disrespectful, lying naked and pressed against David's chest while we searched for death camps and mass graves, for all the places that made my grandparents who they were and me who I had become.

I devoured the satellite images, flipping through one after the other while David began to doze, double and triple checking that we'd made the right connections. His shoulder sleep-twitched under my cheek.

He slept like a child, with trust in his eyelashes and innocence on his lips. His snores were arrhythmic. But they were gentle, and I knew he'd be embarrassed when he woke up, that he'd ask me if he snored. That I could say no; that I wouldn't. I could see his fist clenched, holding onto that balloon string so tight. It felt like the other end was tied around my neck: a thin string, easily broken, sharp.

LINZ, AUSTRIA: 2012

I CLIMBED OVER DAVID and slid out of the covers.

The hosts had left a basket of rolls and apricot jam in the kitchen. I put on a pot of coffee and plucked a roll from the basket. It had gone stale overnight. I cut it in half and put it on a plate beside the toaster.

While the coffee brewed, I ran the bath. I brushed my teeth while I waited for the water to warm up. When I reached for a towel to dry my toothbrush, my knuckles brushed against the heated towel rail. "Shit," I whispered. My skin stuck to the hot metal.

I checked the faucet: cold. There were buttons and dials on the wall without instructions. I pushed a few, twisted the dials. Nothing.

I never liked baths, washing and rinsing myself in dead skin.

Instead of plugging the drain, I stepped into the tub and dampened a washcloth under the faucet, lathered it with soap, washed between my legs, under my arms. I rinsed the cloth in the frigid water and wrung it over myself. I still felt dirty when I stepped out of the tub and onto the tile, when I ran the water in the bathroom sink and washed my face, dried it, carefully wringing the few strands of hair that got caught in the suds.

I wrapped a towel around myself and frowned at my reflection.

The woman looking back at me wasn't the one I imagined I would be.

I put the stale roll in the toaster and poured myself a mug of coffee. My mind was in Ansfelden, in Linz and Belgrade and Vojvodina. I ran the itinerary through my head: twelve days. Eleven cities/towns/villages. Three countries. A crossword puzzle book sat under a plant in the center of the breakfast table. I pulled it out and opened it. The pages were made of the same pulpy, gray-ish paper as the ones Opa had kept, but the letters inside them were different.

Opa had lived in the refugee camp Haid in Ansfelden for six years. He told me stories about flirting at dances with a girl named Katharina and about sketching pin-up girls while he leaned against his family's barrack. He once said he discovered he was good at drawing when he memorized the girls' faces and drew them, shading their cheekbones and cheesecake eyes.

I found a drawing he did in 1946 that survived the trip over the Atlantic. I framed it and hung it in my living room—Heddy Lamar in her dark-haired glory, pouting her lips. She watched over me with eyes that looked alive.

"We could go to Schönbrunn Palace after breakfast," David said, emerging from the bedroom. "There's a park and a zoo on the grounds."

As if I'd come all this way to spend a day at the zoo.

"That sounds nice," I said.

We walked through the museum district, held hands in Maria-Theresein Platz, and looked up at the mirror images of the Natural History and Art Museums on opposite sides of the square. It was disorienting, standing in the space between twin giants. I lost height and sense of direction, as if we were passing through the mirror house at a carnival.

Schönbrunn Palace was uplit even in the daylight with a sheen of unreality. The grounds surrounding the palace had the same effect: perfectly manicured topiaries flanked the pathways in mil-itary-straight lines. A folly of immaculate ruins hid behind them. The palace's name meant "Beautiful Spring."

Its gardens were speckled with dry fountains.

David wanted a photograph. He took a shot and turned the camera around so we could see. Cheeks pressed together, lips too close. It was exhilarating, vulgar. The photograph took away our anonymity: it knew us, it caught us. *Adulterers*, it said.

"I wish I could show everyone how beautiful you are," he said.

"Be careful," I whispered in his ear. "I could turn out to be a madwoman. And after all the money and romance you spent to get me here, I might start collecting locks of your hair while you're sleeping."

"I'll just leave you at the zoo with the other animals," he said, pinching my backside. An orangutan waved from a poster at the entrance. *Willkommen im Tiergarten!*

"And what if you're the maniac?"

"Then I guess you're trapped," he pinned my arms to my side and marshalled me forward, covering my cheek and neck in small kisses.

When we left the zoo, I was amazed how much of the day had passed. Four o'clock had come and gone. Perhaps we'd lingered overlong in the aviary, or in the Emperor's pavilion where we bought fancy-looking coffees and a slice of sachertorte to share.

The air had grown colder, and the streets near the palace were wider and less charming than the smaller streets had been. It was growing dark and overcast. The sun dipped behind the palace, casting a golden halo over the roof. A damp wind swelled between buildings.

We crossed the large streets over the skinny Wien River. Trains rumbled in the distance.

"Are you sure this is the way? It's not the way we came."

"I thought I'd take you somewhere nice for dinner," he said, motioning for me to turn left with him onto a beige stretch of road. The buildings were mostly flat-fronted and modern, post war and bleak.

"After you," he said, opening the door to a large old-fashioned building. Music accompanied the smoke smell wafting through the doorway.

It was dark inside, lit by a large chandelier, a tasseled lamp, and votive candles. The hostess seated us at a small table with mismatched chairs. The walls were covered in dark wood wainscoting. Red velvet curtains hung from the windows. Green and yellow stained glass framed the doors and cast a molten glow. A woman sat at a piano in the corner, with a single rose in a crystal vase perched atop the scratched wood surface. She was playing soft, old jazz.

Our waitress came and took our drink orders.

"Ein Gruner Vetliner," I said. "Bitte."

"Gösser bock," David said, pointing at the menu.

The waitress smiled. David reached his hand over the table and brushed his knuckles over my fingers.

"You okay?" he asked.

"How can people taste when everything smells like cigarettes?" I whispered.

Every table had an ash tray, but only people on the left side of the restaurant were smoking. A thick cloud hung around them.

"It's a bit romantic, in a filthy way."

I smiled and squeezed his hand. "Do you have any idea what this menu says?"

"Not a clue."

I thought I would have recognized something. I knew bits and pieces of things: schnitzel, knödel, salat, apfel, gulasch. Kraut. I thought speck might be ham. Everything looked like it was either pork or beef or fried.

The waitress came with our drinks and we both pointed at mysterious dishes on the menu. I'd chosen the strangest looking words I could find.

David had gone with liver mousse soup and some kind of wurst. I'd picked a different soup that turned out to be beef broth with nockerl and then some kind of smoked pork with buttery cabbage and bread dumplings smothered in gravy. It was warming and heavy.

"No wonder they drink wines like Grüner. You need something to cut through all this pork fat."

I'd only eaten one of my nockerl and half of my main course, and my stomach was already tender. It had been years since I'd had one of Oma's potato dumplings, her pigs' knuckle soup, her schnitzel with buttered noodles. My memory of her food comes with a heavy stomach, but it was a different heavy: overfull and sleepy rather than stuffed and slightly queasy.

Maybe it was the cigarette smoke. The jet lag. The sachertorte from earlier. The lard-fried dumplings.

I was grateful again for the fresh outside air—even though it was cold and raining. David opened his umbrella over us. I checked my watch. Seven o'clock.

"Where to next?" He kissed my cheek and held me close to him. Water ran down his umbrella and onto my coat sleeve.

"Can we get a cab back?" I asked. "I'm not feeling well."

"It's so early," he said. He tried to sound cheerful, but I heard the disappointment in his voice. "Maybe a walk will help?"

No, a walk won't help. We've been walking all day, I wanted to say. But I didn't.

"I'll pay," I offered. The words sounded sour, but I hadn't meant them to.

His eyes darkened. "You think it's about money?"

I looked at the sidewalk. Isn't everything about money? I can't say no to zoos or heavy food or walks when I don't feel well because all these things are gifts, whether I want them or not. Because someone else is paying. It would be ungrateful of me to say no. To say, actually, the zoo is a waste, I wanted to see Vienna, and now I just want to lay down and close my eyes. I thought of the orangutans in their cages and imagined myself beside them, with bars made of David's money. My stomachache was making me dramatic, but I couldn't stop myself.

"So, I'm not allowed to feel sick because you're paying?"

"What?"

"I just want to go back. Please."

"I just wanted us to have a nice night." He said it like I didn't.

"It was a nice night."

I felt his eyes on me, but I didn't look at him.

"Marie." He reached for my arm.

"Don't." I pulled away. "Whatever I say, I'll sound ungrateful."

He stepped in front of me, so close I could smell the pork fat on his breath.

"Forgive me." He kissed my forehead. "I just don't want to waste this."

It took a few minutes for a cab to pass, but when one did, David hailed it.

Back at the apartment, we undressed and got into bed. We laid beside each other and didn't speak. He fell asleep with his lips pressed against my shoulder. I stayed awake a while longer, listening to his quiet snores, his soft breaths, the rustle of his skin against the sheets when he shifted closer.

In the morning, we drove to Linz and checked into a hotel on the Hauptplatz that used to be a nunnery. The receptionist handed David a key and told us that the entrance to our room was outside, down the outdoor walkway that ran parallel to the alleyway below, and off to the right. I peered over the railing and saw signs for a go-go bar hidden below the nuns' old quarters. Rain fell on the overhang and the railing and the cobblestones below: the noise came from everywhere and sounded like whispers.

I covered my left hand with my right so the walls couldn't see the red skin where the diamonds of my wedding band had built a callus. The band was delicate. The bottom points of tiny stones poked through the gold at intervals. It had taken a month for the callus to form: for a month the skin of my ring finger was raw. Shampoo stung my hand in the shower, and scented lotion, peeling oranges over the kitchen garbage can. Since I boarded the plane at Philadelphia International, the band had been in my purse, in a little box with my grandfather's wedding ring.

David and I passed a potted rubber tree and a rocking horse in the open-air corridor. He stopped at room 206 and slid the brass key into the lock. When I stepped into the room, my nose found something sour-sweet and familiar: veneer resin, formaldehyde.

There was a carrot-colored sofa pushed against one wall and veneer wardrobes by the door. Both reminded me of my grandparents' house on Anita Drive, of the orange vinyl chairs in the kitchen, the orange polka dots on the placemats, the erotic orange statues Opa had displayed on the front windowsill. And his veneer cabinet—the one I had always stared at before I fell asleep. His cabinet took up the whole wall opposite the bed in my room, and each door's tiny handles winked in the dark. In our house there were no monsters in the closets, no boogiemen beneath the beds: they were all shut up inside the cabinet, one in each compartment.

The monsters had no teeth, like my grandmother after I was tucked in bed. Their lips were sloppy around their mouths, and they would drool and speak without consonants. I couldn't understand their words, but I knew they were hungry by the way the handles glinted. I had nightmares that the whole cabinet would come crashing down on top of me, that I would be crushed by the weight of the fake black walnut and all the tiny doors would burst open at once and gobble me up.

I wasn't supposed to snoop. I had my own wardrobe. But in the mornings I'd open all the doors to check for signs of monsters that may have come the night before. The cabinet was filled with papers and photo albums, building plans and free things. Bank pens, company calculators, cereal box watches. One door opened to reveal a small box with the name Rosalinde scrawled in Opa's handwriting on the side. I didn't open it, but there were love letters and dirty jokes piled up on yellowed paper inside, and a faux gold ring with a braided band, a welded-on plastic gem, and four crooked letters spelling out l-o-v-e.

My favorite drawer was filled with his used pencils, sharpened down to the metal nubs, with spent erasers. I'd line them all up on the carpet, put the very best looking in my pajama pockets, and return the remaining pencils to the drawer. I'd spend the rest of my mornings kneeling over the coffee table in front of the television, asking Opa to draw me kittens or trees or birds so I could color them in meticulously while he told me stories from his childhood. Like the one where he shouted out an open window at a passerby, "Rascal!" and ran inside to hide behind his mother's skirt when he realized he'd shouted at the village priest. When he climbed the mulberry trees outside the house and carved faces into walnut husks. Or when he snuck through the window of his father's produce shed and sat atop a heap of fruit, biting into the pulpy flesh of oranges and hiding the peels in his pockets—which, he said with a sly smile, made his trousers smell fresh. As he drew, his fingertips pinching the tiny pencils, his skin would grow white, and the contrast made his age spots darken.

Opa was good at drawing trees, but his cats always came out with human faces.

David sat on the bed and leaned against the headboard. I curled into the crook of his shoulder.

"I'm sorry about yesterday," I said. "I was overwhelmed. You're so kind, taking me to these places. I feel guilty for letting you."

"Why do you feel guilty?" he said.

I pressed my nose against his cheek. "Why are you doing this for me?"

"Because I want to. And I can."

What he didn't say, but I wondered if he meant: because I want to win you. I want you to be mine.

We were both hungry for things, hungry like the monsters in Opa's cabinet.

"The rain will stop tomorrow and we'll find your Opa's camp," he said.

"It smells like him here," I said.

Him. There were so many hims, even with the nuns whispering on the bridge. Sid in the little box in my purse. The man at the front desk. The man whose heels clicked while he walked below our window, bound for the go-go bar. David. I fell asleep with my cheek on his shoulder bone. When I woke, my neck and face were sore. My jaw felt punched.

We walked in the rain again, pausing to look inside Austrian Catholic churches. I'd been a girl still, unmarried, the last time I knelt at a pew. But the pews in this sanctuary were blocked off by a gate, perhaps to stop tourists like us from dirtying the ornate tile floors with our sin.

Prayer candles burned in the vestibule.

"Do you have change so I can light one for Opa?" I smiled and held my hands out to David. He pulled two coins from his pocket and placed one like a wafer in my palm. I dropped the two euro into the donation box. He followed, dropping in a coin of his own. I'd never lit a prayer candle before. Oma would have known the proper way to light one: how to begin, how long to pray, whether to pray silently or aloud. In the Alzheimer's ward at Bayside Nursing Home, her bedroom was filled with plastic holy statues and medallions of Saints Michael, Christopher, and Peter. They were kept locked away in her nightstand to keep the other patients from stealing them.

I picked up a large match from a metal cup. There was nothing to strike it on, so I held it over someone else's prayer until it caught. If I stole the light from another prayer to light my own, was I taking power away from it or multiplying it?

The way David looked at me was sweet and skeptical. When I finished, he took fire from my prayer and lit the candle beside it.

The night Opa died, I slept alone on the queen bed in my old room. The comforter was pulled down to the end of the bed, exposing cream-colored sheets. I had a dream that felt like it wasn't a dream. While I slept, a noise came from under the mattress. Unnggg, the mattress moaned. The empty side lifted off the frame until an arm burst through the springs, through the sheets, fingers outstretched. I recognized the age spots. Opa, I moved my lips but no sound came out. I felt a scream in my throat but couldn't hear it. He shouted indecipherable phrases as he reached for me. He reached as if I could grab his hand and pull him up through the hole. As he reached and banged against the underside of the mattress, fibers and feathers flew—white as warm ashes.

"Are you ready to go?" David asked, cupping my hand between both of his and squeezing.

I wanted to watch the candle burn a moment longer, watch the flame twitch, the wick turn black. But I looked at David and smiled.

He led me back out into the rain, past cafés that looked like Oma's dining room. Through the café windows there were lace curtains and doilies, gaudy crystal candleholders and plastic table-cloths. We stopped in one for dinner. The menu was Greek and didn't match the décor they had so effectively borrowed from Anita Drive. The moussaka was good and the wine flowed until my teeth turned see-through, and when the waitress brought the check, she handed us each a shot of ouzo. We clinked glasses and took a sip. It burned my throat. I hid a cough behind my palm and David laughed, plucking my ouzo off the table and finishing it in one swallow.

"Do you believe in God?" I asked.

"Do you?" he asked.

"I don't know. Everything is lonely otherwise."

I thought of Oma standing over holy statues and counting off prayer beads, alone except for her saints and Mother Mary. Her refugee camp was supposed to be on the outskirts of Linz. That's all she could remember. No details. No landmarks. Research turned up nothing about what had been built where her barracks had stood. Oma said that before it kept refugees, her camp was filled with starving Jews. How could something with such a terrible history have disappeared as cleanly from the earth as it had from her memory? Or was I just not looking hard enough?

David ran his finger over the lip of the glass.

"Religion creates bigots and war," he said.

"I'm not talking about religion." I winced picturing my Oma's face if she could have heard me. "There's a difference between religion and wanting to believe in something larger."

"I believe in something larger. I believe in science and progress."

"Do you trust that people will use science and progress for good?"

"There are always bad people," he said. "But the good guys have to win, right?"

"What happens if nobody's good?"

"Then we're doomed," he laughed. "But I don't think that's likely."

I pictured David's soul floating out in space with Sid's thoughts, a piece of dust in a windless blackness. It reminded me of Sid and his belief that when he dies, the scientific equivalent of his soul will go into the atmosphere or the earth and become part of something else: wind or tree roots. He and David were capable of treading alone. Not me. As my Oma needed saints and archangels and holy mothers, I needed an army of lost loved ones watching over me to make life seem less desolate.

David squeezed my hand and stood to leave.

The shot glass left a ring on the tablecloth.

"What a mess," Oma would have said.

It was difficult to imagine my grandparents as children living in barracks just a few miles from where I stood. I tucked my chair under the table.

Back at the hotel on the Hauptplatz, in the middle of the night, I woke up gasping for air. That sour-sweet smell was everywhere. More familiar smells had mixed with the veneer resin: nail polish and pencil shavings. Combined, it was the same smell that had been so powerful in my grandparents' home that it stuck to their plastic bags.

It covered me before I opened my eyes, seeped into my pores, my nose, between the woven fibers of the bed sheets. It pressed down on my chest like two feet standing on my lungs.

I stood to shake the weight and disorientation off; the air was damp with formaldehyde. I walked to the wardrobe and pulled the metal handles. The smell swallowed me. My lungs filled to bursting with it. *Opa?* I couldn't say his name out loud. I couldn't breathe.

I grabbed the keys off the coat hook behind the door.

Outside, I breathed the fresh air deeply. In one-two-three, out one-two-three. Rain pattered against the wooden overhang. I walked in the direction of the go-go bar, but then I remembered the rocking horse. I turned around and found it on the other end of the corridor, resting under the shadow of the potted rubber tree. I stroked the horse's neck. Its mane was rough under my hand.

In a toy warehouse in Northeast Philadelphia, when I was little, Opa watched me ride a whole inventory of rocking horses. Wood and plastic and plush, chestnuts, grays, palominos. Horses with hair growing over their hooves, ponies with pink noses, a bay with a seam running down the center of its mane and neck and tail. I shouted, "Giddy up!" I swung an invisible lasso. He watched me gallop on a squeaking filly on springs until a woman in a red vest with a nametag came to tell us the store had been closed for twenty minutes. I remembered looking from her stern face to my grandfather's sheepish grin. I felt a pang of embarrassment. My face ached from smiling.

Our feet echoed between the linoleum and the metal ceiling as I held Opa's hand and counted the age spots speckling the back like coffee stains. And his fingernails, for the first time I noticed that they weren't the same pink as mine, that they were dull and yellow and ribbed. I looked up into his face and saw gray hair poking out of his ears and nose. I looked up and all of a sudden he was old.

I rocked on the rough horse in the corridor until the contents of Opa's cabinet of monsters fell out: row after row of grinning sharpened pencils, glow-in-the-dark watch faces. The cabinet was still there, in his house, still full. I'd always wondered why he'd kept so many things, so many duplicates of the same things. But of course he'd kept it all. Everything was small and everything was big. It was all at risk of being taken.

OSKAR GEIGER:
TSCHOKA, YUGOSLAVIA: 1944

THROUGH THE FOG, ghostly hunchbacks stalked the dusk, each with a scraggy finger pointing. As the Russians came closer, they looked less like ghosts and more like ogres—hunched backs all lumpy and heads too big. Until they got close enough that I could see their hunches for what they were: backpacks, skinny fingers, bayonets. Their ogre heads only looked too big because they wore fat metal helmets.

Father was conscripted by the German Army. Before that, he had been a soldier for The Kingdom of Yugoslavia. Grandfather told me the kingdom no longer existed and that's why Father had to switch sides. Before he left, Father said, "It's true we speak German, but is that who we are?" When he spoke, his hand was on my shoulder but his eyes were somewhere else.

The Russians were goliath men. Or maybe they just seemed big because I was nine and my father was away in the army and Grandfather had shrunk into a raisin. I was almost as big as him. Even Rosalinde came up to his shoulders. Grandfather held her up to the window, grunting as he lifted her off the kitchen floor.

"You see those men?" he said. "Whatever happens, stay away from men who look like that."

Mother stood by the front door with my baby brother swaddled in her arms.

"Why are they coming?" Rosalinde asked.

"Because we are German," Grandfather said, setting her down on the floor.

"But why?" she persisted.

"Because Hitler is a very bad man," he said. "And we sound

just like him."

The Russians outside were so close they cast shadows on the curtains.

Knuckles rapped on the front door. Mother opened the door just wide enough that I could see one eye and two thick lips through the crack.

"You have twenty minutes," the lips said. "To take what you can carry and leave."

Mother shut the door and walked to her bedroom.

"Pack what you can," she said over her shoulder. "Wear extra pairs of socks under your boots. As many shirts under your coat as you can."

I put on five shirts and three pairs of socks. I wrapped my scarf and my father's scarf around my neck. My sister put on two hats. Grandfather packed four knapsacks full of food. I went into Mother's bedroom and saw her sewing jewelry inside her skirts. She stood in her slip with three pairs of stockings on while she sewed. I could tell there were three pairs because none of the seams matched up. I watched her needle work its way through the layers of cotton. Over, under, over, under. I watched her sew her wedding ring and her mother's wedding ring into one secret pocket and a necklace into another. It was a beautiful necklace, a star sapphire dangling from a silver chain. "It's my Star of Bethlehem," she'd said as it dangled below her throat on Christmas Eve. She sewed away her aunt's choker made of crystal, a bracelet Father had given her, and reached for a tarnished silver brooch with flecks of ruby.

"Oskar, get the blanket from your bed," she said.

When I came back with the blanket in my arms, she'd put on all her skirts. The different colored hems stuck out at the bottom. She reached for the blanket and wrapped it around the baby so many times that none of his skin was left uncovered. He looked like a big woolly bean.

Grandfather put two food packs over his shoulder, handed one to my sister, and one to me. Mother held the baby close to her chest while Grandfather tied the ends of the blanket around her back so she could keep her arms free. She handed me another pack to carry.

"Where are we going?" my sister asked.

"Just away for a while," Grandfather said, putting his free hand on her shoulder.

"How will Father find us?"

"Fathers have daughter detectors." Grandfather opened the backdoor.

"What about Bello?"

Bello was our pointer. We'd gotten him when I was three. His job was to bark at the door when someone knocked, and to scare the foxes away from the ducks. Instead he slept under the kitchen table.

"Bello!"

Bello waddled out from under the table and pressed his nose into Rosalinde's palm.

"He'll have to stay here and keep watch over the house," Mother said, adjusting the baby, whose tiny eyes peeked from the swaddling. The baby wasn't usually so quiet. I was calmer than I thought I should be too. I thought I should feel more like my sister did. She wailed and hugged Bello so tight he could have exploded.

I knew what was happening was bad. I wondered if I should feel ashamed, if we should all feel ashamed—for running away, for wearing so many layers of clothes, for having things in common with a bad man. But I hiked the packs over my shoulder and followed Mother to the door. I tried to act like Father. He would act like he was made of stone.

"Hurry, children," Mother said, putting a hand on Bello's head.

We walked out the door before the Russians came back, out into the yard and into the woods. It was lucky we were so close to the edge of town. The train station was just on the other side of the trees.

I turned to look over my shoulder: empty carts and wagons were coming up our road. I thought maybe they were coming to take the neighbors somewhere, but many of the neighbors were already outside, some following us to the station, others marching toward the village center.

Hans from next door jogged to catch up to us. He was two years older than me and liked to think he was grown up. "Mother heard that the Partisans are breaking the tracks. Are you taking the train?"

I looked up at Grandfather. It was too dark to see his face.

"Yes," Grandfather said. "What choice do we have?"

"In Kikinda," Hans said. "Mother says the Partisans pulled the bolts out of the tracks so the train crashed. And then they shot at it."

Grandfather put his hands over my sister's ears, and my mother moved faster. The baby started crying, muffled by the wool. Mother wrapped her arms tightly around the bundle and bowed her head. She looked like she was praying, but I think she was just taking careful footsteps over tree roots so as not to fall. She grew out of breath climbing the hill through the woods behind our house, tugging at her skirts every now and then so the layers wouldn't slide to her ankles.

I thought it was the Russians who were coming for us. I couldn't understand what the Partisans were doing shooting trains when it was the Russians who had the guns. I saw flyers posted on trees and fence posts in the village calling for men to join the Communist Partisan Movement. I didn't know what Partisan meant, but I knew a Serbian boy down the street who joined. He bragged about it at school last week.

Grandfather looked tired of questions, so I didn't ask.

"She says that some of us had guns and shot back," Hans said.

Rosalinde started to cry again.

"Enough," Grandfather said. "Your mother should know better than to tell you such stories."

"A lot of people are staying." I couldn't understand why Hans kept talking. "They say we've done nothing wrong, so nothing can happen to us."

"They are fools," Grandfather said. We walked, each footstep crunching beneath us like chewing. Hans kept talking, but he fell back as he spoke, back to his mother and the other villagers behind us where he told the same story again and again. He asked many questions.

"When will we be allowed to go home?"

"Are those wagons there to take our stuff?"

"What's going to happen to our house?"

Rosalinde tugged on Grandfather's sleeve. "What's going to happen to Bello?" she asked.

"He'll chase the village cats until we come home."

Everybody talked about coming home. Nobody talked about where we were going.

The train puffed from the station platform. I couldn't see it, but I could hear it, gasping like it was out of breath. My feet felt swollen in my shoes because of all the socks. My toes were numb, and all the shirts piled up under my coat made me wet with sweat. It was hard to bend my arms to adjust the knapsacks. I felt as fat and awkward as Bello shuffling through the sticks and needles.

Poor Bello, waiting under the kitchen table for us to come home.

He would probably still hear me if I called him.

Something in my bones stopped working. I froze in the middle of the woods. Hans caught up and reached for the knapsack slipping off my shoulder. "Are you okay?"

I opened my mouth. My jaw felt stiff and gritty, like there was sand in it. Nothing came out.

"Are you afraid?"

All of a sudden tears started running down my cheeks, with Hans asking stupid questions and my grandfather a few steps ahead, my sister ahead of him, my mother ahead of us all, clutching the baby. And Father somewhere in front of her, with the daughter detectors that couldn't be real because otherwise he'd have already found us.

"No," I said, wiping my face with my undermost sleeve. "I just need to fix my socks."

"We don't have time for that, Oskar," Grandfather said, doubling back to shoo me onward. "We don't want to miss the train."

I saw the station through the edge of the tree line. I could make out red cattle cars linked together, segments of a wooden millipede. The platform stretched out flat ahead of us, but the tree trunks between us and the platform looked like prison bars and I couldn't tell which side was the wrong side—here inside the damp dusk woods, or there on the platform where dozens of other people stood with tiny suitcases.

There were also men in uniforms standing on the platform, with guns and bayonets and metal helmets like the Russians who'd cast shadows on the curtains. Only these soldiers were smaller. The one nearest the tree line was close enough I could see his pimples under the lamplight.

Mother crossed through first, between two skinny oak trunks. Grandfather followed with Rosalinde hanging onto his coat. The pimpled soldier looked at us as if we smelled bad, but he didn't speak. We stood beside our German neighbors waiting for the train, watching another group of soldiers guide a line of horses into one of the cars.

"Are we supposed to ride in one of those?" my sister asked, tugging at Grandfather.

"I think so, dumpling."

My stomach made a loud hungry noise. We hadn't eaten dinner.

I knew there was food in my knapsack, but I didn't dare open it to see what Grandfather packed. I looked at Rosalinde, her full cheeks as rosy as a plum. I hoped there were plum dumplings. Mother made them from potatoes and fried them in browned butter and breadcrumbs. If we were lucky, she served them with cinnamon sugar and sent us to bed with overfull stomachs, so overfull I wasn't even hungry for breakfast the next morning. Sometimes she kept leftovers in the icebox.

"Are we supposed to ride with the horses?" Hans asked, his voice too loud. A soldier guarding the door to one of the cattle cars turned to look at him.

"These horses are worth more than you are," the soldier shouted. "You'll have to wait your turn."

The long line of horses—probably as many as had been kept in fields and stables around the village—included a bulky chestnut with white socks that looked an awful lot like Farmer Brunner's plow horse.

Hans was right.

The wagons back on our road weren't for people. They were for everything else.

The soldiers filled two whole cattle cars with horses, which left only two cars for us. By the time they locked the horses in and started loading people, there were at least two hundred of us on the platform.

"If only you Germans were as easy to herd as sheep," the soldier who shouted earlier said. He jabbed a woman in the leg with his bayonet to make her move faster. Mother and the baby and Rosalinde were herded in next, with Grandfather and me walking close behind to shield their calves.

The soldier banged the butt of his gun on the platform to emphasize his authority.

"Quick, quick!" he shouted, punctuating each word with his gun on the concrete.

I was already in the carriage. My family was huddled by the doorway so we could be closest to the door when it closed, closest to the air because there were no windows in the wooden box. It smelled like a stable. I leaned against the doorway while more people shuffled into the car. We were running out of space.

"Enough," the soldier shouted, but people kept crowding. I caught an elbow in the ear. The soldier banged his gun again—only this time, when it hit the platform, there was a loud tearing sound as a bullet cut the air. It sliced right through the soldier's chin. I saw his bloody teeth burst outward. After that I couldn't see for all the people pushing into the car. Women screamed so loud my ears rang. I caught another elbow. It hit the back of my head and made me dizzy.

Another soldier came who looked like a boy. He didn't have pimples like the one by the tree line, but he had soft features. Eyes that belonged more to a cupid than a soldier. Lips that looked like the pink vetches Mother kept in a milk bottle in spring. He struggled trying to pull the door shut. It kept getting stuck every few inches. When he got to the end, he didn't say anything, didn't make a sick face like the pimpled boy. He just looked into my eyes without blinking and shut us into blackness.

Grandfather leaned against the wall, bending his knees to keep them from getting stiff. It was too dark and crowded inside the car to fiddle with our knapsacks. Also, we were afraid the train would stop and we'd have to get out in a hurry and all the food would be lost. It was difficult to tell time through the hunger. No light reached inside the cattle car except little strips of moonlight that glowed through the door jambs. Even those skinny ribbons couldn't break the shadows.

We didn't speak much. Even Hans was quiet. Rosalinde cried the whole time. I don't know how many hours her sniffling lasted, but she cried so long I thought she would run out of tears. She asked Grandfather how much longer before we stopped. Every so often Mother sang lullabies to quiet the baby, who'd grown irritable in the cold, smelly car. He wailed such high notes that other people on the train complained to Mother, said things like, "Keep him quiet or I will." Grandfather said those people were angry because they were scared.

It was impossible to sleep crunched up with my chin on my knees, leaning against the splintery wall. Mother stood, shifting her weight from one leg to the other, bouncing for the baby. I wanted to know where we were going, but no one seemed to have an answer. One man said, "North." Another said, "Hopefully out of Yugoslavia." Still another, a man who sounded even older than Grandfather, told me I didn't want to know.

I opened my mouth to tell him that of course I wanted to know. That it was stupid to say I didn't because everyone did, otherwise why was everybody so quiet and scared? But instead of my voice, another sound came: hammers on iron.

At first I thought it came from me, but I heard it again when my mouth was shut. It didn't sound like hammers after the first time. It sounded like a giant had spilled a bag of marbles on the train. Screams and flying arms filled the car. I got smacked in the face with a woman's knuckles when she tried to shield her head. Rosalinde got hit in the nose—but she also managed to hit someone else when she tried to cover her ears.

"Father!" Rosalinde shouted, shaking her head back and forth, hands on her ears and elbows swinging. "Father! Father!"

"Shush, Rosalinde," Grandfather said, wincing.

It served him right, thinking he could calm her fears by making up something as impossible as daughter detectors.

One bullet made its way through our cattle car, at one of the top rear corners. It made a hole big enough that a beam of moonlight cut through the shadows.

Instead of the silence darkness had forced on us and the screaming that came with the gunfire, when the moonlight came through the bullet hole, the car filled with a burst of whispers. I never heard grownups make such shaky sounds. Father had never looked afraid. He always looked like a statue. And the only time I saw Mother cry was when Father's German draft notice came. She'd cried so hard she had to brace herself to stay upright. Still, she hadn't quaked like the people on the train. Even now, she stood leaning against the wall with her eyes closed, holding the baby's face to the curve of her neck, singing:

Guter Mond, du gehst so stille
durch die Abendwolken hin
Deines Schöpfers weiser Wille
hiess auf jene Bahn dich zieh'n
Leuchte freundlich jedem Müden
in das stille Kämmerlein

The train didn't stop after the gunfire. It kept churning North or Hopefully-Out-of-Yugoslavia or I-Don't-Want-to-Know. Everyone grew silent again, even the baby. So when my stomach grumbled, it sounded as loud as the guns. I tried to be stone-strong in spite of my hunger, but before I could stop myself I asked Grandfather, "What'd you pack to eat?"

"Bread and bacon," Grandfather said, resting his wrinkly hand on top of my head. Usually he would ruffle my hair, but he kept his hand still. It felt heavy.

I stood up, pulling at the buckle holding one of his bags shut. "Can I open it?"

"You'll have to ask your mother."

"Mother?"

"We have to save our food, Oskar."

"But I'm hungry."

"Me too," Rosalinde said, rubbing her nose.

"Sit back down." Mother's voice sounded tired. "And close your eyes."

"I'll dream of plum dumplings," I said, but the thought of the heavy potato dough and the warm butter and sugar, the soft pitted plum tucked inside it, made my stomach hurt. I couldn't tell if it hurt because I was hungry or if I wasn't actually hungry at all.

I tried to sit back down, but the crowd of grownup feet had squeezed into my sitting space. I wedged myself between the legs and knelt, shifting my weight from one side to the other. I knelt so long I lost feeling in my ankles and feet. My knees felt raw from pressing against knots in the planked floor. Sleep didn't come, only darkness and the single moonbeam that crept its way across the wall until it was swallowed by darkness too.

"Do you feel that?" Rosalinde asked, tugging one of mother's skirts. The train was slowing down. Fast enough that the brakes hissed and screeched on the rails. Fast enough that the whole train lurched when it stopped. For a moment everything was still. No one breathed. Then shouting outside. Angry voices. The sound of someone at the door. It slid open so we could see a platform and a station shack, the Partisan soldier blocking the exit.

Even with the soldier in the way, the station lamps were blinding.

Mother kept her arms wrapped tight around the baby, as if the air outside the car could be any colder than it had been inside, as if someone might rip my brother away from her. There was silence on the platform as we were unloaded onto the concrete, as we saw the cattle car in front of us, the one that had been filled with horses.

The one that was riddled with holes.

"That could have been us," Grandfather said.

He said it like it was supposed to be us.

The door to the horse car was open. I walked toward it until I could see in. There should have been horses in the entrance blowing air between their lips, waiting for hay and apples. But the doorway was empty.

"Close your eyes, Rosa," Grandfather said.

Mother sat down so fast on the platform that her skirts filled with air. The jewelry she'd sewn into the fabric clinked on the concrete, and the different colored hems covered her feet so she looked like she was sitting in a collapsed balloon.

A soldier pointed his bayonet at her.

"Now, now," Grandfather said. "There's no need for that."

The baby started crying again, and Mother held him in his bean swaddling and hummed her lullaby. She looked at Grandfather.

"Please," Grandfather said.

The soldier slid his bayonet against the hem of Mother's top-most skirt and lifted it up. He knelt on the platform and slid his hands up under the second skirt, pulling at the fabric in handfuls.

"Women are so predictable," he said. He counted her secret pockets out loud.

"Leave her alone." I pushed the soldier's arm with both hands. He didn't move. His biceps were solid. The soldier buried his arms deeper into Mother's skirts, tearing holes in her secret pockets until there was a puddle of earrings and crystal and crosses between her legs. Her wedding ring chimed like a tiny bell on the platform. She reached for it, but the soldier smacked her fingers with the barrel of his gun.

His back was rigid. Even his face looked chiseled from rock.

Rosalinde cried with her hands over her eyes, "Father!"

I was too old to believe in daughter detectors. If they were real, Father would have been in the house when the soldiers came. He would have been with us on the train. Maybe he would never have left us at all. He would have held Mother's arm so she didn't fall when she saw the other car. He would have stopped the Partisan from putting her wedding ring into his pocket with her blue Star of Bethlehem, her earrings, her brooches, the crosses that had fallen.

Grandfather grabbed my wrist and tried to pull me away, but I pushed against the Partisan with all my might. He acted as if he couldn't feel me. I wanted him to get angry, to knock me back-wards. Anything to leave my mother alone. But he didn't. It was as if I was made of air. And my father. He made my father seem supple as clay, as if he had never been made of stone at all.

ANSFELDEN, AUSTRIA: 2012

I WOKE UP IN BED beside David, his face pressed into my armpit. My body felt damp. I slid away from him, just a few inches, and kicked a foot out of the covers. Other than my own musk and the scent of David's heat beside me, the room smelled like nothing.

I got up to shower. There was only the faint scent of veneer as I passed the wardrobe.

When David and I walked to the dining room for breakfast, I half expected the rocking horse to have disappeared, too. But it remained.

Breakfast was familiar. Breakfast was lunch from a long time ago. There was a casserole dish filled with liverwurst terrine, deli sausage with cheese inside, fruit cocktail, canned plums with the pits still in, and cottage cheese. There was pumpernickel and rye, and the sort of small pastries that had made Oma wider than the refrigerator. There was even the orange-mango juice I'd found so delicious I bit my glass and spilled shards and sticky liquid all over her kitchen table when I was eight.

"Gott im Himmel!" she'd said. When she smiled, only half her mouth responded. The other half lay flat and slack on her face. I used to think this was because of a car accident that severed a nerve to her lips. When I learned about Rosalinde, I wondered whether her inability to smile came from finding out my grandfather had fallen in love with another woman.

I'd never heard of Rosalinde before Opa died, but I remembered the box he kept in his cabinet of monsters. Oma found it two days after he passed, and it brought back all the old pain. She cried and cursed him for a month. It didn't matter that Rosalinde had been dead for almost forty years.

In the seventies, Opa brought Rosalinde and her husband to the house for dinner on occasional weekends. He danced with Rosalinde at the German-Hungarian club. At the club, Swabian immigrants recreated their culture without shame. They threw theme parties—Viennese nights full of string quartets, waltzes, and multicourse dinners with layer cakes and sweet coffee. They spoke their Swabian dialect and celebrated traditional festivals like Kirchweihfest: an annual fete with centuries' old traditions of pleated underskirts, aprons, men in black vests, a ceremonial rosemary bush auction—and dancing the schuplattler and the polka into the morning hours.

While Opa and Rosalinde danced, Oma sat at a table with Rosalinde's husband. He tried to put his hand up her skirt. "They're doing it, why don't we do it too?"

I pictured Rosalinde and Opa spending late nights in hotel rooms talking about the old country: the town criers, the stove-warm baths, the smell of discharged bullets, the sounds of fear, the refreshing chill of linoleum tile and fluorescent lights in a country so different from home that the Danube seemed a dream. Philadelphia and its paved, littered streets, its brick townhomes, twin houses with plastic siding, sidewalks, neon lights, Chinese restaurants.

But then Rosalinde got sick.

After the cancer took her, Opa never spoke her name.

He rarely had anything to say to my grandmother, but from his chair, the week before he died, he looked at Oma and swore he'd never slept with Rosalinde, that he'd only kissed her, only rented hotel rooms in Center City to talk to her. Because she'd grown up instead of turning inward as Oma had done.

Oma didn't believe him. But forty years had passed. If he had slept with Rosalinde, he could have gone to his grave pretending Oma had forgotten. Maybe he was thinking of that box of keepsakes he'd never been able to throw away, even when he knew it was the end. He knew she'd find it soon.

The family rumor was that Opa only married my grandmother to avoid the draft for the Korean Conflict, that somebody told him if he got married he wouldn't have to go. I don't believe that. Opa had already been through a war. He'd have known better: if a child could be a soldier, there'd be no reprieve for married men. And besides, my grandparents were survivors, two nineteen-year-olds who came from the same place, experienced the same struggle. Maybe they confused their sameness with love.

Opa allowed himself happiness with Rosalinde. It must have been devastating to lose her. But Oma deserved happiness too. Perhaps that was our family curse, that happiness could only exist beside its opposite.

Or perhaps we just misunderstood the word.

"I've never had cottage cheese," David said, pulling a croissant apart and smearing it with jam.

"It's good," I said, filling my spoon with curds and a slice of plum. The spoon rang against my teeth. "You should try some."

"I will," he said, but I knew he wouldn't. He only ate croissants and jam and coffee.

And Haribo candies in the car on the way to Ansfelden.

On the drive we listened to ABBA on the radio because almost every station played disco. David's fingers danced on the steering wheel, and we laughed because we hated disco. The farmland outside the window was muddy, the grass vivid. I tried to take pictures to remember, but they all came out wrong. The earth changed color when it came through the lens, and the feeling of the place was missing.

It was January, but there were crops in the fields—onions and potatoes. Their leaves protruded withered from the soil. David said the crops wouldn't rot if they were kept underground, but as we drove it seemed like fewer and fewer vegetables were still buried. A heap of turnips was piled up along the side of the road, pocked with bite marks that looked as if they came from mouths with no teeth.

Farmhouses speckled the landscape. Made of stone walls and clay roofs, each one a hollowed-out square with a courtyard inside it and religious scenes painted over the doorways—of the Holy Mother, Christ crucified, St. Francis with a lamb at his feet and white doves in his arms. Windows were small and sparse, and the ones I could see were covered with shutters or heavy curtains. There were more fields with abandoned turnips, fruit trees with their harvest wasting on the ground. Three apple trees, a holy trinity of roots and branches and rotting fruit, had dropped so many apples it looked as if they were all released at once, before anybody could pluck a ripe Reinette from the boughs.

The fruit was left for the foxes.

In the village, we followed Haider Strasse, hoping it would lead us to Camp Haid. The road curved and took us down a hill. A newly built, freshly painted café with a wooden patio stood across the street from a block of government housing: a four-story rect-angle with eight chimneys on the roof and mustard-colored balconies. It was the apartment building from the background of a photograph I'd found in a newspaper clipping online, of a girl named Mucki playing with her doll. The photo was a glimpse into the in between time, after the expulsion, before the displaced were assimilated into new life—a child refugee jumping the remains of leveled barracks wearing a pleated skirt and socks up to her knees, her hair wrapped in idyllic plaits, her doll in a basket beside her. For all the hope in the height of her leap and the bright whiteness of her clothing, it was easy to miss the apartments in the background. That complex was her horizon, the promise of something better, a real home, but it would never take her too far from the past to forget.

The girl's white knee socks had no holes. Her skirt had no stains—it was crisply pressed and well-fitted. "Look at what Austria is doing for these displaced people," the photograph said. Mucki wore new shoes, a warm cable-knit sweater stylishly rolled up at the wrists. And did you see the pristine handles on her doll's wheeled basket?

The Austrian government built the apartment complex in the mid-fifties.

Before that, Haid was a displaced persons camp for families expelled from Yugoslavia, Romania, Poland, Hungary, and Czechoslovakia. Alongside Swabians, it housed Jews displaced from Poland and anti-communist dissidents from what was left of Hungary. All the barracks were made of wood except the one Opa had lived in for six years with his parents and his grandfather. Because my great-grandfather had been elected superintendent of the camp, the Glas family were given the singular stone barrack. Opa's father put doors on the latrines, fixed leaks in the wooden rooms, and made better the refugees' meager homes.

One of the wooden rooms was a mess hall where my great-grandmother served small meals to other refugees. There was a field west of the camp that displaced children used for playing handball. I always hated the term, displaced persons. It sounded like people who just happened to find themselves without a home. It didn't sound like a term for people who fled their country to escape dying of starvation or typhus in a much worse kind of camp.

There was a small park beside the apartment complex, with wood and concrete benches from which all the planks had been stolen or else never fitted. Stones were spread across the ground in a disconnected path through the grass. I searched the earth for signs of old barracks.

"Look," David said and pointed toward the overgrowth at the border of the park.

Behind a spread of dried grass: stone after stone, stacked with precision and no mortar.

I crossed through the mud and knelt to look closer. I pressed my hands against the stone. If this had been the barrack, in Opa's last years in Austria, after the Allies had established an education system for the refugees, he would have walked from this spot to catch a train uphill to school. A train so slow, he used to say, he could get off while it was moving and pick wildflowers from the fields beside the tracks. He could fill his arms with spring blossoms and jump back inside the car without having to catch his breath. And he could give his harvest to every pretty girl on the train before the engine crested the hill.

Then there were the things Opa didn't tell me until I asked, just before he died: the flight from Serbia that brought him to Haid, having to work the fields when he was fourteen because the local schools wouldn't accept refugees, being abducted.

"Was it here?" I asked, feeling the curves and edges of the wall with my palms.

"It's possible," David said. His voice came out softer than normal, as if he was nervous to disappoint me. I looked at the government housing behind him and tried to place it in Mucki's newspaper photograph. Not that her position would have made a difference. The photographs that existed of the camp showed nothing that might've told me where the stone barrack had stood.

"It's a foundation-shaped structure, next to the right building, so that's promising," he said, squinting. "I don't want to disappoint you, but it could be anything. The barracks could have been on the other side of the building. The stone barrack could have been removed altogether. It's impossible to know."

"There are houses on the other side of the complex. Do they look like they were built before the war?"

"I don't know. They don't look much older than that, if they were."

I pulled my hands away from the wall and glanced over my shoulder at David. His face was uncertain. He looked displaced, as if the sky had just sucked him up from his fluorescent office and dropped him there.

Assuming he had a fluorescent office. It was hard to picture his life outside of us.

Behind him, in the window of one of the apartments, a woman watched. She stood between two curtains with her arms hanging loose at her sides, mouth open. If I asked her which side of her apartment the camp had been on, I wonder if she'd have known. Over sixty years had passed since the barracks became apartments, but she looked displaced too.

BELGRADE, SERBIA: 2012

DAVID AND I TOOK the night train to Belgrade. The only non-smoking car was first class, and aside from the two of us, a young mother, and her toddler, the car was empty. The little girl knelt on her mother's lap by the window and pressed her hands against the glass. Her grandmother was on the platform making faces. She was the most beautiful grandmother I'd ever seen. Her eyes, somewhere between blue and brown, were almost purple, her gray hair was pulled back in a loose French twist, and her lips were full. She smiled as if she'd never had more joy in her life than in that moment. But while she smiled to keep her granddaughter pressed to the glass, the edges and corners of her eyes were stained pink with tears.

David and I leaned toward each other over the arm rest. He told me he was thankful Serbian Railways had a non-smoking car. He had probably expected first class to provide free booze and leg room like the Eurostar from London to Paris. On Serbian Railways, the train conductor doubled as the waiter in the dining car, and instead of checking tickets, he sat at a table with the chef, several bottles of beer, and schnitzel. When I walked back to the dining car to buy a glass of wine, the conductor said something in Serbian and handed me a menu stained with tomatoes and grease. The menu was printed in three languages: German, Hungarian, and Serbo-Croatian. I pointed to the word "Rot" and held up two fingers. He filled two plastic cups with red wine. Sediment stuck to the ridges.

After David and I emptied and tucked our red-stained cups into the seat pockets, I squeezed my ankles through the six-inch space between the two empty seats in front of us and leaned back against the fake leather seatback that didn't recline. David talked about

couchettes, about sleeper rooms, about the Orient Express and how
his mother had always wanted to travel from the North of England
to the Far East. He told me about old trains with fine dining cars
and beds during the days when the British Empire was in its prime.

He talked about his grandfather building steam trains until he
died. One second I heard him saying something about touching
iron wheels when he was five, and the next he was musing on the
disgrace of the modern train system in the UK. I was hungry for
the details of David's life, what he thought and felt and the stories
that made him. But the night train was hypnotic. I closed my eyes
while I listened to David's voice and the gentle creak of our car
rocking on the tracks.

When I opened my eyes, I was standing in the middle of a fluorescent white room. The white light came from rectangles in an
office ceiling. A drafting desk was pushed against a window that
had nothing outside it. Sheets of paper the size of carpets and covered in eraser flakes filled the desktop, along with a heap of steel
compasses, over-sharpened pencils, and L-shaped straight edges.

A woman leaned against the desk. She looked like a woman in
a drawing I'd seen. Her heel hovered over the pedal that could tilt
the desktop and make everything fall. She didn't smile, but her
face was kind. Her cheeks were warm pink and her eyes welcomed me. I knew who she was, though I'd never seen her.
Rosalinde knew how to lean against the desk and make her hips
look full, her waist thin. Her pencil skirt was covered in wood and
graphite shavings, flecks of yellow paint.

She piled needle-sharp pencils into a pyramid on the desk. She
looked as if she was waiting for my grandfather to come home.
As if his architecture office, where they'd meet before running off
to spend evenings together, was more of a home than his house
on Anita Drive. As if Rosalinde was where he belonged.

I woke up with the back of my head on the window. Conden-
sation from the glass had dampened my hair.

I sat up when I saw the uniforms.

A man in navy blue reached his arm over David and held his
hand out.

"We're at the Serbian border," David said quietly.

"Oh, sorry," I said to the man, but his expression didn't change. I reached into my purse and handed him my passport. David handed him his. The border guard gave mine to a uniformed woman standing beside him, a woman with dark hair and dark lipstick and eyebrows so shiny and thin they looked like they'd been painted on with nail polish. Her fingernails were purple and yellow and silver with a rhinestone on each. Each nail was at least two inches long, and she struggled to flip the pages of my passport. She laughed, and I had a feeling her laugh said, "She's in for a surprise, this one."

The man with David's passport had a different face.

The plastic film over David's ID page had started to peel away from the paper because he traveled so much for business, enough that the border guard walked off the train with the passport and an angry look on his face.

"He can't do that! My passport is legal. I'm a British citizen. I'm allowed to travel without let or hindrance—" I'd never heard David get angry before, and I was still waking up.

"It's fine," I said. "We're not going anywhere until you get it back."

My words made his brow furrow.

"It's fine for you. Your passport's right there." He motioned to the guard across the aisle. If her nail polish eyebrows could have moved, she'd have been scowling. "I'm not getting stuck in Serbia."

"Don't you think you're overreacting a little?"

"No, I don't think I'm overreacting. They could be stealing my passport. And if they steal my passport, I won't be able to leave the country."

"A border guard isn't going to steal your passport, David."

"They could put me in prison."

"Why would they do that?"

"If they think it's a forgery, if they think my passport is fraudulent. That's what this is, isn't it? That's why they've taken it." He was shaking.

"But it's not a forgery. Right?"

"Of course it's not a forgery."

The sky outside the window was dark. The light on the platform was so dim the station was hard to see. The mother and daughter still sat half a dozen rows ahead of us, almost at the front of the car. The little girl slept. I saw her ponytail through the space between the seats, hanging in the middle of her chair and her mother's. She rested her tiny cheekbone against the arm rest. I hoped there was a pillow or a blanket or a mother's arm I couldn't see to keep her smooth skin off the hard plastic.

I didn't recognize David in his panic. I'd only ever seen him measured and composed, wearing confidence and charm in his expression. When had his unease begun? When the trip began? Since we left Austria? Or had it always been there, simmering under the lid of his smile?

The border guard walked back inside the car and handed David his passport.

"So what was that about?" David asked. He meant his voice to sound severe, but it came out anxious. His forehead flushed red, and his nose. The guard didn't look at David, or say a word. He motioned to the other guard, who rubbed her lips together to even out her lipstick, stamped and handed me my passport, and followed him off the train.

"Hey!" David shouted. "I don't have a stamp!"

He ran to the open door at the back of the car and leaned out over the platform.

"I don't have a stamp!"

"UK. No stamp."

Something in my brain clicked: the guards were speaking Hungarian. And if they were speaking Hungarian, we were leaving Hungary, an EU country, not entering Serbia. David didn't need a stamp until the next passport check. Yet there he was, leaning out of the train waving his arms like an American who'd never been abroad. I opened my passport to the page the woman marked and looked at the ink. *Ungarn*. Hungary.

For the first time I understood: for all his talk about adventure and seeing the world, David didn't want to take me outside Central Europe. Austria was far enough. He wanted to take me to Paris or Venice or Rome, places with stamps that Eastern Europeans laughed at on American passports. I was afraid of cursed earth, afraid it wouldn't look any different than good earth. He was afraid of losing control.

The lobby windows at the Hotel Queen Victoria looked out on a concrete building full of closed junk shops. The receptionist was beautiful and spoke perfect English because no one from Serbia stayed there. Her nametag read Radojka, and when we checked in she told us that it was Orthodox Christmas Eve.

Nothing in Belgrade would be open, save the fortress and a few restaurants scattered across the city. But the Hotel Queen Victoria, Radojka assured us, had a great restaurant and would be available for all of our needs.

Our room looked like something out of an old movie, white walls with swathes of mint-colored fabric inside panel molding, a white desk with curved legs and metallic accents, a throw pillow with a gigantic embroidered "V" on the front. The carpet was only slightly darker than the mint on the walls, with a gold braid pattern framing the bed. And a matching brass chandelier cast strange shadows on the floor. In the bathroom, the shower looked more like a teleportation capsule than something to bathe in, with at least a dozen jets that didn't work and a curved sliding door that stuck open.

Outside our window, bus brakes echoed between buildings.

"They sound like whales," I said, pressing my ear to the glass.

Belgrade was an ocean of gray: semi-modern buildings with tinted windows, dingy sidewalks, streets without lines painted down the center. An office building on one corner had a giant gash in its side and jagged edges made of steel and concrete. It wasn't the only one. Buildings with missing pieces hid beside homes and offices with intact facades, with blackened plaster and rubble still strewn through the inside. We passed one with only an iron gate for a front door. Looking in, you could see over a pile of rubble right out the back window. The stairs were intact, but the railing was broken, lying in snowdrift heaps of dust on the floor.

I considered the possibility of asbestos and lifted my scarf to my mouth.

"If it's Christmas, how are we getting to Gašinci and back tomorrow?" I asked.

"Ah," David said, squeezing my hand. "I called the rental car office about picking up our car. The woman on the phone recommended not driving into Croatia. She said it might get vandalized. If something happens, they won't cover the damage."

I stared at him.

"I also read that there are still pockets of mines on unpaved roads near the border."

"Why didn't you say something sooner?" I asked, letting go of his hand.

David adjusted his posture and looked at me. His eyes were as opaque as the concrete office buildings, the ones that hadn't been blown up.

"At first I thought maybe we'd go anyway."

"You didn't think it was something we should discuss?"

"We're discussing it now."

"And?"

"And if everything is closed for the holiday, it'll be even less safe," he said, snatching my hand out of the cold.

"But we're here," I said. "We didn't come to stay in Belgrade."

It was bad enough that I couldn't find Oma's refugee camp in Linz.

I was going to miss her village, her whole home country. It was hard enough figuring out which village was hers. By the time I'd asked her to spell it, she'd forgotten how. I spent months thinking her village was Čačinci until I realized the histories didn't match. I listened to a computer pronounce the name. Cha-Chin-See. Oma had always said Cah-Shin-See. At least I thought she had. What she was really saying was Gah-Shin-See. Gašinci.

Even before I left Philadelphia, I almost got her life all wrong.

But what was the point of coming all this way if we left her story out? The farmhouse she'd talked about so often. The rabbit hutches. Her aunt's house down the street. The school she went to. The road she found a body on. The trees in the yard. The color of their bark. The size of the stones in the road. The smell of the air: wood smoke, manure, ice?

Every destination on our itinerary was in Serbia except for Gašinci and the old camp at Valpovo—where typhus was so deadly that planes dropped DDT to stop it from spreading.

I knew the whole region belonged to both of my grandparents, that Opa's Serbia and Oma's Croatia were both part of the same empire when their families immigrated, and that both became Yugoslavia just before they were born. But I could picture the disappointment on Oma's face if she knew we'd skipped Croatia. She would have wanted me to see the street where her childhood ended. And I wanted to come home to her at Bayside and say, "I went to Gašinci. I saw your home. There are no rabbits in the yard, but the ash trees are the same and the air smells of cold earth and iron—and something sharp, like an oven full of pickled cabbage."

"I'll take you another time," he said, bringing the backs of my fingers to his lips. "I promise. We'll come in summer and drive along the coast with the roof down. Swim in the sea and stay in Dubrovnik and take a day trip to Gašinci."

"A day trip? Gašinci is half a day's drive from Dubrovnik, David."

"I know it's important to you. But should something happen, no one will be there to see. There'll be nowhere to go," he said.

"Who would be out throwing rocks at cars on Christmas?" I didn't want to make a decision based on fear.

"I don't know. I just think maybe we shouldn't risk it."

"I don't want to lose this," I said. "It can't be that bad, can it?" I pushed my hands into my pockets. I had no power—it all belonged to David. David who was kind and generous. David who couldn't bear unknowns.

"Why did you bother bringing me here if you were going to turn around and take half of it away?" I said. The burn of tears blurred my vision.

"That's not fair," he said.

"Maybe," I said, as calmly as I could. "But what do you want me to say?"

"We'll come back. I promise."

It wasn't a promise for keeping.

"Maybe I'll go on my own, then," I said.

"You wouldn't," he replied. And it was true. He hadn't taken my agency. I was free to go on my own, free to be a solitary woman traveling through a country whose language I didn't speak, a country that expelled or exterminated people like me only a handful of decades earlier. Not that anything like that would happen now. The modern world seemed so much safer. Even the war in the nineties seemed a long time ago. As if we progress as humans and become incapable of the atrocities we committed in the past. As if we learn from our histories. It was naïve to believe that anywhere was safe. Maybe David knew that, too. Maybe he knew it better than I did. And what if I talked him into going and something bad did happen, what if we hit a mine on the edge of a field? It would be my fault. The blood on the grass would be festive: Christmas crimson and green. And Oma, from her wheelchair in Bayside, the nurses would tell her and she would mumble: The air never smelled like cabbage. It smelled like potato dumplings. And where was her granddaughter's spine? Did they find it with the remains or had it already been lost?

From street level, the fortress looked like a small garden of topiaries with a statue of Tito and a stone wall atop a steep hill.

Inside, the fortress was the size of a town. Stray dogs ran up and shoved their wet noses into our palms, hoping a pat on the head would lead to food. There were loners, too. Solitary men in red knit hats sat on park benches looking over the Danube, an old man sold painted eggs at the iron portcullis—hollow shells slathered in orthodox crosses and lopsided holy mothers. A dog with mange lay in the shade, and one with a missing leg basked like a cat in the sunshine. David and I sat on a bench beside a man selling Tito hats and former Yugoslavia flags.

Another man, younger, his face shadowed by a brimmed hat, sat down on the bench opposite us. He looked up a lot, when he wasn't staring into his lap. It made me feel like David and I were doing something wrong. David had wrapped his left arm around my waist, pulled me tight to his side. He pressed his lips to my neck when he spoke, whispering things like, "You're everything," and "I wish you were wearing a skirt."

But the man on the bench opposite couldn't hear David. I wondered if he was close enough to see the way David looked at me, the way David's eyebrows lifted and his eyelids drooped a little. The way his pupils dilated and his irises contracted like a camera lens. To see the gold and green lines that ran through the hazel like pen lines on a lie detector. When David looked into my eyes, I didn't think he could tell I was thinking of my absent husband, of my grandmother's disappointment, that the man on the bench opposite was putting me on edge, that when I looked back into David's eyes I had questions.

What else did I know about him, aside from the person he seemed to be? I knew that he needed to feel in control. He called off Croatia without discussion, like the decision was his to make. And the train from Vienna to Belgrade scared me—the red forehead, the pitchy voice, the way he leaned out of the car as if nothing unnerving should ever happen to him. But he was also a man who'd fallen in love with a married woman.

I knew he was from a village I'd never heard of in the north of England, a place I imagined to be made of thatched cottages with casement windows that opened onto unkempt gardens and birdsong. I knew he had both of his parents. A brother. That he was reaching for something more, something bigger. I knew he worked out because those pectoral muscles didn't just happen. He didn't talk about work except where it took him, and to say that he would be in breach of contracts and clearances to tell me anything more than, "I am a defense consultant."

"What is a defense consultant?" I'd asked.

"I solve defense-related issues for companies and organizations."

"Are you an arms dealer?"

He'd laughed out loud when I asked that.

"Jesus, really? No, I am not an arms dealer."

"Are you in intelligence?"

"I'm not involved in anything that exciting. There are just confidentiality clauses in my contract. I could tell you if you were my wife, but—"

But I was someone else's wife.

The man on the bench opposite us stood up. I noticed, but pretended not to. I focused on the constant noise of city dogs howling. He walked in our direction. I put my hand on David's knee and stared at the crisscrossing weave of his jeans.

"Zdravo," the man from the bench said, and continued in Serbo-Croatian. The only words I knew were *zdravo, hvala*, and *živeli*. Hello, thank you, cheers. Though I knew I had to make eye contact when toasting rakija. I wasn't used to making eye contact with strangers.

"English?" David asked, and the man's eyes opened wide into a smile. He pushed a small notebook into our hands and told us he was an artist and had been drawing. He pointed at his notebook. On the top page: a sketch of both of our faces in profile. David looked like himself, stubbled and British. My face on the page looked sadder than I'd like, and my nose was too pointed, lips too full. When I looked at David in this stranger's notebook, he looked like he belonged somewhere else. When I looked at myself, I saw Vojvodina in my face.

EMMA FLEISCHER:
ČAČINCI, YUGOSLAVIA: 1944

THE CARPENTERS OF ČAČINCI pushed wheelbarrows down dirt roads toward unfinished houses. The mothers and grandmothers of Čačinci walked to the market to buy flour and plums for dumplings. Schoolchildren from outside the village center walked their mile and a half home from school alone—girls flipping ink-stained braids against their dress backs while boys lagged behind with grins and smudged fingertips.

In the afternoon, a vegetable cart set up outside the grocer's toppled over, and the onions rolled like single-file soldiers across the street. At five o'clock mass, a wind knocked two brass candlesticks off the altar of the Catholic Church. The few men and women kneeling in pews jumped midway through their prayers. An old nun heard the sound ring in the nave like a warning bell.

All night the wind whistled in window panes and sighed in the eaves of houses. And in the days after, the streets became less traveled. Mothers and children still walked to the church and the schoolhouse and the market. Horse-drawn carts still sidled down the wider lanes, leaving reddish dust clouds in their wake. But the men were disappearing. By the second of October, 1943, even the priest and schoolteacher had gone.

Ten-year-old Emma Fleischer sat on her mother's bed as evening began to settle over their small home on the outskirts of Čačinci. Emma looked down at her mother's collection of Virgin statuettes and sculpted patron saints on the nightstand. Their painted halos blazed around beautiful sad faces. Aunt Anna called for Emma to join the other women in the living room of their one-story home. The dogs lay still on the earthen floor, wondering where their master was. Emma's father had been gone since Thursday night, but she'd heard her aunt say that Mr. Wilheim and Mr. Kreutzer were staying home where they belonged. She said that surely her husband Karl would have stayed home too if he was still alive. Aunt Anna talked about Uncle Karl so often it was hard for Emma to remember he was dead. Once Emma walked in on her aunt in the kitchen and heard her say, "Where's my goddamn handkerchief, Karl?"

It'd only been eight months since Anna moved in with the family, but she had already taken the role of matriarch from Emma's mother. It was Aunt Anna that Emma took walks with to the mill, Aunt Anna who scolded her for being so easily distracted, and that afternoon it was Aunt Anna who gathered three generations of Marzluft women around her on a rug to play a children's game.

"Everyone sits close together except for one, the fox," Anna said, poking Katie softly on the nose. "The fox takes her dolly and sings the rhyme while she walks around and around the circle. When the song is over, she drops her dolly behind whoever she wants, and then that person becomes the new fox and tries to catch the old fox before she can sit in the new fox's seat. Just make sure you stick to running around the circle, girls. No running off into the kitchen."

Emma was annoyed at having to listen to Aunt Anna repeat such obvious rules, even though she knew they were for six-year-old Katie—who was already running in circles, singing "The Fox Goes Around" over and over while flapping her arms.

Emma looked out the window, past the road and the field across the street, to where the woods began, and she thought she heard the forest breathing. She closed her eyes and imagined tree roots lifting out of the dry earth and dragging forward, branches leaning in toward the village center, leaves whispering along with Katie's song, "There's a clever animal round here somewhere. Look behind you!"

Katie dropped her burlap doll behind Emma and squealed as she started running the other direction. But instead of jumping up and chasing Katie the Fox, Emma threw the doll back at her sister and told her to shut up. Katie started to cry.

"Emma, what's the matter with you?" Aunt Anna shouted, pointing at her with a crochet hook. Marzluft Oma pulled Katie into her lap. Mother sat cross-legged and still, as if listening to the distance.

"I'm going outside," Emma said.

"Not so fast." Aunt Anna pointed her hook again. "Milk Margerite while you're out there, young lady. And stay close to the house!"

The door shuddered on its hinges when it shut.

In the lean-to, where the cow was tethered, Emma stroked Margerite's face, relishing her velvet nose. The cow pressed her thick lips against Emma's palm and smacked a fly off her back with her tail. Emma pulled two buckets out of the grass and flipped one over to use as a seat. As soon as Margerite heard the familiar clang of steel, she shifted herself toward Emma and groaned with the weight of her milk.

"At least you're sweet to me," Emma said.

She placed the other bucket beneath the cow and ran her fingertips over the flank and down the udder. Smooth as a baby's backside, her father always said, but Emma thought Margerite's udder felt more like her nose.

The warm milk hissed against the bottom of the bucket—a comforting noise. Margerite shifted her weight from side to side and smacked another fly. When the bucket was full, Emma slid it out from beneath the cow, careful not to spill, and carried it over to the icebox behind the house. She opened the latch and let the door fall open. The icebox was empty apart from the morning's milk bucket and a mostly-melted block of ice—Mr. Geiger, the ice man, hadn't come since Wednesday. Maybe he had gone too. She switched the cold ice bucket for the fresh warm one and carried the chilled milk back to her seat. With her bare toes pressed into the dirt, she ran a hand along Margerite's side—against the grain—focusing on the sound of her fingers passing over hundreds of stiff, short hairs.

Emma peered into the cold milk bucket, gave it a little kick to set the contents rippling. A two-inch layer of cream had settled on top, thick and the color of sweet butter. She wasn't hungry, but her stomach felt hollow. She smelled burning and looked toward the other side of the village. The streets were filled with people again. Smoke hung in the air like dust.

Inside, Aunt Anna was singing over Katie's laughter.

"There's a clever animal round here somewhere. Look behind you!"

Emma cupped her hands and dipped them into the bucket, catching cream in her palms. She brought the cream to her lips and tilted her hands to let the heavy liquid slide into her open mouth and roll down her chin. She thought of the ice man and dipped her hand back into the bucket, drank again. She wondered why all the men had gone. She'd heard the schoolteacher say something about Partisans coming, but she didn't know what Partisans were. The word made her think of skinny night beasts with sharp teeth and lots of hair. She slurped another palmful of cream. Maybe the Partisans looked like upright foxes in people clothes. She swallowed two more helpings from the bucket. Out of breath and sick to her stomach, she slumped against Margerite's front leg. Maybe the Partisans were trees that came to life and whistled along to nursery rhymes. Her mouth hung open. Her whole chin was wet below her lips.

The smoke was thicker and coming closer, a dark mass unfurling over the street. The sun had almost set in the west, but in the east, Čačinci glowed red as if a second sun were rising.

"Emma," her mother called from the kitchen window. "Get inside. Hurry."

Emma stood and wiped the cream from her face with the back of her sleeve, frowning at the wet streak on the cotton. She patted the crown of Margerite's head and kissed the cow on the nose. "I wish I could bring you inside."

Grabbing the bucket full of cold milk, she hurried to the door, shuffling her feet to keep the contents from sloshing into the dirt. Mother, Aunt Anna, Marzluft Oma, and even little Katie had stopped singing and had tucked themselves behind the woodstove. Emma bent to place the milk on the kitchen floor when a sharp bang ripped through the stillness and set the dogs barking. She let the bucket slip and a tiny wave of milk breached the rim and slid down the metal.

"Is someone at the door?"

"Not yet, my little angel," Marzluft Oma said.

Emma curled up in the middle of the circle of women and hugged her knees to her chest. She counted two more bangs, duller than the first, before someone kicked open the front door. The dogs leapt full of teeth and snarls at the strangers in the threshold. A few shots and the dogs went too-still and silent on the floor. Katie started crying as three men entered carrying rifles and speaking Serbian. They wore mismatched uniforms and small dirty hats that made Emma think of butcher's caps. The closest man to Emma was tall and wore pants that belonged to a shorter man. Another had a face like a bulldog. The third was crisply ironed and well-groomed. He'd even found time to wax his moustache.

"Where are your husbands?"

"My husband is not home," Mother said in a hushed voice. "Search the house. You won't find him."

"And yours?" The dog-faced man bent over Aunt Anna and brushed his knuckles over her cheek.

"Dead," Marzluft Oma said from her spot behind the wood-stove.

The tall man walked toward Emma and smiled. "What a beautiful child."

Aunt Anna pulled her niece away from the tall man. He raised a skinny eyebrow, tapped his hand on his rifle's magazine, and crouched down to face Emma. So this is what a Partisan looks like, she thought. His breath smelled sour like fish. She felt a lurch in her stomach. She shouldn't have drunk so much. "Now how about you tell me your name, sweetheart?"

Emma vomited the bucketful of cream onto the tall man's field coat and shoes.

"Pavo scared the German piglet!" The dog-faced man said, laughing so his great belly shook.

"Big strong man you are, picking on the piglets before you take the sows." The man with the moustache ran the tip of his tongue across his lips and stared at Aunt Anna's crossed ankles.

"Careful, Pavo," the dog-faced man scowled. "They're probably rabid."

Pavo gripped his rifle and stood up, bumping Emma's cheek with the butt of his gun.

"Enough," Aunt Anna said as Emma bit her lip and tried not to cry.

"I think the lady's right, gentlemen." The man with the moustache turned around and picked a pitcher off the kitchen counter, measured its weight in his hands. "Nice," he said before dropping it to the floor. Shards of broken glass leapt into the milk bucket.

The Partisans moved around the house, breaking plates and opening cabinets, knocking on walls for hints of hollow hiding spaces. Pavo checked inside the oven. The dog-faced man tore apart the bed sheets and urinated on the pillows. The man with the moustache tapped his gun barrel against the floor. The three men together ransacked Mother's jewelry box. There wasn't much inside, but they tore two sets of silver prayer beads into three equal shares and put them in their pockets.

The man with the moustache put his hand on Anna's neck and pulled her to her feet.

"What has your precious Virgin done for you this evening?" he said.

Anna flinched as he cradled the back of her head in his palm and kissed her, forcing his tongue between her lips. The two other men wolf-whistled.

When he pulled away, there were tears on Aunt Anna's face. Her cheeks were red and she stared off into the corner where the dogs had been lying.

"I think it's time for the rest of you ladies to leave," the man with the moustache said.

"Anna." Marzluft Oma stood and balanced Katie on her hip. She grabbed Mother by the hand and helped her up. "Hold onto your mother, Emma. Come on, Anna. There's nothing here for us tonight."

"She stays." The man with the moustache held tight to the back of Aunt Anna's neck.

Marzluft Oma turned to argue, but the dog-faced man pointed his rifle at her back. The tall man held his gun barrel behind Mother's head. Mother squeezed Emma's hand and looked over at her brother's widow. "I'm sorry, Anna," she said. Anna said nothing, nodded.

The tall man and the dog-faced man marched Mother, Marzluft Oma, and the children out of the house. Emma turned to look at her aunt between the two soldiers and their guns, and saw the man with the moustache reaching his hand up her skirt.

The sky was dark as they made the march toward town. Emma held Mother's hand and watched other women and children and Partisans with guns join them in the street. Mrs. Kreutzer had a bruise swelling on her cheek, and she saw Trudi from class walking barefoot in the dirt and stone. Her feet were cut and bloody. Emma looked down at the dust her own feet kicked up and tried not to listen to the sounds of breaking kitchenware, cracking doors, and rifle shots. The Partisans stopped the march in the center of town at the lawn beside the German Community Center. Mothers, grandmothers, and children filed into the square where carts full of cabbages, beets, and peppers usually stood. Mr. Wilheim and Mr. Kreutzer's families were huddled in a thin patch of grass beside the Marzlufts, and Emma overheard Mrs. Kreutzer say that her husband and Mr. Wilheim had been taken by a troupe of Partisans into the forest, along with a dozen other German men who had decided to stay with their families.

A woman Emma didn't recognize whispered to Mother, "Please God our men are lucky and used as target practice. Or lined up and shot by firing squad. I heard the Partisans in Sissek cut living men's stomachs open and ripped their intestines out."

"Hush, Theresa," Marzluft Oma said. Mother's face had turned the color of milk. Emma heard Mrs. Wilheim sob as little Betty Kreutzer and Katie pulled blades of yellowed grass out of the earth. The women were still talking, but Emma didn't understand much of what they said. Seeing her mother's face so white made her stomach lurch again. She wondered where her father was.

The Partisans set fire to the buildings surrounding the square and the Community Center, including the town hall and the train station, Schiller's store and the schoolhouse, and all the houses in between. While the village blazed, Emma drifted in and out of sleep in her mother's lap. She had a hard time separating the fire from her nightmares: they all seemed the same.

She woke in the middle of the night as a handful of Partisans threw burning wood through the windows of the Community Center, and roaring flames began to drown out the noise of crying toddlers. Emma watched as pillars of smoke rose from the building and the two dozen houses and blackened the stars. The heat coming off the burning plaster and wood made the ground hot. It should have been cold outside, but Emma and the others huddled in the yard didn't need blankets or coats—not that the Partisans would have let them bring any. Half of the children's feet were bare and torn up like Trudi's. Emma's sweat had soaked through the armpits and the back of her shirt. Marzluft Oma's forehead dripped onto her chest as she brushed through Katie's tangled hair with her fingertips. Katie didn't protest, instead she stretched out on the ground like she was making a snow angel.

Emma adjusted herself in Mother's lap and closed her eyes.

The next time she woke up, the sun was blurred and low in the sky. The air was cold. Her face was damp and stuck to the grass. At some point, Mother must have slid herself out from under her.

Last night's fire had burned itself to glowing coals—all that was left of the houses. Emma could barely make out the outline of her family through the cloud settling over Čačinci. Mother and Marzluft Oma were sitting back to back with their eyes closed as if they'd fallen asleep keeping watch. But the Partisans had disappeared with the night. Katie was sleeping tangled with little Betty Kreutzer. Mrs. Kreutzer and Mrs. Wilheim were leaning on each other's smoky silhouettes and sobbing. There was no sign of Aunt Anna.

Emma stood up and walked into the street, rubbing at her goose pimpled arms.

She thought maybe the man with the moustache had let Aunt Anna stay at home and wash the dog-faced man's pee off the sheets. As she walked, she avoided the shadows of inside-out houses. The ones that hadn't been burned down had vomited their contents into front yards. There were busted couches, broken box springs, heaps of clothes and towels dumped out of dresser drawers. Suitcases. Kitchen tables. Pots and Pans. Jellied pigs knuckles in mason jars. Milk buckets.

There's a clever animal round here somewhere.

When she got near her house, she saw Margerite still tethered in the backyard, but her udder looked withered, like she'd been milked too much. Emma rushed to her cow over the foggy drainage ditch and tripped on a log—a soft and rotten log. She licked her palms and rubbed at the grass stains on her skirt. Then she noticed that the log she'd tripped over was wearing a dress. The skirt had been pulled up above two dark stained legs. The fabric was pulled all the way up to where a belly would be if it there wasn't too much dirt and fog to tell. Emma moved closer. She saw arms that were bent too far, swollen fingers, and then Aunt Anna's face.

She had no eyes.

Her shirt was torn open in the front and her chest was covered in the same dark stain that had spread to her legs and arms and made her look like a tree trunk. Someone had cut off her breasts.

Emma's mouth filled with burning.

Sunlight split the clouds and lit a patch of grass behind Aunt Anna. Emma saw a beautiful woman with downcast eyes like the saints on her mother's nightstand. The woman's body was backlit by the sun and glowed as if made of colored glass. In her arms, held out toward Emma, was Mother's silver platter with Aunt Anna's two ample breasts arranged on top, her nipples pointing straight to heaven. Emma stared at the bloody plate and back into the woman's face. But her face was no longer downcast and beautiful. It was Aunt Anna's face with no eyes screaming *look behind you.*

THE E-75, SERBIA: 2012

ON ORTHODOX CHRISTMAS MORNING, we were handed the keys to a beat-up Chevy Spark. The interior smelled like someone had smoked enough cigarettes inside to suffocate an elephant, and one of the rear tires was flat. The rental agent prodded the tread with his knuckles and said it was fine.

As we left Belgrade for Novi Sad, I imagined Oma's village disappearing in the rearview. Even if we went to Gašinci and I brought a photo back to show her, she probably wouldn't recognize it. But I wondered. I'd seen Alzheimer's patients at Bayside lost in their early memories after all the rest had gone. One patient waited every morning by the nurse's station for a bus that would never come. Another cried for a child she gave up when she was fifteen. "Do you have children?" she asked every woman. "Have you seen my baby?" Still another shouted over and over, "Daddy. Daddy!" until her voice grew hoarse.

I pulled out the sketch of David and me, held it between my fingers—carefully because the page was thin and I was afraid of tearing it. The artist had ripped the page out of his notebook and the top edge was jagged.

He'd scrawled his name diagonally across the bottom.

The letters were nearly as illegible as Oma's had been before the Alzheimer's.

When I was a teenager, I would lie in the grass on summer afternoons with her drug store paperbacks, her craggy signature scrawled on the inside covers. While I read, Opa lounged in a patio chair, shaded by a yellow umbrella. Oma watered her crepe myrtles and plucked tomatoes, herbs, and potted strawberries with chemical-blue dishwashing gloves.

Except Sundays. Summer Sundays meant Chinese takeout. Every week, they ordered the same things: chicken and broccoli for her, lemon chicken for him. With fried rice, an egg roll, and crispy noodles in duck sauce. They'd order me shrimp lo mein and wonton soup, and we'd sit at the old dining room table with the windows thrown wide open. The table's surface had grown soft enough I could have carved my name into it with a butter knife. Instead I pressed half-moons into the wood with my fingernails.

"General Lafayette ate at this table," Opa told new dinner guests, as if owning a piece of American history made him less of an outsider. The time he told Sid, he added, "Right after he was stabbed in the leg at the Battle of Brandywine."

He pronounced it "Brandyvine," with a rolled "r."

He said the former owners also had a sofa with Lafayette's bloodstain.

The sofa had never been sheathed in plastic, Opa said. The family who owned it sat on it, slept on it, let their children play on the eggplant-colored stain. I pictured generations of mothers breastfeeding on the dark spot, children napping, drooling lips-down on the ruined fabric.

I pictured Opa reclining against the stain, resting a towering stein of room-temperature Miller High Life on his knee. I imagined it would have made him feel closer to his adopted country. *Look, Puddin', this is a piece of American History*, he said, all slathered in his never-fading Swabianness. A televised soccer match cast a gangrenous glow over the upholstery and his polyester robe, his "Number 1 Lover" necklace cooling his skin. The dead smell of the sofa mingled with the yeasty tang of warm beer as he dozed, as Oma washed the dishes, left his slippers by his feet, and went to bed without him.

They slept in twin beds with a nightstand between them.

Sid and I might as well have done the same. On the rare occasions we shared our bed the way a husband and a wife were meant to, it was sad and gentle, as if we'd forgotten each other's bodies: his bare chest, shaggy blond hair, his always linty belly button; his small soft hands with fingers as thin as my own. He looked down at me while we made love, as if I was precious and delicate. I'd almost forgotten the slobbery way he kissed my ears because his thick lips always got in the way of his mouth. How his chin felt in my fingertips, how oily his cheeks felt under my palms. I remembered his full lips, his beautiful big teeth, so perfect they could have been in a toothpaste commercial. But after seven years of kisses, I couldn't remember his tongue. I couldn't remember him grasping me by the nape of my neck or by my hair like David did.

When we slept, David cradled my face between his chin and his collarbone. His arm held tight to my waist. Some nights I felt like I couldn't breathe. But I liked the way he suffocated me.

The first time we shared a bed, David checked us into an obscure bed and breakfast on Lafayette Avenue in Brooklyn. He was in New York for work. It was September. I hadn't seen him since we'd kissed in my apartment. There was only one door at the top of the stairs—he slid a heavy brass key into the lock and turned it. We stepped inside. I reached my fingers through the buttons of his shirt, felt the spread of hair on his chest, plucked the buttons from their holes one by one while his hands held me close. That first time, when I peeled the clothes off his airplane-sticky skin and kissed his shoulder blades, ribs, the smooth skin above his belly button, he didn't return my affection. He let me move my lips ever lower, let me examine every square inch of him, admire the definition in his belly, the V-shape that started at his hip bones and ended at the beautiful appendage standing erect between his legs. I touched it. I buried my face in the mass of curly hairs around it and breathed in chlorine and sweat and him: his whole body smelled like cedar, sweet pine, and salt.

Sid still slept beside me on weekends. We still took long walks at night to a street where the homeowners wrapped dozens of strings of white lights around the trunks and branches of the Sycamore trees lining the sidewalk. Sometimes the romance of string lights reflecting off warm brick walls made me believe that there was something left between us.

We'd tried to make love twice since I met David, but all that had come of it were tears, tears for how I couldn't make myself feel desire in Sid's arms. Tears for how I thought of David when I was in Sid's arms. Tears for an ending, for a terrifying beginning, for loneliness. In Sid's arms, I'd felt alone. It was hard to pinpoint when everything went empty.

David flipped me stomach-down onto the bed. He gripped my hair and pressed my face into unfamiliar pillows. We made noises like animals. When he finished, he dropped his whole weight on my back, his cheek on my cheek. His ear vacuumed to mine.

I told myself it would be impossible for him to want to hold me so close forever. I'd stopped wanting to hold Sid close. One day David would look at me and think, "I don't remember what her tongue tastes like. I can't recall the warmth of her. What happened to this thing that was once so beautiful and now seems so suddenly empty?"

We showered in the room's raining shower. I admired the details of his beauty: the point of his hairline at the back of his neck, the hair on his chest and lower stomach. The muscles at his shoulder blades. An awkward space between his big toes and his little toes that made the former reminiscent of turtles.

I kissed his neck and his lips and his ears and his chest, his shoulder blades, his belly button, the dimples on his lower back, the backside of his knees. Until we found ourselves kneeling on the sharp tile floor of the shower stall, kissing forgotten parts of ourselves.

We ordered Chinese takeout and sat on our balcony, admiring each other's skin in the late afternoon sun. The last of the summer's glutted bees hovered over a ramekin of duck sauce.

If Opa was still alive, I wondered if he would have sat with us. If his eyes would have told a story of love lost. If they would have told of Rosalinde's cancer, her death, the way he couldn't mourn her out loud because they were both married to someone else.

If, instead, they would have said it wasn't worth it, that it would have been better to stay true to misplaced promises. Because then, at least, when he died, his wife and granddaughter wouldn't have judged his mistakes when they found a shoebox filled with keepsakes from someone named Rosalinde. Because, in the end, he found a different kind of love: a kind that came from fifty years, from sharing himself with a woman who never cringed at ingrown toenails or feeding tubes, a woman who took care of him always, in every way she could.

Opa had a stroke two years before he died. He spoke the same after and his body didn't seem weaker. His motor functions were fine. Except he could no longer swallow. When he tried, he coughed instead. Cartons full of liquid food started showing up on the doorstep and a feeding tube appeared in his shirt pockets. We stopped eating Chinese takeout on summer Sundays. We couldn't eat it without him, just like we couldn't eat zwetschgenknödel or Oma's cherry cake—yellow sponge with canned cherries dropped into the batter like sweet, evenly-spaced bloodstains. Even after he died, we couldn't bring ourselves to eat it.

That afternoon on the balcony with David was the first time in years I'd eaten sweet chicken out of a white paper box. I mixed it up with fried rice and cut up egg roll, and said to David, "This is how my Opa ate it when we sat at Lafayette's table." He said, "What?" And I told him about the half-moons carved into the wood, about Sunday takeout, about the sofa the General had bled on, the noodles and duck sauce. David smiled and kissed me with hoisin lips. Everything tasted old and new, and I ate until there was nothing left but grease stains on the cardboard.

ELSA & LENZ BRUCH:
RURAL BATSCHKA, YUGOSLAVIA:
1945

LENZ SAT IN THE BEDROOM in his nightclothes as usual, having just finished lunch and gone back to work on his latest ship—a 1600's man-of-war with twelve aged paper sails, hand carved gun ports, and a polished walnut, workable rudder—when Elsa heard voices out front. She walked around the outside of the house with her leather gardening gloves balled into her fists and her skirt billowing like one of the sails of her husband's ships. When she saw the three uniformed men coming up the pathway to the front door, she ran to the bedroom window. Lenz was hunched over his skinny tweezers. She rapped her knuckle on the glass and waved her arms toward the stalls.

"Hide!" she mouthed.

He looked up, three pairs of glasses stacked on top of each other so he could see the tiny pieces he inserted into the bottles. The layered glass made him look like a dormouse.

The men knocked hard at the door.

"Good morning," Elsa said from the yard, rushing toward them, out of breath.

One of the men scrunched his eyebrows.

"Is your husband home, ma'am?" another of the soldiers asked.

"I haven't seen him," she said. "Should I tell him you stopped by?"

The men looked at her and said nothing, shifting their weight toward the long-barreled guns slung over their shoulders. One of them frowned at the tile mosaic above the door: the Virgin Mary smiled at Saint Francis of Assisi, who gazed lovingly at a deer that looked more like a goat. Saint Francis's bleeding hands reached out to a flock of wood pigeons.

"Mind if we come inside?"

The oldest soldier shoved past Elsa and reached for the door-knob. He couldn't have been more than twenty-five. She looked closer at the other two. The youngest couldn't have been more than seventeen. They all had baby faces: smooth shaven, unwrinkled, pale as fine china.

The oldest soldier led the way, cracking his head on a bottled ship dangling from the kitchen rafters. It was fat and bottom-heavy like a pot.

"Ouch," the soldier said, rubbing the back of his head.

"They're everywhere," one of the others said. "Look."

Lenz's ships were strewn around the house: some hung from the rafters, others were mounted on the walls, others still sat beneath end tables and cluttered in corners.

A letter had come for him, early in the war: he was required to appear at the village hall for drafting and inspection. In a fortunate accident, their goat had thrown a tantrum. When Lenz's inspection date came, he had a bandaged foot, two broken ribs, and his left arm in a cast. The Sergeant turned him away.

Elsa stood in the hallway while the soldiers searched the bedroom, knocking Lenz's tweezers and strips of wood to the floor.

"You would benefit from cooperating," the youngest soldier said.

She said nothing.

The soldiers moved farther back into the house, down a narrow hall which led to the stall door. The stall was warm and smelled like burning manure and damp. The smallest haze of daylight reached through the windows, just enough to break up the darkness blanketing Elsa's pots. Elsa was in the process of moving her garden into the stalls to save the vegetables from the winter frost. She walked to her sprouting turnips and stroked the heart-shaped leaves. She slid her fingers over the veins and down the stalks to the purple tip of a bulb just peeking through the soil. A huddle of mealy bugs wriggled beneath the largest leaf. She flicked them away and brushed the powdery residue off the stalk with her sleeve.

The soldiers were in the loft above the horse's partition, rummaging through hay and neglected tools. Glass bottles clinked against each other and made Elsa jump. She didn't know her husband had stuck more of his bottled ships up there. He was so sentimental, she thought, squirreling away the vessels of his life's work. They belonged in palaces and smoking rooms, beside carved humidors and crystal decanters of Tokaji.

Elsa saw movement out the corner of her eye. Lenz was in the goat's partition, under a pile of hay soaked with urine.

"Any sign of him?" one of the soldiers asked.

"He's not up here."

They skipped searching near the horse with its shod hooves and nervous ears and peered behind the fire, under Elsa's plant tables, behind the sacks of soil and feed.

Elsa wondered, if she and Lenz had been blessed with a child, would he have become a man not unlike these soldiers?

She would have been ashamed.

They were teasing the goat.

The middle soldier sat down and slid his head under the goat's udder while the youngest tugged the teats. The oldest laughed and leaned in to watch.

It took the youngest soldier a few tries, but on the fifth tug, milk shot into the middle soldier's mouth.

The goat bucked, but the oldest held her still.

The youngest soldier dribbled sweet, warm milk down his chin.

"Germans are filth," the middle soldier said. "Which is perfect for the coal mines. Your husband's face will be as dirty as his insides."

"Yours too," the youngest said.

Lenz's pile of hay shuddered.

The eldest put his finger to his lips and motioned to the other two.

Elsa dug her fingernails into her palms.

The middle soldier kicked the pile and landed his foot against something solid. A yelp sounded as the boot made contact with Lenz's shin. The Partisan kicked again, harder.

Elsa watched what happened next in slow motion. The oldest soldier reached his arms into the hay pile and yanked her husband out by his scalp. Both faces were distorted.

The middle soldier grabbed Elsa by the shoulders and held her still, pressed her so hard into the wall she might have disappeared into the wood grain.

The youngest pulled a bottled ship from the rafter it was tied to. He admired the careful rigging, the thirty-two sails that all seemed full of wind. A replica of the Pisaqua, built in Hamburg in 1893: a four-masted barque with a spanker sail pulled taught at the rear. Thick white paint ran from bow to stern, interrupted by portholes Lenz had drilled into the hull and fitted with miniature cannons. A single boom protruded like a narwhal horn from the bow. He had also made a floss-thin railing that ran the length of the ship. It matched a photograph he kept in his bible, marking a passage from Ecclesiasticus:

Who hath numbered the sand of the sea, and the drops of rain, and the days of the world?

Who hath measured the height of heaven, the breadth of the earth, and the depth of the abyss?

The youngest soldier traced each thin wooden board as it curved along the hull toward the figurehead, which he hadn't noticed until then: a woman, broad shouldered, wearing a breastplate and a billowing shawl. She was blowing into a long trumpet with a bell like an open flower. Elsa had asked her husband to add the figurehead because she'd read stories about men having beautiful figureheads made for the women they adored. Elsa and Lenz were newly married then. She had rested her chin on his shoulder to admire his carving, the folds he had dug into the shawl, the delicate scales of her armor, curlicues in her hair. He had even carved scrolling where her body met the ship so that the vessel itself looked like her skirt, her legs hiding somewhere inside the bow.

When Lenz finished, he sanded her carefully and pinched her small body with his tweezers, tucked it inside the lip of the bottle, down the neck, and onto the ship that had grown painstakingly as the days passed.

The youngest soldier stumbled over the goat.

"Dovraga!"

The bottle slipped out of his hands and fell in slow motion, catching small sparks of sunlight as it overturned. The ship pitched starboard. Its sails, delicate as insect wings, rippled as the fore and main and mizzenmasts collided with the glass.

When the bottle hit the earthen floor, it shattered with a dull noise. The boom snapped in two, the spanker and top sails tore, and the tiny German flag that had flown behind the jigger mast crumpled into itself. Slivers of glass caught the sun and became tiny whitecaps as Elsa and her husband stared at the wreckage.

They were placed in separate freight trains bound for Russia's dead tundra, where they heaved axes into walls made of darkness and wondered at the black grime carved into the lines of their stiff palms until neither Elsa nor her husband could remember much of their garden: not the smell or the sound of the leaves rustling or the taste of fresh greens or plums or turnips. Until the sound of each other's voices became unrecognizable. But they would both remember the two hundred miniature ships trapped in bottles that would never ride the sea or feel the wind rustle over their paper sails.

KIKINDA, SERBIA: 2012

WE PULLED INTO A GAS STATION outside of Novi Sad, fifty-five miles north of Belgrade. We stopped for the convenience store because we didn't know what food we'd find once we checked into our apartment. The gas station had candy, cheese, ambiguous canned meats, bottled water, wine, and the Serbian version of Tastykakes. When I picked up one of the pastries it felt like a paperweight, one of the glass kind that magnifies cockroaches and orchids.

An attendant in a fluorescent vest walked in and started shouting. When I looked at him with confused eyes he said, "Is that your car?" and pointed to the Chevy Spark we'd picked up that morning. He seemed nervous. Or angry. I couldn't tell which. When he asked, he looked at David. He didn't look at me.

"Yes," David said with a pile of chocolate and cans in his arms.

"Just making sure."

"Can I help you with something?" the cashier asked. "I wouldn't eat the purple can."

I pulled the purple can out of David's pile and put it back on the shelf.

"How about this?" I asked, holding up a wheel of spreadable cheese.

"Good."

"Hvala," I said.

A hand gripped my shoulder. I felt thick fingers through my coat and the warmth of a palm. A voice came with the hand, soft and fast. When I turned to find the stranger's face, I saw a green wool hat and farmer's features, wizened where sun and earth and rain had dug trenches into his cheeks.

"That's Brno," the cashier said. "He lives next door. He's trying to tell you Merry Christmas."

Brno held out his hand for me to shake.

"Merry Christmas," I said, but when I took his hand, it had something in it. He pushed a walnut into my palm and shut my fingers over the shell. "Merry Christmas," he said slowly, pronouncing each letter. He kissed me on one cheek, then the other, and I kissed him back. When David put his collection of processed foods on the counter and asked for two bottles of the Vranac behind the register, the old man gave him a Christmas walnut and kissed his cheeks, too.

"You've picked the wrong time to come to Serbia," the cashier said, reaching for the wine, careful not to knock the decorative bottled ships on display beside them.

"Merry Christmas." I pulled one of the plastic bags off the counter and waved to Brno with the walnut still in my hand. "Hvala."

"Srećan Božić," the old man said.

"Zrey-chan Bojeech," I replied.

Aleksander stood waiting outside of his apartment on Njegoševa with a key. He told us the location was great because all the windows opened to the music school across the street. It was two in the afternoon on Christmas in Novi Sad and the music school was silent. Aleksander's English was broken, but he said he'd cook us breakfast even though it was the afternoon, because it was Christmas and nothing was open and he saw the bags of canned meat we brought from the gas station minimart.

He made strong Turkish coffee and sausages, and something called popara that he conjured by boiling stale bread in milk. He sprinkled a pinch of salt in the milk and a dollop of some kind of clotted cream.

Aleksander didn't smile, though he wasn't unfriendly. You could tell from the way he moved his lips that he was glad we had come to Vojvodina. He said, "Serbia is a country in chains," that there was a movie we should watch with a name I couldn't under-stand and a director who had slept on the fold out couch.

He worked in a souvenir shop on the main street—a street with shops full of last year's products and no restaurants. His teeth were yellow from cigarettes. The main street in Novi Sad smelled like his tobacco, and the bars, and most of the cafés that sold little more than coffee, wine, and rakija.

Aleksander asked why we'd come to Serbia, and I told him we'd come to learn about my family. He ate his popara with his mouth open, wearing a shirt that said in English, *Live Forever, Never Day,* and told me it would be easy to find what we were looking for. He told me the villages were small. That this was not New York.

"Were your family Serbs or Croats?" he asked.

"They were German."

"Ah, well, we're all the same at the end."

Aleksander spoke about the wars in the nineties, but not the forties. He talked about the shifting borders between my grand-mother's Croatia and my grandfather's Serbia, about the land mines left by foolish adolescents at the doorsteps of strangers.

There was something that made me uneasy, an empty space where half a million Germans used to be. Everyone in Serbia pre-tended not to notice; they had their own empty spaces. Aleksander filled his void with cigarette smoke. He'd gone through five cig-arettes already, and the air in the kitchen was heavy. He talked about the days before the Balkan Wars with nostalgia. "The Peo-ple's Liberation Front took care of Serbians on Earth, and God waited to take care of us in Heaven," Aleksander said. He said, too, that we were all the same. That Serbs were Croats, that Croats were Serbs. When I told him that my grandfather had grown up in a German village in the Batschka, my grandmother in Slavonia, he didn't compare himself to a Swabian. He just pulled up the cor-ners of his lips a little—as if to say that desperate people are impulsive and superstitious, that it was natural for people to behave like monsters.

Because Serbia is a country in chains.

"You must watch this film," Aleksander repeated, balancing a fresh cigarette between his lips. He lit it on the stove and pulled so deep the ash grew longer than my fingernail. I wondered at how he balanced the gray dust on the tip of his Drina Specials without letting it crumble into his lap. "It is good," he said, "I will bring it tomorrow for you to see."

David smiled, but his eyes were dull. His nose was pinched and I knew he was sick of the cigarette smoke and small talk.

Aleksander could tell, too. He shook David's hand, then mine, and stared at the electric outlet by the coat rack.

"Oh," he said, pulling an air freshener out of his pocket. He plugged it in, smiled, and opened the door. "Until tomorrow."

I rolled my Christmas walnut along the inner spine of *Genocide of the Ethnic Germans in Yugoslavia 1944-1948.* Since finding it in the Philadelphia Free Library, I'd realized it wasn't a perfect text. It was biased and indignant, questionably translated into English. But it left breadcrumbs. And, for better or worse, it was human.

In the central cemetery at Werbass (Vrbas), five mass graves were dug out by order of the Partisans. Afterwards, 570 prisoners disappeared from the city hall. On November 14, 1944, three of the five mass graves were covered. The relatives of the disappeared asked mayor Henkel about the fate of their family members. Mayor Henkel answered, "What do you think is in the holes at the cemetery, perhaps frogs?"

David sat beside me on the sofa and slid his face between my glasses and the book in my lap. His shadow hovered over the tiny print as he brushed the hair out of my face and pressed his lips to my cheek. His afternoon stubble grazed my jaw.

Vrbas was on the way to Kikinda. We were headed there the next morning—where some eight hundred souls were buried under a cold storage depot that was built above an old camp graveyard. Where human bones were uncovered twice before the fall of Josip Broz Tito, and where those who found the remains of Swabian bodies were more afraid of their government than of the angry souls trapped inside the bones.

I closed the book and unpretzeled my legs.

"Alright?" David's voice came from far away, from someplace where there were no secret bones. A haze of dug up earth was suspended in the air between David and me, and it was full of bodies. I saw femurs and teeth and faces, faces that wouldn't leave me alone—tired male faces of gravediggers for the not-frogs, a woman with no eyes, government employees carting skeletons in wagons to potato fields in the dark.

I looked at David. He smelled like sweat and evergreen trees and peat from the scotch on his breath. He scooted closer and pulled my head to his chest. I breathed cedar like the smell of the hope chest Oma had kept in the front hall. It had a secret compartment built into the bottom, hidden under woolen blankets. I always imagined the compartment held cash, heirloom jewelry, passports, emergency clothing. I never opened it.

David laced his fingers through my hair, leaned over me, and pulled my head back. His lips hovered close enough to mine that I could taste the scotch and pine coming off him. I bridged the tiny space between us and met his lips.

When I looked at his bare shoulders, I pictured them swollen and purple, covered in dirt. I pictured one of them dislocated. I didn't want to. I wanted to close my eyes and shake my head clear. I saw an arm dismembered at the elbow as David slid his whole living arm across my thigh, first his forearm, then his wrist, his palm, his strong, soft fingers. His hand was warm, full of life. Not like the Swabians, dead and buried, not like my grandfather, my grandmother's wasting memory.

David was more than alive—he was bursting with heat. His cheek felt hot against my neck when he kissed from my ear to my collarbone. His hands, too, when he slipped my shirt over my head and slid onto his knees in front of the sofa to tug my boots off from the heel and peel off my too-tight jeans, when he tossed everything into a heap on the floor.

He breathed his heat into my belly when he bit the skin below my navel, when he rested his hot cheek on my chest and exhaled the weight of desire into the stale air of the apartment on Njegoševa. I pulled him with both hands by the back of his head until

I could reach his face. I almost tasted the burning in his mouth.

"Can we wait until tomorrow to start searching?" David kissed the hollow at the top of my sternum. "It's already afternoon."

I slipped off the sofa so that we were both kneeling on the laminate floor. I took his face into my hands. "You're terrible," I said.

"For you."

He held me so tightly I could bruise. And I burned for him in spite of all the bodies, to fill the empty space that belonged to them.

The next morning, we drove to Kikinda listening to Serbian folk music. The accordion rang in my ears, and the sad engine shook the floor of the car. The Spark struggled with its almost flat tire and still smelled, like all of Serbia, of stale smoke. I cracked my window in spite of the rain and watched the wind swirl the drops on the glass. Yellow road signs marked a turnoff for Vrbas we didn't take.

The air felt heavier than the rain.

Perhaps the weight came from the sorrow and shame of the last century: multiple iterations of Yugoslavia that had begun and ended in violence. Or maybe the Donauschwaben saturated the space between air molecules so they wouldn't be forgotten—restless dead specimens suspended in the ether.

Oma had been on the waiting list for Bayside Nursing Home ever since the visiting nurse found her outside with no shoes. She had packed a pillowcase full of her things, tied it to an umbrella handle, tossed the sack over her shoulder, and run away from home. She stood at the end of the driveway, waiting, shouting, "Where is the wagon?"

As if her parents were just inside her house, gathering the most meaningful of their things. Her sister coming out the front door, crying with so much force that their father scooped her up and carried her down to the road, to Oma. He looked back at the porch, framed in Oma's once-vibrant hanging baskets that had shriveled and browned because she'd forgotten to water them. And then, there she was: Oma's mother, walking down the concrete steps with a suitcase, leaning heavily on the chipped white iron railing. There were clothes shut into the sides of the case, but not just clothes. There was an arm poking out, a man's arm with hairy knuckles, and hair, a woman's hair—or a girl's—dragging on the paving slabs.

"The wagon will be here soon, schatzi."

Her mother leaned the suitcase on the mailbox.

"It'll take you somewhere safe."

But nowhere was safe.

I caught her smearing Crisco on toast instead of Country Crock and confusing dish soap with laundry detergent. Some days she forgot to eat. Her words made less sense. She stopped showering, started losing control of her bladder and bowels. She mixed up names, called me her sister. Called for her mother and father, who'd been dead since before I was born.

When a space opened at Bayside, I wasn't unprepared. I was sitting on the sofa with Sid when the call came, watching TV and eating lunch. It was almost spring: the icy chill of winter had eased in Philadelphia, and the tips of the Bradford Pear branches outside our sash windows had started to hint at yellow-green.

I hung up, turned to Sid, and said, "Oma's going into the home today." The words came out like I'd said them before. My next words sounded rote too: "We're going to help her settle in. I'm going to get my things."

I got up and put my plate in the kitchen sink, so carefully it hardly made a noise against the stainless steel. I turned on the tap and let it run until the water turned cold, filled a glass, and drained it. I put it in the sink beside my plate. Sid was still on the sofa.

I walked out of the kitchen and back through the living room, to the opening in the hardwood floor where a spiral staircase wound down to our bedroom.

At the bottom of the stairs, I experienced a crash of smells: veneer, sharpened pencils, Brut aftershave, the sour smell of the liquid canned food Opa fed himself after his stroke. Everything came at once, and not just smells. Extra weight in the air, a sense of someone else being in the room, a coldness that pierced my bones.

My knees buckled.

I had a hard time finding my breath.

After what could have been seconds or whole minutes, I heard the stairs creak under the weight of Sid's feet.

"It feels weird in here," he said.

When he saw me on the floor, he knelt beside me.

"Are you okay?"

"You felt it?" I said.

He nodded and put his hand on my knee.

"Did you smell him?" It sounded insane. But I was afraid the smell hadn't been there at all, that I had materialized my grandfather out of thin air because I was incapable of handling the moment without him.

When I looked up into Sid's face, he looked shaken.

"No, I didn't, but it felt like somebody else's space. I don't know how to describe it."

A space filled with so much of Opa's grief that it became his own. Grief for Oma's health. Her discomfort. For the distance between them. For what she had lost and what she will come to lose.

Please, the smell of him had said. *Do something.*

As if there was something I could have done. As if it was possible not to fail them. As if it was possible for one person not to fail another. It was inevitable.

Sid drove us to Anita Drive. We packed as much of Oma's things as we could and piled them into the car. Sid held the door while I helped her into the backseat and buckled her seatbelt. I slid in beside her. On the way to the nursing home, she pointed out the window and spoke unintelligible sentences. She looked over at me and smiled crooked. I took her hand.

"Salz," I said, whispering my fingertip in a circle over her palm.

"Schmalz." I whispered the circle again.

The next part of the game was to say, "Ellebogen," and pinch the loose skin behind her elbow like she used to pinch mine. Flour from her apron would sprinkle my arm. And then she'd reach for my nose and wiggle it between her first and middle fingers, shouting, "Nazale gezogen!"

I didn't finish the rhyme.

She seemed confused about the move, but to make her room feel like home, we pinned photographs to the corkboard beside her bed—a few from Sid's and my wedding, a few from past Christmases and Easter dinners: Oma in a snap-front apron with me in her flour-coated arms; her and Opa when they were young, wrapped in stylish hand-sewn clothing and standing in front of the Philadelphia skyline. My mother and uncle, when they were young. We hung a crucifix above her pillow, propped silk flowers on her dresser, and suction-cupped a hummingbird feeder outside her window.

One of the wedding photos: Sid and I leaning in on either side of Oma's seat at dinner. She wore sequins and Austrian crystal and left a lipstick ring on Sid's cheek.

The chair next to her was empty.

Opa was supposed to waltz with her. He was supposed to waltz with me. I was supposed to close my eyes and remember standing on his feet at the shore. Except he had died and neither of us could waltz without him. We thought our feet knew how, but all they knew was how to follow him.

"Isn't this nice?" a nurse said while Sid tucked an old Huggies' wipes container full of costume jewelry into Oma's nightstand. There were locks on the nightstand drawers so other patients couldn't steal the contents.

We spent a couple hours settling her in, buying her ice cream from the visitor's cafeteria, giving her elbow-squeezes and hugs. We told her everything was going to be alright. That we would be leaving, but she would stay. Just for a little while. We would be back soon.

She looked afraid.

As afraid as she must have looked when the nurse found her at the bottom of the driveway.

Oma was a refugee again. After surviving the expulsion, coming to America, finding a Swabian husband; after having two children, losing one, and raising a grandchild; after keeping a small but respectable home; after nurturing a whole family with meals of goulash, stuffed cabbage, palaschinke, spaetzle, plum dumplings, Black Forest cake, and apfelstruedel, she was destined to be displaced.

I looked out the Spark window again. Red kites perched in perfect intervals along the highway—in trees, on fence posts, half-buried in the tall wet grass. Scattered behind them: one room homes with porches and outhouses, messy backyards and crooked lean-to sheds with tin roofs, rotted hay bales left in fields to decompose beside small orchards of plum and apple trees.

It occurred to me that there were no Christmas lights, no festive trees or red and green tinsel hanging off the bushes.

As David and I trundled down the sloppy main road into the town, we saw a man pushing a bicycle loaded with firewood. His lips made a straight line on his face, and his knit hat didn't protect him from the rain. His hands were naked in the winter air, knuckles white and raw against the handlebars. The firewood wasn't chopped blocks but hacked-off branches, each one longer than the bicycle, all of them tied together with a strip cut from a woven plastic sack. He looked at us as we drove slowly by him, with eyes as hard as steel but with softness in the dark centers.

We drove past a water pump, where old men filled jugs too heavy for their old bones. Where were the younger men? I strained my neck to look closer, but David didn't slow down. He pulled out one of the satellite images we'd marked: he'd drawn a circle around a potential cold storage depot.

In October of 1944, the Milk Hall had been stuffed full of Kikinda's ethnic Germans. The Milk Hall became the central starvation camp of the northern Banat. By the sixties, Tito's regime had ordered the property to be demolished. When skeletons were found close to the surface, no one said a word. In the eighties, a vegetable packaging facility and cold storage depot were built on the lot. Dozens more skeletons were unearthed. Some remains were removed by government officials without comment, some were covered with more dirt. Remains found near the football field on the edge of town were re-buried in sand.

The bones disappeared, but the depot remained. It was under the pen mark, as David had said, with a blue roof and metal cooling ducts and scrap metal heaped in the parking lot.

There was something sinister about the company logo—a red dot at the eye of two swirls, like the eye of a storm. I stepped out of the car with my camera. Maybe someone found a way to leave a clue, a bloody bulls-eye. *Here lie the Donauschwaben, of whom we are forbidden to speak.*

The front of the depot was painted the color of citrus fruits—lemons and limes. As if such garish colors could make people forget what was buried under the foundation. The men who built the industrial park turned it into a 7-Up cool pack. They also turned the backyard into a muddy garbage dump: rusty scrap metal, broken parts, and empty chemical tanks covered the grass behind the buildings. The tanks leaned against the fence and made the chain link buckle. A small apartment building backed up to the gate, with a basketball court set up against the fence and plastic children's toys leaning against the hoop post: a pedal car just large enough for a six-year-old boy, a house with a pink door built for a little girl. The sign outside the depot read Prvi Depo. Beneath the sign, almost a thousand Swabian corpses slept, while skinny children jump-roped on their bones.

A curtain moved in the apartment building.

"I think someone's watching," David said.

I didn't know how to walk away from the bodies under my feet. I pictured a corpse with ears, veins, and desiccated muscle tissue still stuck to the skull. The empty spaces where its eyes should have been stared at me. Its mouth was stretched open.

My stomach felt at once hollow and filled with bile.

I pictured faces like my grandfather's in the dirt. At his funeral, Opa's skin was waxy and thick. I could have pressed a fingernail into his cheeks and carved my initials into the makeup. I told Oma that Opa looked like a soap carving, the kind I did with a bar of Ivory and a plastic knife when I was seven. Oma said her skin looked like soap once, too. Opa had told her so. She said a Native American chief glued himself to her because her house was built on his burial ground. It sounded like something out of a horror movie, but I had an easier time accepting the existence of ghosts than murdered bodies under my feet.

Oma said that during the months she shared her head with the dead chief, she had night terrors with feathers in them. She had night terrors and her skin looked pale and slick. During the day the chief made her angry, Oma said, angry and ill. She had fevers and threw up; she cursed and threw things; she didn't make the beds or Windex the mirrors or have dinner waiting for my grandfather when he got home too late from work.

When the dreams didn't stop, she said, she hired a mystic named Mathilde to read the spirits in the house. The mystic found the chief, the burial ground. Another place in the world where bodies were hiding under the surface. Mathilde left stones in every corner, said prayers in the doorways, and performed some kind of passive exorcism until Oma believed she was cured.

If the phantom chief was real, if he wasn't just a manifestation of my grandmother's anguish that her husband had given his love to someone else, I imagined he was trying to find his way back to his resting place. But what could the dead Swabians with no tombs, no caskets, no headstones find their way back to? The homes that used to belong to them, the loved ones who were buried in mass graves farther east, the children who were raised to forget their parents, the siblings who managed to board carriages and boats to new beginnings?

"What happens when thousands of bodies are buried too close to the surface?" I asked.

"What do you mean?" David said.

"How do they decompose?" Would the moist earth and nutrients of other decaying bodies preserve their faces like soft wax, or would they rot faster?

"Most people in England are cremated," he said, looking at the mud under his feet.

I wondered when someone last stood there knowing the contents of the soil. There could have been remains just inches below the surface.

Did the children who played against the chain link fence know? Did their parents? The woman behind the curtain? I wondered if even half of Serbia knew that when they opened a lemon-lime can of sweet corn they were eating vegetables packaged over a death camp. The assembly line workers carried bleeding soil into the factory in the treads of their shoes. I'd heard of mice and fingernails, band aids finding their way into pre-packaged food. It wasn't difficult to imagine flecks of skull hit by a backhoe getting into the frosty peas.

David opened the car door. I climbed inside and stared at my boots, caked in mud. As he drove back down the main road, I looked for the water pump again, where I'd seen the old men filling jugs. I peered between houses and along the sidewalk, behind store fronts and in the courtyard park by the church. But the pump was gone, and the old men with their too-full jugs gone with it like a window had been opened and shut in midair. The empty space had swallowed it up.

"You're such a gentleman," I said as he pulled onto the road. The village grew small in the side mirror. "Opening doors."

David caught my eye and smiled, but said nothing. My words came too late. Raindrops unfurled like tiny glass ferns on my window.

I thought of Sid, my sometimes husband, of the times he explained to me exactly what made the rain move in swirls around the side mirror. *The front of the mirror has a higher air pressure than the back of it, and the difference in pressure creates vortexes, which create the curls on the window. So now you've got this whipping tail of swirly wind behind your mirror called the wake. Like a boat's wake, it expands as it goes farther back. Combined with the generally upward flow of air coming from your car hood and windshield, you get flares behind your mirror, on the window.* On the rare occasions when I drove us home in the rain, I caught him staring at the vortex swirls, marveling at the science of them with his forehead pressed against the glass.

Home. When I followed David, there was no such thing as home. We moved between B&Bs, holiday apartments, and hotels with concierge desks and room-service menus, minibars filled with overpriced 50ml bottles of booze and half-sized soda cans. Hotels were all the same—they all had the same windows, the kind that didn't unlatch, the ones caulked in black around the edges. They were predictable. They had no risk, no inconvenience. They weren't villages without running water, with wind chills and scabby mud and food that tasted like iron and guilt.

"I'm famished," David said. Once the words left his mouth, my own hungry stomach stirred. All either of us had eaten were Haribo candies and pre-packaged walnut bread.

I couldn't cry, but I could eat.

When we got back to the apartment on Njegoševa, we ordered takeout from a menu Aleksander had left on the kitchen table. Not knowing what anything was, we ordered half the options and filled our bellies with palacinke and sopska salad. Our shoes still on and heavy with mud because we were too tired to pull them off, we sat on the bed and leaned against the wall with glasses of wine in our hands and an empty bottle on the floor. I leaned forward to pick at the crusty corner of a pancake David had left in his takeout box. I forgot the glass in my hand for a moment, trying to pull the pancake away from the Styrofoam with my fingers, fighting with the chocolate that glued it tight. I heard David breathe in fast and looked up to see my wine slosh in slow motion over the rim.

The deep red color of the Vranac on the sheets was the same human-colored stain as the soil. So were the other foods of the Pannonian Plains, the foods my grandmother used to cook before she was diagnosed with Alzheimer's: plum dumplings with plum brandy, pork in red wine sauce, soups the color of spoiled red peppers. Beets.

Then there was the smell of burning cigarettes, of ash and decay.

There was mud so thick and wet it stuck to the bottoms of our boots. While David washed the bed sheets, I sat at the kitchen table with a cup of Turkish coffee and a soapy towel and waggled my heel back and forth, trying to free the dirt from my sole.

I remembered a photograph of a starving girl in a sleeveless polka-dot dress, an inmate at one of the camps. She was missing a lot of hair and her arms were hardly thicker than my thumb. She could have been a toddler, except her arms were too long and there was knowledge in her expression. Her face hadn't grown into her eyes: two black orbs filled with despair and the tiniest shine of hope, as if the man behind the camera would have saved her.

What could he have done, with the guards and a room full of skeleton children?

The towel was cold against my palm. I scrubbed at my boots until my fingertips pruned. The dirt on my shoes looked like blood under my fingernails, blood on the towel—wet and slippery, it smelled like iron.

I scrubbed and wiped, folded the towel over to a clean corner, and started again.

David dropped a plastic bag full of wine-soaked toilet tissue on the floor and sat beside me with wet hands. I slid a cup of coffee toward him. He reached his hand across the table.

"It's okay," he said.

I drank too deeply and the grinds stuck in my teeth like earth.

BAČKI BRESTOVAC, SERBIA: 2012

WE SET OFF AGAIN after breakfast.

We'd been driving for an hour when I saw a shadow from the car. A black dog stood broadside with his legs spread across both lanes, his head turned to face us. I couldn't find his eyes in the mass of dark fur, but I noticed a white sock on his left front foot.

"David!"

The Spark breaks squealed like a wailing peacock. David swerved onto the shoulder. A cloud of dirt swallowed the car as he jammed the gearshift into park.

"Jesus," he said. I could see the stray dog beside the car in spite of the dust. His nose rested on the bottom of my window, and he breathed fog onto the glass. I cranked the manual handle and watched the car door swallow the pane. "Be careful. He might not be friendly."

"Hello, you." I reached my hand out the window. The dog panted with his tongue hanging out, dripping slobber. He didn't look like a dangerous animal. He barely looked like a stray at all. I reached to let him sniff me, and he shoved his wet nose into my palm.

"Marie? You want to see this." The dust had settled, and when I turned to look at David's face, I found the back of his head. He was staring out the window.

A marble cross, at least fifteen feet tall, erupted from a sheet of flagstone in the middle of a field. I'd read about the monument, seen pictures of it on Donauschwaben websites. But I didn't think we'd find it. There was no town called Filipowa anymore, and the photos I found were taken by tourists who didn't caption a street name or address. They were mostly family photos of smiling

Swabian-Americans standing on dead ancestors.

Americans couldn't help but smile into a camera lens. I wondered if it was easier for us to smile, because even when we heard about war crimes and genocides, we were incapable of comprehending the enormity of it. People from Vojvodina must have felt the history in their bones: it was in all the elements—the old men pumping water, the smoke-heavy air, the blood in their earth.

We stepped out of the car and headed into the field. The dog followed us to the monument. He sat beside us like a guardian of souls.

Two-hundred and fifty men and boys were brutalized and thrown into a pit dug in a hay field on November 25th, 1944. One of the Partisan guards, a draftee who held ropes around the condemned to keep them from escaping, told a nun that before they were killed, the victims made the sign of the cross over themselves. Fathers made crosses with their thumbs on their sons' foreheads before they were stripped naked, beaten with knives, and shot. I put my hand on the marble. Most days I believed in a god, or at least I wanted to, but when I thought about the things men have done to each other, I couldn't understand how any god would create something with a capacity for so much hate. I knew Sid and David didn't believe in gods or afterlives, but both said the same thing to me, whispered softly in my ear first thing in the morning, with sour breath and soft noses on my cheek: "We were made for each other." Made for each other because when we spooned, we fit together perfectly, when we made love, our bodies felt like we were the same person. Made for each other because we could talk about everything and nothing and kiss until our lips were chapped.

To say I believed in fate would have meant I believed I was predestined to marry Sid and betray him to get where I was supposed to be. That didn't sound divinely inspired. But both of them, both disbelieving, practical-minded men, believed in "the way things were meant to be," even while saying they didn't believe in a higher power. They didn't see what I tried not to see—that all bodies were made to fit together—knees were made to fit behind other knees, the crooks of shoulders were made to cradle faces.

If I had asked Oma and Opa what they thought of fate, I wonder what they'd have told me. *God gave me your grandfather, and I am grateful,* Oma might have said. But would she have thought of Rosalinde? The keepsakes in Opa's cabinet? Would she have pictured the bodies left behind in Croatia and Austria while she spoke, the lost limbs and families with empty spaces?

I wanted a photograph beside the memorial to take home to her, but I was afraid of those American tourist photos. I was afraid of smiling, too, as if history was a spectacle rather than something living on our shoulders.

A bus drove past the Spark with Ikarbus painted on the side. It looked old, tired, and it was filled with people in dark clothes with deep lines around their mouths. I didn't know what Ikarbus meant in Serbian. All I saw when I read it was Icarus falling out of the sky with melted wings and the crash of water as he hit the Danube. It seemed in bad taste to name a bus after a mythological crash victim.

"I think that's it, up there," David said, looking toward the village on the gray horizon. Vojvodina had been cloud-covered since we arrived. But as we drove onto the main street in Brestowatz, a few rays of sunshine poked through. As we drove down the muddy street, all I could see were abandoned shops with gates over the doorways and weather-bleached signs hanging on the windows that read Затворено. Closed. David sounded out the letters; it sounded unforgiving. I wondered if the Serbian word for "open" sounded softer.

"Which house is his?" I asked, pulling a glossy map out of the glove compartment. The map had belonged to Opa. It was printed with the layout of the village as it was when he'd lived there, compiled by the Brestowatz Swabians who migrated to Philadelphia. It had a square for each Swabian home—each square held the surnames of the extended families who'd shared it. One ink box on Kirchegasse, a block south of the Catholic Church, held the names Glas and Feiter. Opa's father's name was Glas. His mother was Apollonia Feiter. But the streets on the map were written in German. I didn't imagine the Serbs of modern-day Brestovac would have made it easy for us and translated Kirchegasse into the Cyrillic version of Church Street, especially since the Orthodox Church was on a different street than the Catholic one, on the other side of town.

"I'll drive to the northernmost tip. You look for the church steeple." David placed his hand on my knee and squeezed. "It's a small village. We'll find it."

As we trundled down the uneven roads, the barks and howls of village dogs chased our bumper. A man stood on his stoop watching us, frowning.

"There." I pointed to a bell tower rising behind rooftops, and we followed a street with no name to the church. It stood on the left side of the road, surrounded by an iron gate. It looked as if someone had renovated it. It was shiny and disused like a toy still sealed in its box. Of all the buildings I'd seen in Serbia—the graffitied, the run down, the shacks in potato fields, even the soot-stained Orthodox churches, the Catholic church in Brestowatz was the most immaculate. Painted yellow and white, it towered like an Easter egg over homes made of chipped plaster walls and metal shutters.

We parked on the side of the road, and I handed David the map. When I opened the car door, there was no noise and no movement.

I headed for the church gate.

"Wait," he said, pulling me back. "It's locked."

I shook his hand off my elbow. "Who would lock a church?"

"Maybe they don't want it vandalized."

As I approached the gate, I saw a thick chain wrapped around the entrance with a padlock jammed through the links.

"I'm sorry," he said. I felt the pressure of his hand on my lower back.

I shook the gate. It banged against itself and against the chain holding it shut.

"Hello?" I shouted.

David pulled me toward him. "Come on, nobody's inside."

"How do you know? Shouldn't there be a priest?"

I peered through the bars.

"It looks more like a monument than a church," David said. "Are there even any German Catholics left here?"

I didn't respond. I had no idea if there were German Catholics left in Brestowatz, but if there were, there were few.

The church looked suddenly familiar. I'd seen it in a painting on my grandparents' wall. On the street in front of the painted church, shadows of men in black hats looked skyward. Gray clouds made everything dark. The church alone was light.

Had surviving expellees turned the church into a memorial? A reminder that they'd existed—that they'd built homes and churches and schools, the shops that lay empty on silent streets. That their blood was in the soil. Opa wasn't the only Brestowatz native at the club in Philadelphia—there was Mr. Stampfer, the Albrechts, the Merkls. Had they helped with the renovation somehow? Had he?

"Your Opa's house shouldn't be far," David said.

Walking down the side of the road, we saw no one. A closed-down convenience store stood at the corner with canned goods still on the shelves, knocked over like someone had been inside and filled their pockets with death camp vegetables. There was a boarded-up place called Flora with naked headstones in the window. I couldn't tell if it had been a flower shop or a funeral parlor. The houses down the street looked vacant. The grass outside the doorsteps was dead. A burned down home leered from the next corner. We walked toward it. The whole north wall had crumbled. Charred paint ran the length of the interior walls, giving way to older paint jobs beneath it: forest green, powder blue, coral. Black blown-out light switches had left round holes in the plaster. Surviving carved moldings in the doorways reminded me that Serbia had been different when it was still Yugoslavia, different still when it was Austria-Hungary. The dirt floor was littered with rubble and twigs.

"Looks like it burned down years ago," David said. "It must have been beautiful."

Nothing falls apart as remarkably as beautiful things.

I looked at the home across the street, with fruit trees and a ditch out front, and a makeshift dirt bridge running over it. A story my grandfather told me: when he was eleven, he pushed a wheelbarrow full of flour over the bridge outside his house. He'd gone all the way to the miller's by himself to fetch it.

I pictured him thinking he looked pretty smart, taking his left hand off the handle and waving it in the air while he balanced the heavy load with his right.

The wheelbarrow lurched. He twisted to catch it and fell head-first into the ditch, wheelbarrow and all.

The bucket landed on his arm and a cloud of flour engulfed him.

I heard my grandfather's voice retelling the story, laughing, describing the look my great-grandmother had on her face when he opened the front door looking like a ghost.

"This is it," David said, checking the map.

"I know," I said, walking up to the bridge.

Most of the houses along the street had their shutters closed, but not Opa's. In the window beside the front door, a curtain moved. The heavy picot at the bottom of the lace rippled. It had jaundiced from age or sunlight or cigarette smoke. A shadow crossed behind it: a woman, heavyset and short.

I walked the length of the house until she couldn't see me anymore. I pressed my hand to the wall. I looked at the one-story plaster and brick L-shaped structure, the courtyard hidden behind the tin fence, the brown clay shingles, the few small windows, the dovecotes, the attached storeroom in the back where my great-grandfather would have stored fruit for his shop. At the way the roof sagged in the middle, how on the edges of some of the shingles something that looked like oxidized copper grew. There was a yard off to the side, barren fruit trees fenced in with chain link and rotted wood posts. I pictured Opa sitting in the branches of a plum tree with a small knife, cutting bits of branches off and throwing them for his dog, who would fetch them and bound back to the tree, front paws stretching up the trunk.

Later, Opa would slip into the storeroom, flip an empty crate upside down for a seat, and spit cherry pits into his hand until his palm was full or until his mother called from the kitchen at the front of the house: "Jakob, get your father for dinner!" He would sneak out of the storeroom, walk through the inner courtyard, pass the outhouse and the rabbit hutches, the chickens roaming loose in the dirt, blow his mother a kiss through the window, and find his father standing behind the counter of his grocery shop—the shuttered one down the street perhaps, with the aggressive-looking sign on the door.

I imagined Brestowatz was beautiful in the summer: lush grass and sweet-smelling trees. Bees hovering drunk and lazy over windfallen fruit. Sunshine spilling inside, breaking the winter must. Children playing in the streets. If there were any children. So far there had only been quiet schoolyards, old men, women peeking from curtained windowpanes.

Children should have been riding bikes down small lanes, testing out Christmas gifts in their yards, hanging out by Ikarbus stops, and leaning against vending machines at the gas station. But there were none. As beautiful as the summer sun and plentiful harvests would be, I got the feeling that Vojvodina was dying. I had more sympathy for the land than I had for the people. The woman behind the curtain was probably old enough to remember the Feiters and the Glas family, the Wirags and the Merkls down the street, the Aments from the edge of town. How long had the house been vacant before she moved in—pushed by Partisans to relocate to a home filled with someone else's things? Had she moved from within the village, from somewhere nearby, or had she come from Montenegro or Herzegovina—somewhere far enough away that she wouldn't have known the people who'd owned the house before her?

"What are you staring at?" I wanted to shout. My face was the same shape as my grandfather's, whose photographs had been left behind for the new family to find.

Anger hit me like an ambush. The people we had seen were as old as my grandfather would have been. They were alive for the expulsion. They hid behind their shutters, behind wrinkled frowns and blank eyes. They said nothing. They didn't smile or wave. Maybe they were ashamed. Maybe they were angry because my presence reminded them of something they'd worked hard to forget.

Or maybe they didn't remember at all. More than sixty years had passed. Germans weren't the only ones who died badly here. Everyone died badly here in the forties. And then there had been the civil war. I was just a stranger standing on their lawns. When they looked at me, they didn't see me. They didn't see my grandfather, how the earth here was a part of him as it was a part of them—rubbed into his scraped boyish knees until it was in his blood. The smell of grass and fruitwood blowing on the breeze like pollen, osmosing into his skin so deep it was still there, years later, when he was old and his skin had gone soft and thin.

They couldn't have been much more than children when it happened. Under Tito, it had been verboten to speak of German deaths. I read accounts from Serbs who waited until Yugoslavia broke to share what they saw or did because they were afraid they'd be jailed or killed or worse.

But Tito had been dead for a long time. For every man or woman who had spoken, how many had remained silent?

David looked at me as if I was made of glass.

"People are starting to stare," he said.

"I know. I saw her." But then I saw them. A child sitting on the handlebars of an old man's bicycle, leaning back against his chest.

She watched me while the man pedaled slowly. He whispered something in her ear. Who did they think we were? Hooligans? Someone's family visiting for Christmas? Tourists? What would tourists be doing in rural Vojvidina in January? But if someone had asked me who I was, standing there, I wouldn't have had an answer.

The girl had a pink puffer coat that looked like one I used to wear—except hers had stuffing coming out one of the elbows. The man didn't have a coat on at all—instead he wore layers of hoodless sweatshirts piled on his thin torso. He looked at us too, frowning. I looked at David. He styled his hair like a businessman. He wore leather shoes, tailored jeans, a tight overcoat. And me: warm knee-high boots and a dark khaki parka.

No wonder the sketch artist pegged us as tourists in Belgrade.

No wonder the woman in the window kept her curtains shut.

I waved. It seemed rude to just stare back.

The house on the other side of the ditch was no longer my grandfather's home. I had hoped being in Brestowatz would bring me closer to him. Instead I was overwhelmed by a feeling of not belonging. There would be no homecoming in Vojvodina. Only feelings of horror and unease, of being watched, of something I'd never felt before but couldn't express. Like the ground was more alive than the villages.

NICOLA ILIĆ: KIKINDA, YUGOSLAVIA: 1980

EVERYONE HAS BEEN TALKING in hushed voices about Marshal Tito's health: *There's something wrong with the blood in his legs.*

They're going to amputate, they whisper.

I read he gave his New Year's speech from his seat.

Not long ago, the Marshal shot a bear in Karađorđevo. His photograph was in the paper: the Marshal propped his foot on the animal's spine, and the dead bear eyed the camera.

My room looks out over the neighbor's pigs.

He has been letting them into his orchard to eat the fallen, fermented apples.

My windows watch the pigs bump into each other under the apple tree. They watch me, too. The windows pass the things they see onto other windows, who pass it on to walls, onto thresholds and door handles until the Marshal himself gets wind.

My room has an infestation of lady beetles. They scuttle across the glass in hordes. The windows aren't the only ones who watch. Each black dot on the red shells stares.

I remember the day my family moved into the house in Jabuka. It had four rooms and a courtyard. Our first house had been a small apartment outside of Jagodina; I was too young then to remember much, except that we moved from a place named after strawberries to one named after apples. Everything was the same only bigger—and my father wasn't a janitor anymore. He wrote pamphlets for Marshal Tito. *God is make-believe created by the ruling class, he wrote. The monks with their false vows of poverty live in fine monasteries while men like us clean their toilets.*

I saw caravans full of Germans moving up the highways toward Hungary. *They are being sent back where they came from*, my father said.

The house in Jabuka used to belong to a German family.

I found envelopes full of letters under the floorboards. One of the letters was a family tree, each name a leaf dangling from the branches. Another letter was from a woman named Gertrude. *Dear Usurper, it began, You will find a dozen letters in this house. Each letter, each comma, each sentence, each period on the page is a curse. I put the weight of our family's loss on your spine.*

A new building is going up in Kikinda. A big one. I heard about it from a friend: *The new depot needs a digger.*

I needed a job.

I don't know how many I lifted out of the soil before Stevan shouted up at the cab and waved his arms. I turned off the engine. A muffled word came through the cab windows. I opened the door.

"Bones," he said as I stepped off the machine.

He pointed to my bucket.

One poked out of the dirt like a stick.

We will not be destroyed, Gertrude had written.

The foreman shook his head. "Jesus shit."

"Get the boss," he told Stevan. To me, he said, "Don't let anyone see this."

"What am I supposed to do?"

He handed me a pack of cigarettes and a lighter.

"Look like you're taking a break."

I chain smoked six cigarettes before Stevan returned.

"You and Stevan are the only ones who saw this? And Boris?" Vlatko asked, rubbing his forehead with his palm.

I nodded.

There was a long silence. It was pregnant. Full of bones and full of watching. The sun was a spotlight. Even the bones had eyes. I could feel sweat pooling in my armpits.

Stevan shifted as if he wanted to speak, but said nothing. It's always best to say nothing.

"I called the authorities," Vlatko said. He looked tired. "They told me to send everyone home. But we need you to stay, Nicola."

Five officials showed up and ordered me to keep digging. I climbed back into the cab and turned the key. This time I didn't need Stevan to tell me they were there. I saw them: ribs and skulls and femurs, hip bones, spines dangling like Jacob's ladders.

When one of the men motioned for me to stop, I stopped. The headlights on my backhoe were watching.

The officials counted fifteen bodies. Pieces were missing. They found fifteen sets of collarbones, twelve and a half fibulas, thirteen elbows, fourteen skulls. The missing skull drew the most concern. The skull is the human bone.

With the whispers of Tito's illness, I wondered: if a symbol of a thing dies, does the thing die with it?

The men loaded the bones into wheelbarrows and took them away. I was told to go home.

The sky is turning black outside my windows, but the pigs still gorge themselves on rotten apples.

I pour myself a glass of rakija. There's a pear at the bottom of the bottle that I want to eat, but it won't fit through the top. I drink until there's nothing but the fruit. It smells sweet. It also smells like cleaning agent.

My mother found the family tree under my bed. She took it from me and said, *Don't let their filth contaminate you. Germans are animals.* After she took it, the leaves filled with names remained. They burned like eyes inside my head.

I can't see the pigs anymore, but I can hear them.

Two hogs are fighting. I've never heard them growl before.

When they scream, they sound like people.

Your walls are filled with our dust.

The ladybugs watch like soldiers.

We hide in all the cracks.

While the windows stare like passersby, the neighbor comes outside in the night with a lantern and a stick the size of a human femur.

He beats the swine until they stop screaming.

GAKOVA, SERBIA: 2012

THE AIR IN VOJVODINA smelled like burning. A blanket of smoke spread across the streets, stinking of wet burning hay and manure.

The sky was too dark for four o'clock.

A defunct railroad ran parallel to the road. Naked tree silhouettes stretched their branches to the dimming sky—desperate arms reaching upward. Hundreds of small black birds hovered in flocks over occasional houses. Everything was shades of black and blue. A busted recliner rested on the tracks with the footrest extended. A permanent man-shaped depression had formed in the seat and back, discolored at the headrest from hair grease. The armrests had turned grimy from invisible palms.

Roosters crowed the end of day and dogs barked in return. There were men on the road in Gakowa: a man pushing a wheelbarrow full of garbage, one hobbling on mismatched crutches, another dressed in full camouflage with a black knit hat pulled down to his eyebrows.

All their faces looked the same.

David pulled off onto the side of the road and held a satellite image against the steering wheel.

"What are we looking for here?" he asked.

"There should be a monument behind the cemetery," I said, leaning over and pointing at a tiny white rectangle on the southern edge of the village.

The cemetery in Gakowa was crowded with black marble, plastic flowers, and shriveling bouquets. Three old women in rubber boots pulled dead blooms from the graves and piled them in wheelbarrows. They didn't look up at us as we passed, only at the graves, the spoiled gifts for the departed.

How much sadness must there be in a person, in a place, to care for a cemetery so well? I'd never seen a place like it—so many graves overflowing with candles and ribbons and wreaths, those horrible artificial blossoms. Even the marble headstones carved with Orthodox crosses shined as clean as glass, so clear I saw my reflection staring back at me.

"This is a big cemetery for such a small place," David said.

"Yes. But it doesn't account for everyone."

David and I looked at the names: Borojan, Kovic, Vasković, Andrejević. There were no Gartenmeyers or Fischers, no Dietrichs or Müllers.

When they thought we weren't looking, the old women snuck glances at us, then buried their arms in the flowers and lowered their heads again. They wore black headscarves to match the marble. Like sad angels who ferry souls, collecting memorial gifts in return for safe transport.

"Where are they?" he asked. "The Germans."

"Most of the German cemeteries were leveled during the expulsion."

"What's the point of that?"

"Dehumanization?" Or to erase proof of their existence, which made no sense: even if you removed hundreds of years of German bodies by plucking up tombstones and ruining graves, the evidence of the Donauschwaben remained. The footprints of whole towns, the width of the streets, the carefully ordered homes. All those things were, for the most part, designed and built by German settlers and Austro-Hungarian subjects. Another thing I didn't understand: what had happened to the bodies? Were they removed and thrown into a single pit? Into the river? If I lay a flower on an Orthodox tombstone, would it mark two graves—the Serbian body in the casket and a Swabian one below it?

We followed the path past rows of silk flowers and black marble. Farther back, almost invisible from the cemetery, a twenty-foot monument sprouted out of dead grass with inscribed plaques translated into eight languages on the sides. The English inscription read:

THE DURATION OF THE CONCENTRATION
A ΛP AKOVO WAS FROM MARCH 1945 T
JANUARY 1948.
AKOVO 2004

Even monuments in Vojvodina obscured the past.

A spread of tall bushes hid the mass grave from view. I wondered if every time a villager passed the hedgerow he thought of death until one day he walked by and thought of nothing, and it was as if the bodies had never existed.

"How many people died here?" David asked, picking a prayer candle off the monument and looking at the weather-damaged photograph of a woman glued to the front.

"Over eight thousand," I said. The words sounded like they came from someone else.

"Jesus," he said, putting the candle down as if it had burned him. He backed away from the cross and began reading the names on the closest headstones: more Novaks and Jovanovićs.

There were dozens of red glass prayer candles, most of them only burned halfway. One candle had burned all the way to the bottom and cracked—the red glass bled white wax. On one, the Virgin Mary cried. Another had the Lord's Prayer printed in German. I recognized the words from a wooden bread plate Oma kept on display in her kitchen. *Gib uns heute unser tägliches Brot.* On yet another, scrawled in permanent marker: miene Mutter, Wilhelmina Knebl.

Something rustled in the hedges.

From the cross, only sticker bushes were visible, and something that looked like skinny bamboo. I walked toward the noise.

"There's a path cut here," I said, but David didn't follow. He had moved back to the monument and was rifling through other items left around the cross, straightening windblown flowers even though they were dead.

The three old women clearly didn't clean this part of the cemetery. Did they only ferry Orthodox souls? What happened to the Germans buried here—were they still waiting for their angels to arrive?

I stepped into the opening. The brush was tall and dense, and the flattened stalks crunched beneath my feet. Great green walnuts the size of softballs littered the path. It was difficult to step without disturbing them.

"The piths of walnuts are made of brains," Opa had said once, smiling. "Make sure you eat the big ones."

The path broke into a small clearing. A concrete cross the size of a small child reached out of the earth—a headstone covered in moss, bearing Deutsch, Magdolna, 1895-1945. At first I thought I'd found a German cemetery. I peered through the overgrowth: nothing but fallen nuts. Magdolna Deutsch's headstone stood alone. A basket of silk flowers sat at the foot of the cross, brilliant as the lime green walnut hulls. The basket overflowed with bright fake daisies and roses and sprays of plastic baby's breath. The color of dusk in the clearing turned the walnuts and the mossy headstone a surreal and lurid green. I looked back at the trail and realized how worn it was, how flattened the dead grass and stalks were, how perfect the edges of the path had been cut by whoever still visited Magdolna's headstone to replace the silk flowers when the sun dulled them, how the path stopped sharply at the tree line, and how far I'd followed the walnuts.

I could see the path, but not the entrance anymore.

The walnut trees shuddered and a twig cracked.

David stepped into the clearing.

"You scared the hell out of me," he said. "I had no idea where you'd gone."

"I'm sorry," I said, but I wasn't.

David picked up a walnut, scratched at the hull with his thumbnail, and brought it to his nose. He held it out to me.

"Smell it," he said. I breathed in. It smelled as new and crisp as freshly broken maple branches, under ripe bananas, and sweet oil. In such a damp winter, it shouldn't have been possible for a walnut to smell so clean.

David kissed the space between my neck and my ear. His breath felt warm and perfect. He whispered, "Your grandfather's house had walnuts like these, too."

JAKOB GLAS:
BATSCHKI BRESTOWATZ,
YUGOSLAVIA: 1945

"RUN, YOU SWABIAN DOGS, before we kill you!" a Serb shouted in the dark as the Glas family fled.

At dinnertime, a voice had come through the kitchen window: "Gerhardt," it said.

Jakob recognized the voice of Javor from down the street.

Javor used to come to dinner every Thursday night to talk about exotic fruit with Jakob's father. Whenever a shipment of oranges came in, Gerhardt set a dozen aside. Javor would come and peel them all at once to smell the sharp citrus. He would bring his honey rakija, and while he ate the fruit and spit the seeds, Jakob would sneak sips. One night, Javor taught Jakob how to chew orange rinds like gum. "It'll keep your breath fresh for the ladies," he said.

But Javor hadn't been over for dinner in months. Not since joining the Anti-Fascist Council for the National Liberation of Yugoslavia.

Jakob smiled and waved to Javor. He hadn't used the orange peel trick on any girls yet. He was saving it for when they started to get breasts. He spent most of his free time climbing trees or going to the movies with Mischi Wirag and Johann Niklos. Just that afternoon they went to the matinee—Tarzan der Affenmensch—and joked at watching Maureen O'Sullivan in sheepskin underpants.

"Gerhardt," Javor said from the window. "We're coming in the morning to send able-bodied men to Russia. Everyone else will be marched to Gakowa. Run."

He paused.

"It goes without saying, Gerhardt, I didn't come here."

Three hours later, the Glas family was packed and clambering onto a wagon hitched to a farm tractor. Jakob's father drove a roundabout route to the Hungarian border. Ordinarily it would only take a couple of hours to get to Hungary, but there were Partisans and Red Army men everywhere, setting up makeshift checkpoints.

Jakob heard a line of tires and horses bumping through the mud from inside the wagon. But he didn't peek outside to see the wagon train. He shut his eyes and dreamed the Partisans were Wild West railway thieves like in the movies.

Around midnight, a man with a Mauser stopped their tractor.

"Šta se ti nosi?" the man asked Gerhardt Glas.

"Proizvesti," Jakob's father replied. When the stranger pulled back the fabric and peered inside the wagon, all he saw were heaps of fruit—oranges, apples, plums, grapes, a few bananas. Jakob and his mother hid with their suitcases beneath the produce. They held their breaths, careful not to move so much as a toe in case the pyramid stacked around them tumbled. The man grabbed a banana and bit into it without removing the peel. When the ripe mush within burst out the sides, the man licked at it, and then sucked the guts out of the yellow fruit. He waved the tractor on.

When they crossed over into Hungary, Jakob's father stopped to put fuel in the tractor. A man walked up to him and said, in German, "You aren't safe yet. There are men waiting in the woods to take you back. Don't stop until you get to Austria."

At the refugee camp Haid, an unfamiliar man sits across from Jakob and his father in the mess hall at breakfast. Jakob looks back at his mother ladling thin potato soup into bowls for the other refugees and looks down at his own untouched broth. He's been at Camp Haid for weeks and still isn't used to the nutrient-poor meals and sleeping on a military cot and getting up at dawn to work the local farms like a man.

"You're from Brestowatz?" the man asks.

Jakob's father nods.

"Did you leave before it happened?"

"I'm sorry?" Jakob's father says.

"I wish I wasn't the one to tell you. The Partisans took twelve men and boys into Farmer Ament's field. They made them bury each other up to their necks in the dirt, save one. Johann Niklos buried his father and then got a bullet in the back of his head."

Jakob puts down his spoon. Acid burns his throat.

"As for the rest, the Partisans beat their skulls in with shovels until they were dead. Some had the heads cut—"

Jakob rushes out of the mess hall before he hears another word.

Both the men and women's latrines are the same giant hole in the ground, with wooden planks balanced across it.

Johann is dead.

Jakob vomits into the hole. When the vomit hits the pit, it splatters. He retches again, but there isn't enough food in him to bring up anything else.

Jakob feels emptiness in his stomach and his chest. He knew there'd been violence back in the Batschka. He'd heard of Partisans ambushing wagons along the way, of men getting shot in other villages' woods. But not in Brestowatz. Not his friends.

Jakob follows his father to work in silence. In the fields, he hacks his mattock into the ground, stabbing and tearing the soil. He's supposed to fill the tilled earth with the turnip seeds in his pocket, but he doesn't. He rips the brown apart and thinks how heavy Johann's shovel must have felt.

"Jakob," his father calls. "It's getting dark."

The sun hangs low and dim, as if God plucked a red plum and placed it in the sky.

"Coming, Papa."

The field workers, covered in mud, walk a tired road toward the camp and their dinners made of the same broth as their breakfast. The group grows larger as other men join the ranks from other farms. They talk about news they've heard, rumors of extermination camps made out of whole German villages. They talk about what happened in Brestowatz. His father comforts a man Jakob doesn't know.

Jakob lags behind, watching the sky darken, kicking his toes in the dirt.

He kicks dust over an apple and stops. His stomach grumbles, and he wonders if the apple is a mirage. He glances around. There are woods to the left full of Austrian pines. He bends down and wraps his fingers around the smooth, firm skin. He tugs the stem off the top and sniffs the tart flesh peeking from the apple's belly button.

Pebbles crunch in the road, a clumsy footstep.

Jakob feels something hard press against his spine and drops the apple. He looks up at the road. He squints to find his father, but in their muddy clothes and wide-brimmed hats, all the men look the same.

"Keep moving. Don't say a word or I'll shoot."

The gun barrel guides him toward the trees.

Jakob walks slowly through the brush.

"Move," the stranger says.

"Where are you taking me?"

The man presses the barrel harder.

"Shhh. I'm not afraid to shoot anyone who follows us."

Jakob keeps his eyes on the earth. In the spread of naked pine trunks, the ground is all dead needles and sticker bushes.

The day before Javor's warning came, Jakob climbed a giant oak with Johann after school. They carved faces in the hulls of under-ripe acorns. Faces and women's nipples. They laughed and cracked the shells and tried to eat the pith. The acorns might still be inside Johann's unmoving belly if the two boys hadn't gagged on the taste and spit the bitter nuts to the ground.

Thorns catch on Jakob's trousers.

"Enough," the stranger says once they're out of earshot of the farm road. "How old are you, boy?"

"Fourteen."

"And what's your name?" He shifts the gun from his left hand to his right.

"Jakob."

"Surname?"

"Glas."

"Wrong," the man says, pressing the tip of the shotgun against the boy's forehead. "Your name is Lukas Sholz."

Jakob looks beyond the barrel. The man's eyes are swollen.

The gun presses harder against Jakob's skull. Jakob feels the stranger's hand shaking through the metal. "I am Mr. Walter Sholz," he says. "The mayor of Ansfelden. And you're my son, Lukas. If you say anything to the contrary, I'll have your family killed."

Mr. Sholz drops the barrel. Jakob circles his fingertips over the indent on his forehead where the gun had been. He looks up at the mayor and then down at his feet. "Why are you doing this?"

"March," the mayor says.

As they walk through the woods toward town, Jakob hears the mayor breathing behind him. The mayor is overweight, but his heavy breaths sound more like hysteria than exhaustion. The gun shudders against Jakob's spine.

When they get to the edge of the wood, the mayor lowers the shotgun again. He looks around and kicks at the ground, mumbling under his breath until his foot finds what he's searching for. Jakob imagines his own head peering sideways, unblinking and bodiless, from a shrub.

The mayor pulls a dead hare from the dirt.

"We should be thankful for our fruitful hunting trip, son."

Mr. Sholz carries the gun in one hand and the hare in the other, by its ears. The animal has patches of fur missing, and tiny holes of torn flesh where the pellets hit. Jakob stares at the smooth red holes and the dead hare's eyes as he follows the mayor out of the woods and onto Laaher Strasse.

Jakob thinks of running as they turn left onto Ansfeldner Strasse, but Mr. Sholz holds the shotgun tight. The mayor leads them up a pair of concrete steps to a red front door, turns the lock, and steps inside.

"Come along, Lukas," he leans the shotgun against the wall and tosses the hare on the kitchen countertop. The house smells like cedar and dish soap. Furniture sits on throw rugs on the floor—a plush sofa, an armchair, and a foot stool. There's a wood-stove like the one Jakob's mother used to cook on, and an arched doorway separates the kitchen from the sitting room. "Marthe,"

Mr. Sholz calls. "We're home."

"Oh, thank goodness," she says, rushing down the stairs.

"Where is he?" The mayor looks at his wife.

"In the attic. Walter, we've got to get this one cleaned up." This one. Jakob shudders as Mrs. Sholz leans over him, licks her thumb, and rubs at a spot of dirt on his cheek.

He pictures a drafty prison in the attic with no windows and a slanted roof, where terrible things are done to refugee boys.

"Should I bring my gun up, Marthe? In case the boy gives you any trouble."

"He knows you'll be listening," she replies. "Don't you, dear?"

Jakob looks down at his feet.

"Come on, then." The mayor's wife guides him upstairs with her hand on his shoulder. Her palm is warm and damp through his shirt, but her fingers rest softly on his collarbone—they don't dig into him like the barrel of her husband's gun had done.

She leads him to the bathroom at the end of the hall.

The porcelain tub looks slick as bone. Mrs. Sholz turns the hot water on and plugs the drain. Jakob looks at the toilet, the first one he's seen in weeks, the first one he's ever seen indoors. Its glinting silver handle hangs like a broken wing.

"What do you say we get you freshened up?" She smiles. Jakob says nothing.

"Would you mind getting in the water, then?" Her eyebrows crease in the middle. "My husband is just downstairs."

She walks to the open door, facing away from the tub, and leans against the molding. "Please forgive my husband, dear. This whole situation has got him in an awful state."

Jakob puts the toilet lid down. It clonks against the seat. He lifts his foot up and pulls his shoestrings one at a time. After his shoes come off, he slips his socks from his feet with his thumb, folds them in half, and tucks them beneath the tongue of his shoes. He pauses and looks up at Mrs. Sholz, at her shoulders, her hair pulled into a bun at the nape of her neck. Her left hand has turned white on the door jamb. He sees her flushed cheeks in the edge of the mirror. Jakob pulls his shirt over his head, unfastens the button of his trousers and lets them drop to the floor with a quiet thud, shielding his privates with both hands. A turnip seed rolls across the floor like a tiny black eye, a shotgun pellet. It rolls across the checked tile and behind the toilet.

"Mrs. Sholz?" Jakob asks, sinking himself into the bathwater.

"Mother," she corrects, leaving the doorway and kneeling beside the tub.

"What are you going to do to me?"

"We're not going to do anything to you, dear." Her voice wavers. She lathers soap in her hands and runs her fingers through his hair, scrubbing at his scalp. "But I'm sorry. I have to keep my son safe."

"Safe from what?"

She doesn't answer. Instead, she points to a shelf near the edge of the tub. There's soap on one shelf, a towel on the one above it, and a lot of empty space where perhaps there had been trimming scissors and razors and heavy jars of shaving cream. He watches a thin froth appear on the surface of the water as he rubs the soap over himself.

Jakob washes his face and buries his head under the water, releasing the air from his lungs and wondering what it would feel like to drown.

"You have soap left," Mrs. Sholz says, pointing to her hair. He submerges himself again. Something brushes his scalp, presses the crown of his head. Jakob kicks out and breathes a mouthful of water. He pulls himself to the surface, coughing and covering himself.

"Forgive me," she says, stepping away from the tub. "You had soap left. Please forgive me."

"My name is Jakob, Mrs. Sholz."

She holds her hand up to quiet him.

"My name is Jakob Glas. I am not an orphan. My mother and father live at Haid, in the barracks with other families. They'll know I'm missing. Please let me go home. My mother will worry."

"Enough," she says, pointing to the towel on the shelf and closing her eyes. When he's outside of the tub with the towel around his waist, she hands him a fresh pile of pajamas.

"Put these on, Lukas."

He brings the clothing to his face and breathes the clean smell. The bathroom tiles wave back and forth. Jakob grips the tub for balance.

"Please," he says.

The mayor's wife pulls the shirt from him.

"Arms up," she replies. He inserts his arms through the shirt-sleeves. The room is too bright. Jakob blinks. His knee bends as the mayor's wife guides a pair of underpants over his ankles. He feels a tingling sensation in his groin. Mrs. Sholz looks away before slipping the underpants up under the towel. She tugs the trousers up one leg at a time, lets the towel drop. The tiles wave in front of Jakob. It looks as if, if he took a step, the floor would ripple like water and he'd fall in.

Mrs. Sholz's face is the color of red clay. She walks toward the hallway and looks over her shoulder. Jakob meets her eyes and knows he's supposed to follow. *If you say anything to the contrary, I'll have your family killed.*

He shouldn't have given the mayor his name. He shouldn't have given it to her either.

She was supposed to let him go.

With her hand on the small of his back, she guides him inside a room down the hall. It's a boy's room, with white walls and a wooden bed wrapped in a blue bedspread. There's a poster of a football team, a desk shoved against one wall with schoolwork on it but no pencil. The navy curtains are drawn. The wardrobe is shut. A pair of slippers sits at the edge of the bed in front of a nightstand with nothing on it but a very small lamp.

Mrs. Sholz follows him inside and pulls the bedspread down.

"Get comfortable, Lukas. I'll bring you up something to eat."

She locks him in. While she's gone, Jakob looks around the room. He checks the desk drawers for scissors or a letter opener, for a photograph of the real Lukas, the one locked upstairs in the attic. He pulls the chair away from the desk, stands on it, reaches up and beats his fist against the ceiling. The floor creaks as Lukas moves above him.

"Can you hear me?" Jakob asks, just above a whisper. He asks again, a little louder. No answer. Only footsteps above moving away from where he knocked. "Please," he says. The footsteps stop.

Jakob hears a stair creak. He steps back onto the floor, pushes the chair under the desk, and sits on the edge of the bed with his hands in his lap.

The lock clicks, the knob turns, and the door swings slowly open. Both Sholzes are standing in the doorway, Mrs. Sholz with a tray of real food—milk and goulash and bread, a shiny red apple—and Mr. Sholz with his gun on his shoulder.

"I'll be right out here," he says, leaning against the hallway wall.

"Be nice, Walter. He's been a good boy."

The mayor sighs and shifts out of view. Mrs. Sholz shuts the door so only a crack of light comes in, perhaps so that her husband's gun might feel farther away.

"There now," she says, balancing the tray on the desk and moving toward Jakob. "Tuck yourself under the covers. You've got a big day tomorrow."

Jakob pulls himself up the bed with his arms and slides his legs under the sheets. The mayor's wife places the tray on his lap and hands him a spoon. Her eyes are red and the corners of her mouth look tired.

"Goodnight," she says.

He hears his mother's voice. She calls as she did the day he left the house to buy her flour, a few years before they fled. "My Jakob, such a good boy!" He felt so proud then, so tall pushing a wheelbarrow all by himself for the miller to fill. He tried to show off his strength by steering the load one-handed. But then everything tilted sideways. The flour and wheelbarrow lurched and fell and Jakob's arm got caught underneath. He heard the bone snap. His blond hair was doused with white, his clothes, his bare skin. He doesn't remember pulling himself out of the wreckage and walking home, but he remembers leaving white powder footprints on the floor. His mother shrieked when she saw him. There were clumps of blood on his arm, tears caked into the powder beneath his eyes and the flour on his cheeks.

"What have you done?" she cried.

Jakob will wake to knuckles rapping on the front door and the sound of Mr. Sholz's footsteps in the hall. He'll hear soft conversation, another man's voice.

"Hurry up, hurry up!" Mrs. Sholz will whisper, bursting in and shoeing him out of the bedroom. "He's early!"

Jakob will picture one of Tito's men, come to drag him back to the Batschka, as the mayor's wife guides him down the hall.

"Make yourself at home," Mrs. Sholz will say to the guest as she rushes down the stairs and into the sitting room, pulling Jakob by the hand. Jakob will count the cushions on the sofa. Three, plus four pillows.

"Would you like an orange?" Mrs. Sholz will pull a bowl of fruit from the sideboard and thrust it forward.

"No thank you, ma'am. This is your son?"

"Yes, sir."

Mr. Sholz will nudge Jakob. "Stand up straight, son."

His wife will drop the bowl and sob into her wrist. Jakob will watch the oranges tumble across the floor.

"Your name?" the soldier will ask, handing him a stack of folded clothes.

Jakob Glas. I am not their son.

Mrs. Sholz will blow her nose into a handkerchief.

"Show respect to the Lieutenant, son."

"It's all right," the officer will say, lifting Jakob's chin and smiling. "It's a big day for him. But he's going to be a strong man and fight for his Führer and his country, isn't he?"

The mayor will thrust his left arm forward. "Heil, Hitler."

The soldier will tighten his grip on Jakob's chin.

"Your name?"

NOVI SAD, SERBIA: 2012

DAVID WAS PRESSED against my back so firmly the thick, dark hairs on his chest felt like they belonged to me. The light sweat collecting on his skin from the warmth of us felt like mine. If it weren't so dark, I could have seen the heat rising off his chest like summer on asphalt.

Sid's chest was smooth, his skin always slightly cool, always dry. But he held me the same way, his arm draped over my waist and bent at the elbow so his hand rested joyfully between my breasts.

"How are you always so delicious?" David whispered.

I rolled over to face him.

"I don't know what you're talking about." I kissed his soft, thin lips. His tongue tasted of felled wood and smoke.

His hand moved between my legs.

I tried to pretend I wasn't thinking of Sid, of earth filled with corpses, that I wasn't picturing my grandfather frowning, saying, "Sid is safe. Your Oma was safe. For a while I thought of leaving, but Rosalinde died. If I'd left, I'd have been alone."

Was I as afraid of the unknown as David was?

I thought of the dream I had the night Opa died, the one where he reached through the mattress. I thought of the way his smell washed over me the day Oma went into Bayside, and again at the hotel in Linz. I thought of Magdalena Knebl, Madgolna Deutsch, prayer candles, walnuts falling from trees and startling the dead.

"I can't," I said. "I'm sorry."

He looked at me as if I'd said, "You're not enough."

I knew my grandparents. But I didn't know them as Jakob and Edie. As a husband or a wife. A friend. A neighbor. A sibling.

I only knew them as Oma and Opa.

One Easter, Oma shouted at me for staying up past my bedtime to watch Charlton Heston play Moses on TV. She gave me the silent treatment for a night and a day. She didn't talk to Opa either, for letting me stay up.

"Sure, you can break the rules," she'd said to him before the silence began. He didn't respond. Neither did he respond in the morning. He didn't say, "Eds, please," to soften her anger. He didn't get angry in return. Instead he got himself a warm can of Sprite and sat in front of the television.

She shut herself in the kitchen, peeling leftover eggs and putting them inside tiny meatloaves.

And I knelt on the carpet, coloring, dripping tears on the crayon that didn't absorb into the paper.

I thought Oma had stopped talking to me because she didn't love me anymore. Not because grown up life was complicated and she was lonely.

And now, if she didn't have Alzheimer's, would she speak to me? Would she see Opa in me, whatever was in him that made him unfaithful?

Maybe she'd look at me and realize she didn't know me at all.

But maybe she already knew that, that no one knows anybody. Not really.

What else would you learn when you woke up one day and your neighbors wanted you dead.

Sid and I got in a fight once, at two in the morning. We were tipsy. We had each drunk a bottle of wine, and I was coming off my buzz, my eyes refocusing on the mess around the living room. Dinner plates stacked up on his computer desk. A garbage can overflowing beside it. Beer bottles on the coffee table, fleece jackets and socks on the floor. There was cat food all over the breakfast bar because we had to keep the cat's dish off the floor so the dog wouldn't eat from it. Four pairs of shoes in front of the sofa, one of which I tripped over when I got up to pee.

"You're so fucking lazy," I shouted from the toilet.

"Nothing ever changes," I screamed through my toothbrush. I spat into the sink, using his toothbrush to scrub crusted toothpaste out of the basin. In the kitchen, I heard the faucet turn on, the sound of dishes clinking and a soap bottle thudding against the counter. *Why do I always have to get so angry before he picks up after himself?* I hated the nasty screaming version of me—I'd never seen that part of myself before Sid.

That night I stood in the bathroom, crying into the mirror, rubbing at my mascara-stained cheeks until they were raw. I raged at his silence, as I often did, and he responded predictably: he stared into the sink and said nothing.

We'd only been married for two months. He came out of the kitchen carrying clean wine glasses, still dripping wet. He stood in the bathroom doorway, bare feet on the porcelain tile, and the look in his eyes was both hateful and sad. His mouth was turned down and his knuckles were white on the glass stems.

"Stop being such a fucking bitch," he said. I felt my heart throb in my intestines. "Fuck you," I said and raised my hand to slap him. It happened in slow motion. I saw his hands moving to shield his face, still holding the wine glasses. *Move your hands, move your hands, I can't actually hurt you.* But I couldn't stop my hand from swinging.

The impact felt like a porcupine. Skinny shards of glass buried themselves between my fingers, in my palm. It sounded like a bell breaking. Tiny pellets of hail rained on the hardwood. I looked down and saw blood. On my shirt, on the floor. Mostly below Sid's hands. I looked up at him. His face was the color of wet concrete. He looked at me with his mouth open, and then looked at the back of his right hand.

A piece of glass that must have been one-third of the whole had wedged itself between his thumb and forefinger. He pulled it out slowly, and I took the shard from his fingers. I squatted over the blood and started picking up the larger pieces. I shooed the cat and dog away. Both animals seemed to know better than to come too close.

"I'm sorry," I said, but I don't know if any sound came out.

"I'm sorry. Oh God, Sid, I'm so sorry."

I cried and shook as Sid walked to the bathroom sink to rinse the gash in his hand. I hugged the back of him while he turned on the faucet and let the water run. He leaned over his hand as he held it under the flow. When the cold water touched his skin, the cut opened deeper—his muscle showed through like raw meat. He let out a groan and got heavy in my arms. I stumbled backward and caught myself, guiding his unconscious body to the floor. I leaned against the bathtub and pulled him to my chest. "Sid," I said.

I shook him gently, kissed his cheek.

"Sid, please wake up, or I'm going to call an ambulance. Should I call an ambulance? Sid, please. I'm going to call 9-1-1. Wake up." It felt like minutes had passed, but I knew it had been only seconds. I just didn't know how many seconds. Or how many seconds was bad. And his hand was so bloody. And he wouldn't wake up. I slid my hand into his front pocket and pulled out his cell phone. "Sid, wake up or I'm going to call."

As soon as I'd hung up with the dispatcher, Sid woke up, and we had fifteen minutes to concoct a story that didn't sound like we'd been fighting. When the EMTs showed up, they separated Sid and I and asked us if we had been victims of spousal abuse. We said, to separate EMTs on separate sides of our apartment, that we were tipsy. I was brushing my teeth and Sid was washing up. I had been talking with my mouthful of toothpaste and Sid couldn't understand me. So he came, wet wine glasses still in hand, to hear me closer up, while I, after quickly spitting the toothpaste into the sink, came rushing out of the bathroom to talk to him in the kitchen. And then the craziest thing happened. We collided in the doorway. We both put our hands out to brace ourselves and ended up with glass all over the place. We went to the sink to clean his cut, and then he fainted. And I caught him. And he wouldn't wake up. So I called 9-1-1.

The EMT I was speaking with looked at me like I was an idiot. After Sid finished telling the story to his EMT, the two men met in the hallway and whispered for a few minutes. Sid came over and leaned his head on my shoulder. His hand had been wrapped in gauze. Mine too.

Finally, one of them said to Sid, "You're going to need x-rays and stitches. Are you alright to walk to the ambulance?"

We spent a total of seven hours at Temple University Hospital. Six and a half in the waiting room. "I'm sorry," I kept saying between uncomfortable naps on the waiting room chairs, my head on his shoulder, his cheek against my forehead. "I broke you. I left a mark." *I'm going to have to look at that scar every day for the rest of my life.*

"My hand looked like when you carve a turkey, when you separate the leg from the body," he said. I couldn't tell if he heard me.

"I'm sorry," I said, over and over.

They pulled out a few small pieces of glass from between my fingers. A med student sewed Sid's hand up, eight stitches. She did a sloppy job, without enough Lidocaine. And then they sent us home, hands bandaged like catcher's mitts. There were no cabs because it was rush hour, so we walked three miles, through North Philadelphia, with no sleep, in silence, looking like we'd just spent the night beating the crap out of someone, or each other. While we walked, Sid called his boss and said he wasn't going to be able to come to work because he spent the night in the ER and he couldn't type for all the fresh stitches in his skin. His soft, perfect skin. I loved those soft hands. They were softer than mine. Mine were always dry. His had been hands that were polished by model airplanes and PlayStation controllers. I gave him a hard time about those things, but I loved him for them.

When we got home, the dog and cat were sitting by the closed bathroom door, looking at us with scolding eyes because it was us who messed on the rug this time, not them. Sid went to lie down while I swept up the glass and scrubbed dried blood out of the grout.

When I finished, I curled up behind him and molded myself to his body. I pressed my face against his back, my knees against the backs of his thighs. I draped my bandaged hand over his side and kissed him through his shirt. He turned his head to face me and kissed me. Again and again we kissed: his big lips tasted like hospital air. We kissed and I thought, *I'm a terrible person.* We kissed and I thought, *I'm a terrible wife*. We kissed and I thought, *I don't think I can rely on this soft, beautiful man*.

After the stitches came out and the scar healed, it looked like a crooked smile. He had three moles in a triangle above the pink curve.

"It adds character," he said. "Besides, I don't really notice it anymore. It doesn't hurt."

I took a felt tip pen and drew a circle around each one of the moles. I drew a hot dog shape around his scar. I dotted two of the moles like eyes and connected the dots. It made an alien face with thick lips and a little antenna sticking out the top of its head. We named him Hubert and pronounced it in a French accent.

Sid would wiggle his thumb so Hubert's mouth moved. He would squeeze his thumb to his forefinger and make Hubert pucker his lips and kiss my cheek. He would press Hubert to my ear and whisper things like, "Sid thinks you're pretty. He wants me to tell you he misses your kisses."

I often thought, "Hubert, you selfish alien, you swallowed everything."

I don't know what happened. When we started dating in college, Sid and I would lay naked in my extra-long twin bed and count stars. Every time we made love, we added a metallic star sticker to my dry erase board. Afterward, we'd lie together, talk about rocket science, what I was going to do when I grew up, what our life would look like if we managed to get old together.

"You'll be a sexy GILF."

"You'll be a fat old man. But I'll love you anyway."

Our best days were spent pretending we weren't growing up. I don't remember exactly when those days stopped—whether it was when he was in grad school or after we moved back to Philadelphia to start what we used to call real life.

So much time passed between being intimate that I got nervous of what he'd think about my body, that he'd forget my too-soft parts in the interim and frown at the rediscovery. I'd done the same to him. Hair grew in funny places on his upper arms—not dark hairs, but long ones, dense enough I could stick Velcro to it. And the pores on his nose were so deep, with so much dirt buried in them. His teeth weren't as white and shining as I remembered them. His lips, they were perfect, too big for my thin ones; they swallowed me when he kissed me, and I loved it. Only, once he stopped acting like a lost boy, his kisses tasted more like pickles.

He worked all day. I worked evenings. He made money and I spent it. On wine and clothes, shoes, apartment decor. When he got home from work, on the days I wasn't working, we ate dinner in front of the television. Afterward, he played video games. We'd go for a walk if the weather was nice, down the tree-lined streets or to the river where we'd sniff the tide and follow bridge lights and lampposts for miles. I'd walk ahead while he lagged behind, and it felt like walking alone. But when I slowed down and he caught up, I'd look into his eyes and see something that made me think maybe so much hadn't changed. I'd hold his hand and lean my cheek on his shoulder. He'd say, "I want a house with you." And I'd say, "I want that one," and point. The houses I pointed at were always corner lots with slate roofs and arched wooden doorways. He'd say I love you and I'd say I love you too, but I'd still feel alone afterward.

On weekends, we went into Center City and tried to bring the romance back. I'd ask him to take me out to eat truffled egg toast and drink champagne, or else pile cheese onto baguettes with mostarda and drink reds so heavy I couldn't see through them. We talked about the food and the wine, mmm-ed over the flavor combinations, and otherwise said nothing. Sometimes he'd say he was unhappy at work because it didn't feel like a challenge. I'd want to say something like, "I'm unhappy at home because this loneliness is too much work."

But I didn't.

I didn't tell him that the wine and cheese and truffle oil, the fancy beer, the expensive dinners with more than three courses, the shoes and skirts and dresses I bargain-hunted on sadder days, the jackets, the overpriced haircuts, I didn't tell him that I was making a Sid out of those things to fill the distance between us. I didn't tell him I didn't like having sex with him anymore.

I asked him if he was happy. His voice came out like a bad

transmission from a satellite news station.

"Yes," he'd said. "Yes, I'm happy."

When we only made love dutifully, I started getting angry. I started locking myself in the bathroom and crying. I didn't know why I was unhappy. I should have been happy. I was married to my best friend. We had a grownup apartment—one with hardwood floors and high ceilings and crown molding. It had a dishwasher and south-facing sash windows and a Juliet balcony off the living room. We were living in the city, our city. We had artwork on the walls, flowers on the kitchen table. We had a wine habit and a walk-in closet, a cat, a dog, and if I wanted, we could have kids.

"Are you happy?" I asked him again, when I couldn't remember how long it had been since we'd been intimate. We were at dinner at a seafood restaurant that served seared scallops in a saffron broth, gorgonzola with walnuts and lavender honey, and pork belly rendered in duck fat. Sid had always been a quantity of meat kind of guy—Red Robin burgers with bottomless steak fries, whole thin crust pizzas, full bowls of gnocchi with cream sauce. He looked up at me from his three-ounce portion of pork belly and said, "I don't know."

I looked at him.

"I think I'm happy," he said, "But I can't be happy if you're not happy."

Happy. The word sounded like balloons and confetti and rainbow jimmies on soft serve ice cream. It sounded like Ferris wheels and candy apples. It didn't sound like anything real.

For our wedding, we wrote our own vows. We promised to make each other happy forever. I didn't know if I'd ever been happy. I didn't know what happy was supposed to be. Sitting at that too-small table in the corner of that restaurant, I'd had such high hopes. And there at the table, they all burst like blue and red and yellow latex. I felt the pieces smack my face, like when you blow a balloon up too big and it explodes and rubber-bands back on your cheeks.

"I'm not," I said. "Happy."

ZRENJANIN, SERBIA: 2012

WE STOOD IN A FOREST OF PINES. The trees were half naked—bare at the bottom, needles at the very top. The needles made a blanket on the ground, and the blanket killed the grass. Twenty feet up, a black and white bird perched in the branches. I asked David what it was. He said, "Hello, Mister Magpie, how are your wife and kids today?"

The bird's slick feathers contrasted the matte gray sky, the dull green needles in the tree, and the dead brown needles on the ground. He looked at me and made a noise like a dial-up modem.

"It's bad luck to see a magpie on its own," David said.

The magpie wore a mourning cloak and cried because the insects he plucked out of the dirt tasted like dead people. There were people in the dirt, and the plants ate the people in the dirt, and the bugs ate the plants full of people, and the frogs ate the bugs and became full of people too.

Something was wrong with my throat. It felt full and it itched. I opened my mouth and reached my hand back, knuckles against teeth, fingers slipping over my tongue.

Something was in there. I pinched the end of a piece of twine, and when I pulled, it chafed my tonsils.

"Be careful not to break it," David said. "You know what's at the end."

The magpie said it too, "You know what's at the end."

I pulled and pulled.

The string coiled on the ground like skinny intestines.

When I opened my eyes, David was lying on his side, staring at me.

"You were breathing funny," he said. "I almost woke you."

I reached for the glass of water beside the bed.

"What time is it?" I asked. My throat felt like sandpaper.

"Five-thirty," he said, climbing out of bed and pulling open the curtain. "Are you okay?"

"Fine." But I could feel the dampness of my skin and the sheets beneath me. "Come back to bed."

"I'm awake now." He held his hand out for me to take. "What do you say I make breakfast and we get an early start."

David made scrambled eggs and piled them on two plates next to smoked fish and dry toast. He sprinkled pepper over the eggs, salt over the eggs and toast. He boiled coffee in the small Turkish pot on the stove. We ate in silence. David had overcooked the eggs. The coffee was hot and strong and burned the charred egg taste off my tongue.

"You said something else while you were dreaming," he said.

"What?" Oh God, what did I say?

"You called out for your Mum."

"I did?"

"Can I ask—what happened to your parents?"

"I never knew them," I said.

"I'm sorry. Should I not have asked?"

"No, it's okay."

He pushed my plate aside and took my hand.

"When she was a kid, my grandparents dressed my mother and her brother up in dirndls and lederhosen and taught them all the German dances. The polka. The schuhplattler. The maypole dances. They spent most of their time either at the German Hungarian Club or at church.

I don't think my mother wanted to be the daughter of immigrants. She wanted to be American. She'd go out after school with her skirt rolled up to meet kids who didn't know her as "the German girl." I know this because Opa saw her outside the 7-Eleven smoking cigarettes with an American boy. He dragged her home by the wrist and forbade her from seeing the boy again. It's a funny thing parents do with teenagers—forbid them from doing a thing. Because you know they'll do it anyway. She kept seeing him. If you listened to my grandmother, he was the worst kind of boy:

back-talked, smoked cigarettes, didn't go to Catholic school. But even if he had been polite and Catholic and German, my Oma would have hated him because my mom got pregnant. She was seventeen. There were complications. She died just after I was born."

"I'm sorry."

"After everything they'd been through, trying to raise a family in a safe place, my grandparents still lost their daughter."

"And your father?"

"I never met him. And my uncle left for California after graduating college. But my grandparents were more than enough. I was loved. I had everything I needed. They didn't push me to learn their culture the way they did with my mother. I don't know if that was because going through all the teaching again would have reminded them of her. I didn't even have a dirndl. Though I wore one of hers to school for Halloween one year. I went to the public one and became what my mother wanted to be: separate from my Swabianness."

"I was close with my grandfather," David said. "I don't think I told you, but he died the week before we met. I was traveling for work, and I didn't make it home to see him."

"Oh, David," I squeezed his hand. "That must have been terrible."

"Maybe that's why I wanted to bring you here, when you told me about your grandparents in your apartment that day, when I saw all the photographs and books and how much you loved them."

"What was your grandfather like?"

He shook his head.

"Everything a grandfather should be."

After we cleared away the dishes, I showered. Aleksander hadn't been in the apartment since the day we arrived, and the towels he'd left smelled strange. I couldn't tell if laundry detergent smelled different in Serbia or if the towels were dirty. I skipped drying and walked naked and sopping out of the bathroom.

David balanced on one foot in his underwear, tugging his sock up. Even standing like a flamingo, he was beautiful. I couldn't help feeling that I could never let go of something so perfect and kind. So much more tender than I expected, so much sadder. We were both grieving. Maybe that's what made us so hungry for each other. Whenever I looked at David, I wanted to touch him. I could forgive anything for the beauty of his face, sideways, looking at his feet while a gray morning light snuck in through the window behind him and illuminated the stubble on his chin.

"Where are we going today?" he asked, looking up. "I can't remember."

"Zrenjanin," I said. "The old sugar factory."

When we started planning the trip, I found postcards and old photographs from when the sugar factory was the face of Gross-Betschkerek—renamed Zrenjanin after the Swabians were expelled. The factory was made of brick and plaster. Parts of it were five stories high. I thought it would be easy to find, that the towering brick chimney would erupt like a skyscraper over the rooftops. Except when I searched for it on Google Maps that morning from Aleksander's apartment, it didn't exist.

I searched the Serbian web and found an economic report. In 2006, it produced six thousand tons of sugar a day. I also found a company called The Sophia Group, but their page was in Serbian and the Google translation was vague. All I could gather was that The Sophia Group had purchased the sugar factory in 2011. I searched for Sophia Group, Sophia, fabrika Sophia, and Sophia šećera, Zrenjanin, and found nothing.

The absence of information felt purposeful.

It couldn't have just disappeared. A man had visited the property in the fall and had his photograph taken with the chimney stack. I'd found his blog back in Philadelphia, but that also didn't seem to exist in Serbia.

We followed the skyline in the Spark, looking for the factory. I was thankful it was winter: no leaves obstructed the view between branches. We drove circles around town. From my postcards, it looked like the factory was built to be on display. But there was no sign of it.

Then: a tiny sliver between two prone limbs.

"There!" I pointed.

David saw the chimney too and turned down a small stony lane.

The lane dead ended onto a paved street. Tall stacks of hay bales ran along the roadside behind a brick wall—hay bales stacked so high we couldn't see past them.

"Shit," he said.

"I know, the hay, it blocks the view. How weird is that?"

"Not the hay. The barbed wire."

"What?"

"It's facing the wrong direction."

"What do you mean?" I asked, taking in the steel posts holding up three rows of sharp wire.

"If you want to keep people out, you point them toward the outside," he said, his face the color of oatmeal. "If you want to keep them in, you point them like that."

Inward.

My insides coiled. David kept driving. Both the barbed wire and the hay continued the length of the wall. I pictured the bales burning: a great fiery ring cooking all the sugar down to hardened sludge.

A stone driveway with a gate appeared to the right. David stopped in front of it. It looked like a construction entrance, with tracks the size of digger tires scoring the mud, but there were no men in hard hats, no machines running.

A break in the hay let us see in:

The chimney stack thrust itself into the air behind a white plaster building. No steam or smoke emanated from the top. Along the road, on the other side of the gate, shacks the size of small sheds backed up to the wall. Not big enough to fit a grown man lying down, they looked like chicken coops. Except beaten footpaths wound from each shack through the grass and mud to the road. There were wooden posts and wire fences between them, and doors and garbage out front. I pictured a man sitting inside each one, peering through gaps in the wood, watching for people like me.

"Maybe we shouldn't stop here so long," I said. "What if someone sees?"

"We're not trespassing."

I'd written to a Chicagoan named Thomas in the months before the trip, looking for advice. Thomas was the president of a Swabian-American organization. "If you manage to get to Serbia," he'd said. "Be careful. You're allowed to ask questions, but they'll make you believe you're not." I hadn't thought of his advice once since we arrived in Serbia—until we found the sugar factory.

David drove around the perimeter. Cyrillic signs surrounded the property.

I assumed they translated to *No Trespassing*.

We pulled around a corner and found a platoon of park benches and pine trees standing guard at the front entrance. The park was beautiful, even in winter, but there was no one inside it. The asphalt shone beneath the needle canopy. Empty benches lined immaculate paved pathways. The garbage cans had no stains, as if no one had ever spilled coffee against the sides, or soda, or sandwich grease. The fence around the factory was taller by the park. In spite of its height, it looked friendlier—happy blue chain-link ten feet tall. We pulled into a parking space near the gate.

David and I stepped out of the car and walked up to the fence. I aimed my camera lens at the chimney stack. I photographed through the links: a fountain in the courtyard, not running because it was January, surrounded by perfect brick and plaster walls.

You'd never know from looking at it what it used to be.

"Vi!" a man shouted. "Vi! Vi!"

I looked around. David's mischievous expression had changed.

The man appeared at the fence out of breath in a navy-blue uniform, slicing his arms through the air. I couldn't understand his words, but his frown was deep. I could hear Aleksander saying that in Serbia, men's lips were heavy because chains hung from the corners of their mouths.

I lifted my arms above my head with the camera tight in my fist to show that I wouldn't take any more photographs, that I'd stop whatever it was I was doing to offend him. He shook his head and pointed toward the road, shouting.

"I'm sorry," I said. At the sound of my voice he scowled. "Nosy American," his scowl said. "Foolish woman."

The guard retreated to a small building, clean and well-kept like the larger buildings behind it, the ones that used to house sick and starving beaten Swabians. Dying children. The recently deceased. The guard shut the door and watched from the window.

"I think we'd better go." David's voice was quiet.

"We have a right to look," I said. "We're on the right side of the fence." I wanted to be on the other side, see what the factory looked like on the inside, if they'd gotten rid of the stench of eight thousand unshowered bodies living in their own refuse.

"Maybe we do. But they can still make this really unpleasant." He pulled at my sleeve. "Please. We can get some lunch and figure out what to do next."

My stomach remembered that it hadn't been fed since before dawn. I felt sick that some part of my body thought food could fill the emptiness in my belly. I'd stirred a teaspoon of Serbian sugar into my coffee every morning since we arrived in Novi Sad. It had tasted like coffee and sugar were meant to. Because the sugar factory was sleeping. If it woke up and made sugar again, would the sugar taste funny—or would locals and consumers as far away as Austria sip their sweetened coffees and smile without tasting the bodies in their mugs? As they must have done for all the decades the Zrenjanin sugar factory was operational: 90,000 tons of sugar left the factory to be consumed in 1977 alone.

"Okay," I said, and walked toward the car. David backed out of the parking space before I had a chance to shut my door, and by the time we passed the park, sirens were sounding. Not sirens from the factory, sirens ahead of us, police cars. It sounded like at least two.

"Is that for us?"

"I don't know," David said, "It might be." He sounded calm but his knuckles were too tight on the wheel and he shifted the gearbox more roughly than normal. He pulled the car into an apartment complex parking lot. "We need to park where they can't see our plates from the road. We have Belgrade plates."

I thought he was overreacting, but my heart raced. I also thought he was too good at concealment. David parked the Spark behind a garbage can, where we could still see the street. He turned off the car and double checked that the lights were off.

"David." The sirens' shrill echo screamed between the apartment buildings. "David?"

He reached his arm around the back of his seat, grabbed our plastic grocery bag lunch, and pulled out two cans of tuna fish salad, bread, and cheese wedges. I took a slice of bread, one can, and cheese. David made the grocery bag look like Mary Poppins's carpet bag—pulling out bottles of water, forks, knives, paper towels, and an oversized bag of walnut crescent cookies that looked like the kipferls Oma made every Christmas.

"Shouldn't we wait to eat?" I asked. David opened the bag of walnut crescents and popped one in his mouth. Air hissed out of his water bottle as he unscrewed the cap. His eyes didn't leave the road. When he popped the second cookie into his mouth and chewed, flecks of pastry and powdered sugar stuck to his lips. Police lights reflected off the apartment windows. Three cars drove past, toward the factory. When they were out of sight, David started the car and pulled out of the lot, still chewing his cookie.

"What do you say we get out of Zrenjanin?" he said.

The plan for the day had been to look for the other city camp at the oil factory and to search for the German Catholic cemetery as we had done in Gakowa, even though all the cemeteries in Vojvodina looked the same—as if only Serbians had been buried there for the last two-hundred years.

I'd learned, at least, how everything stayed hidden so long.

"Okay," I said. My heart thudded.

I popped the tab on my tuna can and slid the lid back. Inside, mixed with flakes of fish: black beans and corn. I looked at the can for signs of Prvi Depo but didn't find any. I slid my fork into the can and took a bite. When the fish and corn hit my tongue, I was both hungry and sick to my stomach. Seven hours had passed since I'd eaten eggs with David in Novi Sad. I swallowed every last kernel of corn from the can, smeared cheese on my slice of bread, and forced it down with the oily flaked tuna.

My stomach lurched on the bumpy side roads out of Zrenjanin. It lurched when we hit potholes, which we did often, and with each change from asphalt to gravel and back again. The Partisans had starved Swabians in milk halls, in sugar factories, in vegetable canning facilities. They'd starved thousands of human beings where they made food for themselves. They swallowed hidden genocides to destroy the evidence of death.

"Would you like a crescent?" David held out the bag.

UNNAMED: GROSS-BETSCHKEREK, YUGOSLAVIA: 1945

THE VIEW THROUGH MY WINDOW is of men in the mud. It's hard to tell that's the view because my room used to be part of the sugar factory and my window is covered in a sticky film. My room isn't my own. I have a bunk. There are fifteen other bunks. They belong to women. My bed isn't warm, but it feels safer than other places. Except when I sleep. Then the nightmares come.

The men outside the window are rolling in the mud, but all I see are prison guards trampling on their bodies. I can't see the guards' shoes, but I know there are nails on the bottoms because of the screaming.

At nightfall, all the women are locked in my room—the sixteen of us plus dozens from other rooms facing out over the yard. We're locked in while the men are brought one by one into the room next door. We hear the guards' throaty voices through the stone. The commandant speaks Serbian. I can't understand him, but I understand the pleading in German from the inmates.

"Please God, have mercy," the woman beside me says. It's her husband. I know because when his voice echoes, she falls to her knees. The Partisans have chipped away gutters in the interrogation room floor, an old man told me the day I arrived. There are whispers that the gutters are used to catch German blood. We all know the room is used for torture, that the men who go in don't come back. The guards tell us they are merciful, that they free the men who disappear because they've denounced their Nazi heritage and have promised to work for the Anti-Fascist Council for the National Liberation of Yugoslavia. But we are not stupid. We hear ragged breathing through the stone when the guards are done. We hear the gunshots in the yard before dawn.

The woman has dampened her blouse with her tears, but she hasn't made a sound. The guards like it when the wives of the tortured cry out.

I was a wife. But my husband is dead, and my children. I lost them in Lazarfeld, before I was brought to Betschkerek. I prayed for God to take me with them, but He did not.

The commandant's voice grates against the wall. The woman beside me is trembling. The others keep their distance, as if she's cursed. I pull my skirt up and kneel so that our arms touch.

She digs her teeth into her lower lip. I press my palms together. As the tips of my fingers meet their mirror image, I close my eyes and pray without words. For grace. For mercy. For the suffering man. For my husband and my children. I pray for the women around me, for the crying woman, for myself. I pray to the Blessed Mother to help me understand what He has planned for me, why He brought my family to His bosom and left me behind.

A door slams. The husband has grown quiet next door. There are footsteps in the hallway, men's boots on stone. The women are silent. The only noise in the room is the woman beside me sobbing through her closed mouth. A drop of blood falls from her lips and sinks into the weave of her dress.

Time moves slowly waiting for what's next. The footsteps stop outside our door. A key works the lock, tripping one pin at a time. The lock clicks. Every woman holds her breath as the door opens. The commandant steps inside with half a dozen guards, and the air is thick with the smell of rakija—the tang of fermented plums stings my nose.

We call the commandant The Boxer. He calls himself Bog Batina, God of Beatings. He is the worst of men. When he enters a room we must stand at attention, but we're not allowed to look into his face. I saw a man make eye contact with him at breakfast on my second day. The Boxer threw one punch straight into the man's face and broke his neck. When the man fell, The Boxer leapt on his belly and said, "Are you dead yet?"

To the other inmates in the mess hall he said, "You worthless fascist swine. How dare you raise your eyes to meet me."

It's easy for the commandant to kill a man with one punch. His fingers are made of gold. If you look closely, you see the gold consists of many pieces. Golden rings run the length of each finger—from the butts of his pinkies to the tips of his thumbs, with space left only for his knuckles. He pulls wedding bands from the hands of men and women who disappear from camp. It's hard to know how many have disappeared. Empty beds are always filled with new faces, and no one dares to ask. The Boxer polishes his golden hands with the skin of Swabian faces. His fists gleam in even the dimmest light.

All of the women stand upright—shoulders back, feet together, eyes to the floor. I rise and pull the crying woman off the ground. It's a mistake. When I lift my chin to see how much slower I am than the others, The Boxer is before me. His eyes are dark.

"What is this?" He grabs my jaw. His neck is splotched with rage. I try to look down at his shoes, but all I see are rings shining on his fingers. When I close my eyes they're still there, as if I've been staring at a bright light for too long.

"Napolje! Brze, brze!" one of the guards shouts, pointing to the door. "Run, you fools!"

The guards laugh as the other women rush for the hallway like cattle. The Boxer smiles and pushes me away. "Move!"

My bare feet are heavy. The floor is out of focus. And the guards follow us like wolves.

"Here, piggy, piggy!" they shout. The other women are far ahead. I hear them stampeding around a corner. Their bare feet beat the stone until the distance between us muffles their steps.

No one is safe. Other guards may be waiting to catch the women up in their arms, hold them close like lovers, close enough that the women can smell the blood on their hands, the drink on their breath, the hate on their tongues.

My toe catches on the stone.

I lurch forward in slow motion, throw my arms out. The floor rises to my face. My arms hit first, then my knees, my chest. I feel the hem of my skirt up too high. I feel cold air on my calves. I feel the quake of heavy boot steps behind me.

Hands grip my ankles and tug. I turn to look at the man pulling me, but he jerks hard and my cheek knocks against the floor. Iron and salt flood my tongue.

There are gutters, and they're filled with more than blood.

A wave rises in the back of my mouth.

In the center of the room, there's a dark, stained table. It looks damp.

Someone grabs my wrists and grunts.

I'm on the slab, belly down, legs dangling over the edge. I can feel the dampness beneath me.

Rough hands scratch my skin. Then something soft.

Silk.

The stockings feel familiar, from someone else's memory.

"Look, pork meat in casings!" the guards say, mouths stuffed with laughter.

The guards are drunk and hungry. My legs are sausages and my skirt is up too high. Hands pull at the silk, one pair after another until the stockings tear and dig into my skin. I feel veins pulsing behind my knees. The stockings twist like twine around my legs where the guards have torn them. Like the rope their men fixed around my children before they hung them beside my husband from the rafters of our barn.

They hung me too, tied the rope so tight I felt the fibers in my throat. I watched my family kick until everything faded. When I woke with my face in the straw, the rope still around my neck, I saw my children's feet above me—toes down, pushing away from the devil. My son's mouth was open. My daughter's eyes were bloody and too big. And my husband, at least he couldn't see them. I couldn't stop looking.

There are dead men in the gutter. Their blood on the table is like oil.

My body slides across it like a cut of meat.

A hand grabs my shoulder from behind me: the hand of a statue, not a man at all.

My mouth is shoved full of stockings.

They taste like men's hands.

Please, God, Mary. I appeal to your gracious mercy. You have taken my loved ones home to you. Do not forsake me. Do not leave me alone in the darkness, full of sweat and blood and corpses. Full of men and the stink of liquor.

Empty of your Holy Grace.

But wait, there's a light in the distance.

Golden. I see it.

It's shaped like a boy.

He looks at me with eyes I know and smiles.

There's a crown of thorns around his neck.

I hear him whisper, but I can't understand the words. They must be in the language of angels.

He grabs me by the waist and lifts me with the strength of a grown man.

"My child, take me home."

I feel the angel's cold hard skin against my knuckles.

And then the light is gone. My left ring finger is naked and cold.

"My child, where are you?"

No one answers.

BAČKI JARAK, SERBIA: 2012

SLEET SPECKLED THE GRAVESITE at Jarek like dip n' dots.
My stomach reeled.

Day after day we sought death camps, mass graves, forgotten people buried under mounds of dirt with not enough crosses for all the bodies. It was hard to separate the days and too big to swallow it all so quickly. Especially when everything looked the same.

Jarek was empty. All the German-style homes were shuttered, and there was no one on the streets. It was unreal how alike the villages were. From the rundown houses with peeling plaster and the roughly paved roads, to the mulberry and apple trees, the black marble cemeteries and peripheral mass graves, it was as though David and I hadn't travelled at all. We'd been walking the same empty street over and over. I thought movement was proof of time passing, but if the same movement repeated, what did it prove?

I could count on my fingers how many people we'd seen since we arrived in rural Vojvodina. There were more stray dogs than people. The villagers were probably tucked inside because of the weather. Twenty-six degrees Fahrenheit had never felt so cold. Or perhaps it was the abundance of political graffiti we found on shop walls: circle-As, swastikas, anti-Bosnian poetry.

You can't take our hearts, one wall had read.

Whose hearts could be taken?

Another mass grave belonging to three thousand ethnic Germans lay on the outskirts of Jarek. The stables across the street were abandoned and surrounded by barbed wire sagging from steel and concrete posts. I wondered if there, too, the wire was meant to keep people in. People and pigs and sheep and cows for milking.

Dirt had been piled in a mound on top of one-by-six boards to

mark the grave. I didn't understand the purpose of the lumber—
was it to keep the three thousand bodies from rising up? Or to
keep the muddy mountain from sinking into the ground from the
rain? One weathered cross balanced perfectly atop the heap. Brass
characters read: *Jarek 1944-1948*. Another cross, with the same
mailbox-style lettering, had fallen face-up beside the grave, thick
mud caked to the pointed bottom.

The identical crosses had once been joined to mark the grave
from opposite angles.

Part of me wanted to stand the cross back up, hammer it into
the dirt out of respect for the dead, but it seemed appropriate to
leave it where it had fallen. Indifference was heavy.

There was violence everywhere: barbed wire and broken roof
tiles, sharp stone roads and jagged gaps in plaster walls. There
was so much blood in the earth and so much shame. *So what if
our grandfathers buried yours naked and broken. So what if their
bodies provide minerals to the soil that feed our crops. So what if
we live in their houses and find heirlooms under old floorboards.
We've got enough history on our plates without thinking of bodies
in our peas.*

David stepped behind me and put his hand on my shoulder. I
suddenly felt very tired.

"Are you okay?" he whispered, pressing his lips against my
ear.

It began to rain harder. The damp leeched through my parka.

I wanted to say, "No." But I didn't know why. I didn't know if
it was the enormity and sameness of day after day of gravesites
and ghost towns, or if it was the guilt of my selfishness weighing
heavy on my chest.

"I don't feel well."

"Get out of the rain," he said, reaching for my camera. "I can
take pictures for you."

Inside the Spark, I pulled off my muddy shoes, my socks, and
put my bare feet on the dashboard. I reclined my seat, closed my
eyes, and breathed the stale cigarette air.

The radio crackled as heat blew through the air vents. I looked
at the console.

The feedback came again. Something about the noise made my skin ripple. It sounded like dry throats choking on mud. There were pauses in the noise where punctuation might have been, where words might have rested and shallow breaths might have been taken. Vocal chords grated like rusty cymbals. I felt it in my bones. It made my teeth ache.

I put words in their mouths:

"Are you listening?"

"Can you hear me?"

"Do you know my name?"

"My name is Hans."

"Adam."

"Walther."

"My name is—wait, your nose looks familiar. Hans, doesn't it look familiar? Are we related?"

"Klaus, you're twelve years old. You never had kids."

"No, but my sister could have had a family. We can't all be dead."

My grandfather had no siblings, but his father had eleven. Opa never spoke of what had befallen his aunts and uncles and cousins. I had a feeling he didn't know.

"Hey, you, in the car, with the familiar nose, what's your name? We'll remember."

"Will you remember ours?"

Sleet hammered down. David looked toward the car and blew a kiss. Ice pellets had gathered in his hair because his hat was sitting on the backseat—it made him look salt-and-pepper handsome. The radio wheezed.

"He's a good-looking one."

"Yeah, but he's not one of us, is he?"

"No, but the other one is. Sid. His name is Kohler."

David opened the door, climbed in, and buckled his seatbelt.

"Thank you," I said, reaching for the camera.

"You look unwell," he said.

"It's nothing."

David reached for the radio dial.

"No, don't," I said. "I'm enjoying the quiet."

It was vain, imagining that the bodies under the earth would want to speak to me. I kept looking for a sign that I was meant to be there. That I was meant to forget my Opa's books, find them again, go to Vojvodina with a stranger. If I was meant to be there, it was okay to leave Sid to travel with David.

If I was meant to be there, I was allowed to be unfaithful.

"You ready to go?" David asked, shifting the car into gear. He waited for my nod before pulling away from the gravesite. Rocks kicked up from the road and knocked against the bumper.

The dead in those graves were old men and women, mothers, children, the sick, the dying. What sins were they paying for? Because if they were still there, they'd found a life after death, and if there was a life after death, there had to be a god. And if there was a god and if the dead were still in Jarek, screaming through a Chevy Spark radio, what would happen to me?

"Walther, she looks like your type."

"I'll pass, Klaus. She's already discarded one husband."

"I bet it runs in the family."

"Lay off, guys, you're upsetting her."

I didn't know what Rosalinde looked like. She probably wasn't as beautiful as I imagined her, but I pictured her looking like Heddy Lamar in that sketch Opa drew in 1946, when he was still at Camp Haid. I pictured her with flowing black hair that caught the light and reflected graphite. A pert little nose, tight round lips, perfectly manicured eyebrows, and skin the color of paper.

I pictured Opa renting lavish rooms at the Bellevue or the Loew's or the Ritz for her. In reality, he probably rented rooms at cheap bed and breakfasts without air conditioning or room service.

But he said he'd never slept with her.

If he had loved her, did it matter if it was consummated? The love existed. They were together in those hotel rooms without regard for how warm and properly seasoned Oma's dinners were, spread out on the table and getting cold while the children sat in their chairs with napkins spread over their laps, waiting for their father.

Oma waited beside her children, overweight in her mismatched vest apron that snapped in front, with her matte black perm and her house slippers, no makeup and elastic khaki pants with ironed creases. She plucked bits of spaetzle from the pot while they waited, arms crossed, for Opa to come home. She dipped a burnt spaetzle in the butter gathering at the bottom of the dish. And when he finally came home, at nine o'clock, there was a woman with him. A woman with graphite hair and gray eyes, with parchment skin and a narrow waist.

When Oma came to the United States, she became a seamstress to help her family make ends meet instead of going back to school. Even as she grew older, she read very slowly, sounding out the words. She could hardly write. When I was young, I admired Opa's geometric handwriting. I was shocked by Oma's hesitant letters. She couldn't balance a check book, drive a car, send a letter. She could cook, sew, dance, and watch *The Price Is Right* with me asleep on her ample belly, her apron still on, soft and warm under my cheek. She could iron. She could laugh. She could bake. She could throw tantrums like a child and not speak to anyone for days. She could suffer fits of sadness, when the weight of all the things she lost held her down. I used to think those fits were mostly about my mother, before I knew the rest.

Oma loved me in ways more grown up grandmothers couldn't have. She loved me with giggles and naps and an unparalleled desire for sweets. Our love was mint chocolate chip ice cream. It was curling each other's hair with our fingers late mornings. It was carefully measured bowls of cream of wheat with tenderness in the balance of water and milk and cereal. It was baths for hours in so much froth I smelled like Mr. Bubble for days. It was brushing my hair in the bathroom while we both stared at her varicose veins like they were tiny purple worms living under her skin. It was playing with ceramic and plastic Catholic statues—like Mary in all her white robes and delicate incarnations and Saint Michael with his gleaming sword. It was making our own whipped cream and sticking our fingers in the bowl. It was maraschino cherries. Butterscotch candy wrappers hiding under sofa cushions. It was costume jewelry and dress up and an overabundance of pillows she'd made herself, clothing she'd made herself, while I played with paper dolls and scraps of inexpensive polyester lace.

She made me a Christmas dress out of deep red velvet and white lace that I wore until I couldn't fit into it anymore. She made me flowery Easter dresses, chocolate cakes, linzer cookies, strudel. She gave me everything she loved, everything that was herself.

It was easier to show gratitude to Opa for his articulate words of support, his boyish smile, the similarities in our characters and circumstances. But perhaps it was only easier because he was dead.

David and I were always on the road. Always in the car. Always going somewhere and never getting there. The people who buried my ancestors naked in the dark soil with no headstones, they acted like monsters because they blamed other people for their unhappiness.

There was always distance.

Opa was somewhere unknowable, with my mother. Oma was at Bayside—even if what was left of her mind was here, in a village I might never see. Sid felt far away. David felt displaced. But maybe he wasn't. Maybe Sid never was. Maybe it was always me.

NOVI SAD, SERBIA: 2012

THE HOST LED DAVID and me to a window-side table at Dama Reka, a restaurant at the foot of the old fort's walls, at the edge of the Danube. It was decorated for Orthodox Christmas: a baubled tree on display in the corner, a wood fire roaring in the center, string lights hanging vertically like radioactive snowflakes. Even the bottled ships propped above the windows were resting on Christmas garland. We ordered two bottles of Serbian Vranac along with smoked fish, roasted red peppers, a plate of Balkan cheeses, and boiled veal to drown our weariness.

The restaurant was full of smoke and ethnic folk singers—cigarettes, ash trays, accordions, stringed instruments, and men in black vests with white shirts. There were a few other customers, but the waiter told us that in the summer Dama Reka would be Novi Sad's most frequented dining establishment. He poured both bottles of Vranac into an oversized decanter and said that the wine's vintage had been a beautiful year for Serbian viticulture.

While he decanted, and while we waited for our food to arrive, another man brought a bottle of honey rakija and poured us each an aperitif.

"You will eat at Dama Reka until you can drink rakija like a Serb, yes?" the man with the rakija asked, showing all of his teeth when he smiled.

"Of course," David said, sipping from his tiny glass.

I slid mine across the table.

"Shh," I said, "I don't want them to think I can't hold my liquor."

"They already know you can't hold your liquor." David swallowed half the glass in one gulp, leaving a sip at the bottom.

"Which is a good thing for me." He winked.

I swallowed what was left of the honey spirit: it burned like rocket fuel.

"That tasted nothing like honey." I laughed and pulled swigs of sparkling water from the glass to my right. The waiter came back and refilled our waters from the bottle on the table.

"How did you enjoy?" he asked, taking our empty shot glasses and putting them on the aperitif man's liquor cart.

"Very nice," I said. The waiter smiled and lifted the decanter, swirling it again before filling our wine glasses.

"Perhaps this is more for you," he said. "Best Serbian wine."

He'd left the empty bottle on the table. The vintage read 2009. The year I married Sid. David and I lifted our glasses over the candle in the center of the table and clinked.

"To adventures together," David said. I repeated the words.

In the fall of 2009, Sid and I honeymooned in Paris. It was our first vacation in years. It was also our last.

The afternoons were perfect—we ate Muscat grapes and soft cheese and drank wine on our iron balcony, stumbled tipsy until we got lost in new neighborhoods, ogled stained glass windows and fountains and the smell of a city at once butter-sweet and sandy. We lingered hours over dinner with carafes of inexpensive rosé and glistening droplets of truffle oil suspended in our soups. We took the escalator to the top of the Eiffel Tower, kissed in the wind whistling through the metal, and rode the carousel beside the tower when we were too windswept to keep staring at the Paris skyline.

We got drunk in the gardens at Versailles and pretended to be statues. We slept on benches, frowned at signs telling us to keep off the grass. I stared at my wedding ring a lot. Something about the Paris sunshine made the tiny diamond chips sparkle more than they had in Philadelphia. I touched as many things as I could reach with my left hand to hear how my ring sounded against new surfaces. Metal railings, stone railings, park benches, spoons, plates, tablecloths, bus seats, plaster walls. Each sound was beautiful, whether my ring chimed or fizzled.

In the mornings I woke early, snuck out from under the sheets, slipped into jeans, and walked down five flights of winding stairs and across the street to a patisserie. I bought croissants and pain au chocolat and some mystery pastry. One particularly delicious mystery had half a glazed apricot perched face down in the center.

We sat on our balcony and dipped our pastries in hot chocolate and Nespresso coffee. I don't remember our conversations, but I remember them being sweet and thoughtful.

Something happened after that. I couldn't tell if there was something in the pastries, some strange kind of sugar that turned us into monsters or so much butter that our arteries clogged and our hearts grew hard and cold.

We fought.

We fought because we got lost in the city's winding streets. We fought because not speaking good French made everything awkward. Because tickets for the museums were expensive. Because it was our honeymoon and it was supposed to be perfect and it wasn't. Because it was. Because my feet hurt in the peep-toes I wore to be fashionable in Paris and we didn't check the time the Bateaux-Mouches stopped running. Because he wore sneakers that frayed the hem of his jeans and threw a sport jacket on top of wrinkled dress shirts. Because sand from the parks got stuck between my toes. Because Paris was beautiful. Because we were out of place. Because we were where we were supposed to be.

We didn't make love our whole trip except once, the first night, with the fluttering lights of the Eiffel Tower coming through our window like flickering candles. Sid's love-making was quiet, and he whispered, "I love you, Mrs. Sid," in my ear over and over until he came. The feeling of his lips on my neck, just below my ear, sent goosebumps across my skin. "I love you, husband," I said, feeling the weight of his body and the breeze from the open window.

He fell asleep quickly.

I watched the tower flicker every few minutes until it shut off at one o'clock.

David and I were different. Sex and high energy and footsie under the tablecloth. He talked about fast cars, smoking cigars in Mexico, about business trips to Dubai and hotel stays on the coast of Israel that no longer allowed him entry into the Middle East. He talked about the sports he played, the people he'd met: the director of the new Batman movies once in a bar in London. David and Victoria Beckham at a petrol station off the motorway. One of his ancestors had designed some kind of machine gun in the Great War, he said, and, of course, the Spitfire was the most glorious machine ever created by man. He did it skillfully—somehow it didn't sound like bragging. This is what I have and maybe you can have it to, don't you want it?

I talked about the Allied Forces playing a role in the Swabian genocide. How Churchill and Roosevelt sanctioned the removal of all ethnic Germans from Eastern Europe. How a museum in London—the Imperial War Museum—listed what they called all the occasions of genocides and crimes against humanity of the past century, but left out the Swabian genocide in Yugoslavia.

"The way the museum shows it, it's like they're saying the British aren't capable of doing what those other people did," I said. As if anyone could say they knew what they'd be capable of if they lived in a society in ruin, what they would do for security. "Good things were done in the name of justice, but awful things were done for the same reason."

"Justice is absolute," David said. "Those who do wrong should pay."

"But the ideals behind justice are changeable."

David said nothing. His whole demeanor had changed. He chewed his veal, stared at me, and cut another bite-sized portion. To me, his eyes said, "England can't be blamed."

"Churchill was right," he said after he swallowed. "Those countries all lost so much because of the Nazis. How could Germans exist there afterward?"

I put down my fork.

"They didn't know what else to do." He said it as if it was obvious.

"That doesn't make it right, David."

"I don't think about that kind of stuff as much as you do." He looked at me as if he was seeing me for the first time.

"Then what are we doing here? Aren't we here to think about that kind of stuff? Isn't that the point?"

He said nothing.

"How did you know to hide the car in that apartment complex?" I asked, picking my fork back up and pulling my fish into flakes across the plate.

David looked at me with eyes that said so many things he would never say out loud: *How can you question me when I'm giving you everything?*

It was hard to know where my perception of him ended and the real him began. How could he see things in such black and white? Right and wrong. Justice and injustice. Where did traveling with a married woman fall on his scales of good and bad? It was a beautiful gift, to connect me with my past, to stand beside me while I found these places that are both mine and not mine. But what did that mean to him? Was it to ease the grief he felt for his own grandfather, to give someone who was dealing with the same grief an opportunity he didn't have? Was it because he loved me? Because he wanted to give me what Sid couldn't, as if this was some kind of game where I could be won.

"I don't know what else I'm supposed to do," David said, gripping the edge of the table with his hands and then letting go. "I've brought you here. I'm taking you to all of these places. I'm trying to understand. I don't know the details you do. I haven't read the books you've read. And you don't tell me anything unless I ask.

"I have no idea what you expect from me. And I'm trying. I'm really trying to be what you want me to be."

We sat in silence. I chewed my fish. My fork made a blunt clunk on the tablecloth.

"You're right," I said, reaching across the table and grabbing his hand. "I'm sorry. I shouldn't expect you to understand. But our countries aren't blameless in this, David. It's not okay to defend something blindly."

"England didn't kill those people."

"No, but they knew. America knew. There is no such thing as innocence. Nothing is that simple."

"Of course nothing is simple. America didn't suffer like Europe did. Rationing went on in the UK for almost a decade after the war ended. We couldn't buy bacon. Even potatoes were rationed. And we spent sixty-one years paying America back for its aid.

You think you can just walk in and pass moral judgements on countries where people weren't allowed to eat more than one egg a week, where populations had been devastated by two wars, where the men who came back weren't the same as when they left. Where people were just trying to do their best."

"You say America is my country like it's the only place that's part of my identity, like there's only one American identity. And not to diminish what your country went through in the war, but England fared much better than France. No one was rounding up Jewish communities in England like they were across continental Europe. And look, I'm not here to stand on a pedestal and say that what happened to my grandparents and the ethnic Germans was more or less wrong than what happened to anybody else. Just that it's part of the history and that makes it important. How are we supposed to do better if we don't understand the whole truth? But you want to talk about the devastation of a population because of wars—where do you think we're sitting?"

"I saw what the war did to my grandfather," David said, his voice soft. "And he hated Germans after. But he was a good man. How do you go through something like that and not put a face to the horror?"

"I don't know," I said, trying to flatten a wrinkle in the table-cloth, first with my palm, then the back of my thumbnail. It was easier than looking up at David, and it helped calm my mind enough to speak softly in return. "But that's what's wrong with people, isn't it? All of us simplify things down to easy prejudices. Even when we're good people, or at least trying to be."

Everything broke with Sid because I was too stubborn to keep trying, and I was too stubborn to listen to the world around me telling me that David would be no different. I shouldn't have been able to leave someone like Sid.

Oma and Opa would probably have said the same: "How could you leave him? He took such good care of you." But the two of them and their twin beds, separated by a large nightstand, an answering machine, and an art deco lamp, they didn't know mar-ital happiness. Maybe they would tell me I was foolish to expect to find it.

I might have had different expectations if I'd experienced life as they had.

Oma always had a jar of whiskey cherries sitting on her kitchen windowsill. She'd plan a Black Forest cake two weeks in advance and prepare the cherries by pitting them and dropping them one at a time into a mason jar full of rum. She called everything whiskey if it was stronger than wine. While my Opa knocked back beer and schnapps at German-Hungarian Club parties, Oma would sip club soda with an orange slice on the rim. When people asked her what she was having, she'd say, "That's my secret."

She thought she was clever, but everyone knew she was teetotaling and quietly begrudging the drunken men—most of all her husband. When he got drunk at the club, he kissed Rosalinde on the lips.

I was my Opa's granddaughter.

Only Sid didn't give me the silent treatment and stomp around the house like I didn't know he was upset. He didn't huff and cry and tell me I didn't love him. He should have told me I didn't love him, but he wouldn't because he knew he loved me more. It hurt to know he was the most loving. And it must have been painful for him to know that I wasn't capable of giving as much.

He called me an unloyal wife once.

I teased him for using a word that doesn't exist.

The folk musicians shuffled to our table, drunk and laughing. They started playing, the accordionist fat and red-faced, older than the rest. The violinist was young and thin—young enough to not be old enough to drink at the bar. The music made me forget it was January. It made me forget the frigid wind in Novi Sad as we sat beside the Danube, a draft whistling through cracks in the windowpanes. There was sadness in the notes, in the slow pull of the accordion, the soft kiss of an over-rosined bow on worn strings. You could see it in the musicians' painted smiles, in their alcohol-reddened foreheads, their sweaty necks.

The notes sang, "Our world is imperfect, but we don't give a damn. Our world is imperfect and we love the bitter wind on our ungloved fingers, turning our knuckles numb. We love the cheapness of our dinars, the power of our graffiti, and above all the taste of wine on our tongues, the savory warmth of smoke on our plates, infused into that prime fish on your fork, the warm blood of the veal on his, the satisfying smush of potato between your tongue and the back of your teeth, the slick buttered richness of those greens as you grind them in your mouth and let the salty-sweet fat run like a river down your throat and into your belly.

Our world is imperfect but we have the comfort of Vranac and meat, of Vranac and paprika, of Vranac and palacinke, of Vranac and kisses. So kiss and be sad in the Dama Reka, kiss and be sad' because Serbia is a country in chains and you are shameful."

At the end of the song, David's face was blank from drinking his rakija and mine, from our bottles of wine, from only hearing the notes and not the words beneath the musicians' song. The men bowed and looked at us expectantly, smiling and speaking short bursts of English—"You like violin, I teach you;" "You have pretty smile;" "I see you drink rakija."

David smiled at the compliments they paid me, but he didn't get the hint. I pulled several hundred dinars out of my purse and handed the bills to the accordionist. I smiled so long my cheeks ached. My lips were dry from being stretched so tight. I knew when I released them they'd resemble accordion bellows.

Back at the apartment, David made two small cups of Turkish coffee and sat beside me on the edge of the sofa.

"You know how we're supposed to meet Mislav tomorrow in Apatin?" I said.

Months before the trip, when I couldn't find locations for the camps and gravesites, I searched for Danube Swabian groups on Facebook. I found one based in Apatin. The page was written in a dialect of Serbo-Croatian that didn't translate easily. A man named Mislav Pavlović posted often—mostly photographs of monuments and Swabian ruins with grand statements like, "The Devil's servants in action."

I reached out to him, asked him if he knew anyone who could help me find what I was looking for. He said he could help, that he knew a man who ran a Swabian museum in Apatin. That he could show me Apatin's German cemetery, the museum, and—if I wanted—the monuments I sought.

He told me his life, that his ancestors were expelled from Frauendorf and sent to the camp at Batchki-Jarek. His father was only a child, but he survived. A Croatian man adopted him, changed his name to Avram.

When Avram grew up, he worked for the Communist government. He had two children by a Croatian woman: first a daughter, then a son.

Mislav never met his father. He didn't learn his family's history until 1990—when someone told him about the camp at Jarek. He said the truth ripped through him like rushing water. And then, he said, he made problems trying to prove his identity. *There are still people who think all Germans equal Hitler. Austria-Hungary made roads and railways, canals and factories. They made jobs for three million people, and now it all rots. In the nineties, was still not good to be German. I could not succeed. In Vojvodina there are many poor, yet also the most millionaires in Europe. It is corrupt. In God no one believes.*

He echoed, too, what Thomas from Chicago had told me. *It is not forbidden to explore. Only most will not admit it because they need to blame for their failures.*

We kept in touch as weeks passed, planned on meeting in Apatin when David and I arrived. We would meet at the museum, which he'd give directions to, and then we'd visit the German cemetery.

"He sent me a strange message," I told David, sipping at my coffee. "He wants us to pick him up from his sister's house in Sombor. He said he can direct us to Apatin from the car."

"Are you kidding? I'm not letting a stranger in the car."

"He says he doesn't have a car to get back to Apatin."

In the message, he wrote that his New Year was not off to a good start, that he was poor, had no job and no prospects. He wrote that David and I should be careful, that many Serbs were out to make money off people like us.

"He's not dangerous, David," I said. "Do you think he wants money?"

"He could be anybody."

"I know. But he can show us so much," I said.

"How can he expect us to drive to a stranger's house in a city we don't know in a country where we don't even speak the language?"

I said nothing. I didn't disagree, but I didn't want a repeat of Gašinci.

David drained his cup and propped it on the windowsill. Piano notes and a tenor voice whispered through the pane. The music school went on. Restaurants still served food, bars were always full, men bought pastries from the cart at the corner. But the rural villages were impoverished and Serbia was a country in chains. What happened to a man after being chained? What happened after his identity was taken, and when he found it again too late to make a difference?

"We don't know anyone here," David said. "We're looking for places the locals don't want us to see." He paused. "It's not worth the risk."

"And you're the one who gets to decide," I said. My voice came out cold. He didn't say anything. He didn't have to: his eyes said it for him. *Yes, I am the one who decides.*

I sent Mislav a message saying that I was sorry, but that our plans had changed and we could no longer meet. That I appreciated his help and how candidly he spoke of his past. That I wished him all the best and hoped he found himself in a better situation soon.

Mislav's response came quickly. *I do not want such friends. It is not fair. I wanted to lead you many places.*

I pictured Mislav sitting on the sofa at his family's home, talking about how great it was going to be to show the American woman he'd been talking with all the things he'd learned too late about his life. Maybe he said to his sister, "She'll help me." And maybe she replied, balancing a child on her hip, a boy with tiny clenched fists, "Mislav, don't be foolish." And maybe when Mislav read my message saying that I couldn't meet him after all, his sister had looked at him, put a hand on his shoulder, and said, "See. No one is going to undo what has been done."

David slid his shoes off and pulled me by my fingertips toward the bedroom.

"I'm sorry," he said. He opened the window. The music had stopped.

It smelled like snow.

He warmed my forehead with his breath and rubbed my brow with his thumb. When he smiled, his teeth were dull.

"I'm tired," I said, laying down and turning away from him. We never seemed to find the light switch. But there was something about rooms lit only by windows: the lights of every city shined differently. So many places in so few days, I needed the subtle differences in brightness to tell me where I was. That I wasn't home.

I woke in the middle of the night, checked my phone: two o'clock. No new messages. Air blew through the crack in the window, so cold my nose was numb, and the toes of my right foot, which I'd left outside the covers to counter David's warmth. Ice crystals floated into the room and caught in the cold light of the street lamps. I was afraid for a moment that they weren't snowflakes at all, that instead the stars had come crashing out of the sky to show me I'd lost something. To dance over the empty floor, my empty shoes, my naked hands.

I slipped out of the covers and stood. I walked to the window and exhaled a cloud into the night. It wisped like cirrus before fading to nothing. The rooftops looked like clouds, too, covered in enough snow to disguise the uneven crests and chimneys. When the rooftops were bare, the crests had undulated like light waves, the chimneys had leaned like tiny Pisas.

Lamplight reflected off the snow onto David, sleeping on his stomach with his face pressed into the corner of my pillow. His shoulders pulsed with each breath. Only his right leg and lower back were covered. The hair on his exposed leg glinted silver instead of chestnut. Looking at him, my frustration and disappointment faded.

He was so afraid. Of what I didn't know. Losing control. Doing the wrong thing. Because to him everything was as simple as control and chaos, right and wrong. Yes and no. But just then, looking at his body in the blue light of the night, it didn't matter. I imagined

growing old with him. I could cook meat pies filled with pork jelly.
We could make love after our features had fallen into Picasso
shapes—when my eyelids dripped under my eyes, when my
cheeks melted down my chin. And the homes we could share, the
anniversaries, the Christmases. A Christmas tree, six-feet-tall and
fir, with short prickly needles and sap on the branches. David could
string the lights nearest the trunk until his arms smelled like sap,
like fir tree, like Christmas, like he could be wrapped up in ribbon
and paper and stuffed under the bottommost branches.

I slipped into pajama pants and David's dirty t-shirt and left
the bedroom. The hallway was dark: it smelled like air freshener.
I followed the smell to the coat rack, pulled my boots over my
pajamas and my coat over my shoulders, grabbed the key from
David's coat pocket, and walked out the door, down four flights
of concrete steps to an unglazed atrium. The sound of water running gave me the urge to pee. I stepped into the courtyard. Snow
had collected on a small patch of grass around the fountain—a
leaking water pump made of concrete, painted yellow. I lay in the
snow with my arms outstretched, making triangles with my limbs.
I was a small part of many shapes, a lot of pieces of too many
things instead of one whole.

The snow felt cold through my pajamas. I waved my arms and
legs through the powder as if it could take me back to when life
was bursting with becoming. Opa stood beside me in his backyard
while I made snow angels. He stood there like he stood at the
beach, waiting to make sure I got back inside before I sunburned.

"We don't want you to catch cold, angel."

When Oma tucked me in at night, she folded me into the sheets
as tight as an envelope and kissed my cheek. Her bedtime kisses
were the softest because her teeth were in a cup. When Opa tucked
me in, he tucked the sheets under my shoulders, my elbows, my
knees—so I was vacuum-sealed. "Sleep tight, Puddin'," he said.
"The angels will guard you until morning."

Guard me from what?

Mislav's message ran through my head, *They need to blame
for their failures.*

The courtyard darkened. The darkness was a shadow. For a

moment I saw my grandfather in the silhouette, but when I looked again, it was David standing in the way of the floodlight.

AVRAM PAVLOVIĆ:
TEMERIN, YUGOSLAVIA: 1948

WHEN I WAS ELEVEN, I ate lice off the dead girl beside me. I don't even know how long she'd been dead. In the starvation camp, in Jarek, Yugoslavia, all the children looked the same. We all looked dead. Louse exoskeletons cracked between my teeth and her stale blood spread over my tongue.

"My child, what is your name?" The voice came from a man I hadn't seen before.

I could not speak. None of us spoke.

The man pointed his right index finger to his chest. It was dirty. "Doctor Jan."

My surrogate father's name is Jan. This father is from Temerin; he took me in a year ago, when I was thirteen, and we live alone. Jan Pavlovič sells potatoes on the roadside, and he doesn't ask for help to gather leftovers from the others' fields. It's amazing how many potatoes are abandoned. Sometimes you can even find them piled up for hunting bait. The ones on the outside of the piles are half eaten by deer, but the potatoes buried within are fresh-skinned and unblemished. I know this because Jan told me. I told you, he never asks for my help.

I was born cursed by the sins of men I do not know. I am of the same blood as Hitler, but I can get better if I try. I can get better if I forget. My bad blood is what made me sick at Jarek, not the soup with no salt, the cold with no heat, the excrement in the straw by my head, not the typhoid. My memory is wrong. I thought the man who shot my birthfather in the throat was a Serb or a Croat because of the way his voice sounded. But my ears were funny. They heard wrong because I was sick. Only Nazis are capable of such things, Jan says.

This is what Jan taught me, Jan the potato thief.

My mother lived in the room with the other mothers instead of the room where I lived with the alien children. Alien children don't have homes. It's one thing to have your home taken from you. It's another to have your soul taken. The shame is acid in my throat. Even if I remembered, I don't think I'd know the name of the dead girl who slept beside me. Maybe she was only dreaming, maybe she'd wake up. Then I'd ask her name. Because she was pretty before she died. She didn't have the scabs on her mouth that made the other girls' lips swell so much their teeth showed like animals'. She had bad blood too.

I can count on one hand the number of times I saw my mother in the sixteen months we were prisoners. She said we'd stayed in Jarek because it was our home, but after the neighbors moved out one by one and the houses were all empty and the silence in the village was loud, like wind screaming in all the hollow spaces— in the corners of rooms and streets and courtyards, beneath empty beds and through kitchens with cold ovens. Uuuuuuuuuu, the wind screamed. The wind also said that it is big and I am small. I've had dreams in which I am an infant and my mother walks me down the road in a pram. There are warm blankets the color of milk, and there is a shade, a beautiful black canvas shade that makes the Earth seem knowable. All the edges are close and there is no fear because there is no horizon. But then she folds back the shade. It's terrible. The sky goes on forever. It goes up and up, and out and around, it goes sideways and forwards, backwards and in directions that don't exist.

When there was only one other German family left in Jarek, I wrapped my things in a towel and stood by the front door. "We've done nothing wrong," she said, "We won't be run out of our home."

The Partisans turned the village into a camp. They marched parades of ethnic Germans from other towns through our streets, single file. They marched some in their nightgowns, others with no shoes. The neighbor's house was filled with old men. The stables were filled with German children. Mothers were herded into our own empty home. There was a house full of mattresses. One full of ladies' underwear. Another full of stacked up furniture—chairs piled crooked on upside-down tables. My mother slept two years on straw in her kitchen. But she didn't understand. We had done wrong by existing. I had done wrong by being born into a kingdom that no longer belonged to my people. My people of the rotted blood.

Jan says this was never the land of my people, that it had always belonged to his. But before the Habsburgs it was the Turks, and I know Jan hates them as much as he hates me. He tries not to hate me. He wants me to be good. My mother tongue is forbidden in his house, and when I slip up, he throws the potato pot at me. Sometimes the pot is still on the fire and the water inside is boiling. Sometimes the potatoes are still in it and leave hot red welts on my arms. The water burns through my pant legs. One time the pot hit my stomach and I threw up on the floor. But it is not so bad. I can eat as many potatoes as I'd like, and he reads to me before bed, while I lay on my cot by the woodstove. He used to read translated Russian pamphlets to teach me Serbian. In those days I was mostly silent. The pot was always on the fire. I remember one of the pamphlets he read to me most often. I don't know how long it took before I understood it. *We are continuing Pasteur's work, who discovered the serum against rabies. We are continuing the work of all scientists who have discovered methods to destroy deadly microbes.*

I'm not bad, he says, only my blood.

There's a drainage ditch in front of the house that's full of water. When Jan goes to steal potatoes, I submerge a jar in the ditch. The jar fills with dirty water and leeches, and while Jan is away, I put leeches on the welts where potatoes have burned me. I put them there so he can't tell. I put them on my belly and my legs. I put them on my chest, my back. I put them on the backs of my knees. I put them under my arms. There's a bucket under my cot where I keep them once they've fallen off. I fall asleep with them behind my ears. I put one in my palm like a wet dog's nose.

I am trying to forget. I'm trying to be better.

Now he reads proletariat newsletters about Comrade Tito and the good he is doing for Yugoslavia. There is a photograph of Tito on the kitchen table, and another beside my bed. The one in the kitchen is from the neck up. Tito's cheekbones and his nose and his chin and his forehead shine like those of the Holy Mother. His eyes look out of the frame as if he can see the whole of his country and all of his people at once. His face has hollow spaces at the corners of his lips, and the shadows tucked inside those spaces make his mouth look too big and hungry. He looks out at everything from his tiny frame and threatens with those shadows to eat you alive. He looks at me and I say in my head, *Don't eat me, I am trying to be good.*

My blood would make a poor broth, he says, my scarred skin would be tough, he says, and I have no heart, so I would be bland. The photo beside my cot is different. In it, Tito sits at a chessboard with shining leaf-skeletons embroidered on his lapels. The chessboard is made of onyx and mother of pearl. He's holding a black pawn between his right thumb and forefinger. His fingers are well-fed, and the way his hair is slicked back crooked makes him look unconquerable. The shadows in the hollows of his lips are so deep he must have spent his whole life frowning. My mother had hollows there, too. I noticed dark pits at the corners of her lips after my birthfather was shot. But they spread while she lived in the room with the other mothers. Sometimes the sun buried such big shadows in her face that she looked like she'd grown a moustache.

The day I lost her was the day the doctor asked my name.

He was there when it happened.

A guard said, "There's a woman in the field."

And another, "She won't move."

One of the guard's wives made fun of the children under blankets, the ones who were dead or barely breathing. She said things that made the guards laugh. There weren't enough blankets for all of the blanket children, so boys and girls were stacked on top of each other. The parts of the room where the blanket children were kept made no sound. But the rest of us, the ones who might live a while longer, our sick bodies sounded like motors. I heard one of the mothers say once that you could hear the hum of children from every street in town. I tried to listen to my hum, but I couldn't pick it out from the rest. The girl next to me, for a while her hum sounded like an exhaust pipe: she rattled when she breathed. But at least she made noise.

The doctor had no medicine and no blankets, no food or water. The doctor only had cold compresses at room temperature. He said things to the guards that I couldn't understand. But I heard something familiar.

It was her.

I stood up. It had been a long time since I had stood. The skin on my feet was swollen with rat bites, and I couldn't feel much of my legs. It was like walking an invisible tight rope, taking step after step without knowing where or when my foot would find the line. Several times I stepped on parts of bodies because there wasn't enough space between us. The guards stared at me and said nothing. The wife spat. Her saliva landed on a girl lying on the floor with her feet up on the trough. She'd put her feet up to stop the rats from biting, but instead of eating her toes, they'd stolen the skin off her elbows.

Outside in the field, my mother sat by the fence, with her knees pressed to the concrete cylinders holding up the posts. The rest of the town wasn't surrounded in barbed wire. Just men with guns every hundred feet, watching for runaways. My mother watched runaways get shot from her window, children mostly, trying to sneak away at night to go begging. Or to hunt stray dogs. Jarek used to be filled with dogs. Every family had two at least, and they all wandered loose, except mine. When everybody left, when the Partisans came, the village dogs became no one's dogs. Five boys killed mine with stones. I didn't see it, but I saw them holding him tied to a stick over a cold fire. When I told them he was my dog, they offered me some of the meat off his thigh. The meat was mostly raw.

My mother's knees were pressed to the concrete, and she had no stockings on. Her legs were bare, and when she'd sat, she pulled her skirt up to her thighs so she could wrap her legs around each other. Her legs were red and caked with dirt.

I pulled on her arm. *Mother*, I wanted to say. *Go back to the house.*

She didn't move. She didn't even look at me. I half expected her to turn her face up at me and smile like she did in those dreams, with wide eyes and only sunshine around her lips because she wasn't sad enough for the shadows.

My mother was humming. Her ribs rattled. Maybe they were speaking something for which there are no words, but I couldn't understand. She stared ahead at a barb on the wire. There was a little patch of fabric caught on the barb, and the metal was rust colored even though it was made of steel. I put my palms on her cheeks so I could turn her head to face me. Her skin felt like an earthquake. Her motor shook the fence. She wasn't moving forward or backward, her legs weren't sinking into the mud, and her body wasn't in the sky. Maybe she was moving inward, so far inward that she'd fade away like the blanket children, or pop out somewhere secret where no one could follow her.

The doctor came while I studied our humming. He looked at me and his eyes were shadows.

He picked my mother up off the ground and carried her back to her kitchen. I followed the doctor and stood outside my house. There were more than two hundred mothers inside, but they were silent. Except you could hear my mother humming from the street. She hummed until she disappeared.

Jan says he took me in to save me. He says my blood is not my fault. When the Partisans closed Jarek, it was almost empty. Men came to take the leftover children. The men sometimes came with wives, sometimes with other children—tall children with no shadows in their faces.

When I first saw Jan, he was the color of dirt.

A guard grabbed my wrist. He held out my arm for Jan to take.

I don't know how long it took before Jan saw my bloody feet. I'd left raw footprints on the road. When he saw, he stopped and bent toward me. He put me over his shoulder so my belly hugged his shoulder blade.

Inside his house, he handed me a knife and a bucket of vegetables and said, "Guliti," to which I did not reply. I did not move except to look at the knife in my hands, at my dirt and blood caked feet, at the shoes Jan was wearing—boots with the soles peeling away from his toes.

If he said it now, I'd know he meant me to peel the potatoes.

He put the potato pot on the stove, filled it with salt broth. He took the knife from me and pulled a potato from the bucket, slid the blade over the skin, and handed it back to me. Where he had cut, the potato felt spit on.

He smiled, Jan the potato thief, and said, "To nije mnogo."

My memories bleed. I can see the horizon, but I can't make out the edges of the pram. I can taste the dead air in the stables at Jarek, but I can't place the smell. I can feel the slime of that first peeled potato, but I can't remember anything more than bitterness on my tongue when I brought it, raw, to my lips and bit down.

It feels late in the afternoon. I lift a pot of salt broth onto the woodstove. I light the fire and wait for the broth to boil. I drop yesterday's leftover carrots in, old potatoes, a parsnip, and half a cabbage Jan found frozen inside a heap of rotted onions.

While the vegetables soften in the water, I pull the filled-up leeches from under my cot. I've collected so many the bucket is full. I place them on the hot top, beside the potato pot. I burn my fingertips turning them until they shrivel and hiss like pig skin. When I cut the leeches into thin slices, burned liquid leaks onto the stove. It bubbles and burns to soot.

I set two soup bowls and a pair of bent spoons on the table, on either side of Comrade Tito's hungry mouth. I don't know if I've found a way to destroy my blood, or if I'm damning Jan with my microbes. But when Jan comes home to the hot soup on the stove, he hangs his coat on the back of his chair and says it smells wonderful.

APATIN, SERBIA: 2012

SOMETHING FELT BROKEN in Apatin, like a widow with lipstick on her teeth.

The homes were cleaner, but cracks in the plaster walls curved like the sad, soft wrinkles of resigned eyes. Grass grew in whole lawns instead of patches, although it grew yellow instead of green.

Driving into the village, I smelled the Danube. It smelled like life—fish and river weeds, sunshine heating bankside branches, pine sap thawing sweet.

The water looked mercurial.

On a narrow dirt road flanked by pine trees and a manicured hedge, we found the Swabian Catholic church. Set back from the road, a concrete fence blocked off the grounds.

"Maybe the cemetery's in there," David said.

"Can we see if it's open?" I asked as he pulled over and shut off the engine.

It looked serene from the road, but up close, the church was ruined. Sun shone through broken windowpanes onto the burned insides of the sanctuary. The walls were covered in black splotches. Fallen plaster curled like paper on the window ledge. Rotting pews, burnt to charcoal in places, rested on the floor like discarded lumber. A spread of ash covered everything like sawdust.

It looked unfinished instead of undone.

Oma put on lipstick on Sunday mornings. I stood beside her in the bathroom, rifling through her makeup bag for eyelash curlers. She blotted her lips with toilet paper and dropped her kisses in the bowl. She wiped the edges of her mouth so the line of red was clean, but it never stayed for long. While she smiled and checked her teeth, I flushed the toilet and watched a cyclone of used up kisses spiral down the drain.

At my grandparents' church in Philadelphia, all the women painted their lips the color of communion wine. I stayed in the pew while Oma walked up to the altar. I was too young, Opa told me. He sat beside me while she knelt with her hands cupped, waiting to be filled.

What did it feel like to have nothing and then to have everything and still be afraid?

The mural on the ceiling had survived the fire in almost perfect condition: pale pinks, mauves, and reds, unyellowed by smoke, not blackened by flames, a sacred heart cradled in scalloped filigree at the center.

"It's strange," I said while David hoisted me up to get a closer look. I grabbed the window ledge, careful not to catch myself on glass shards. Burned plaster crumbled into dust and left black ash on my palm the shape of a flower petal. "Someone comes to trim the hedges, but no one's touched the church."

The church fire wasn't as old as the 1940s. Mislav had mentioned something about arson in the nineties. But why? Was it residual hatred toward Swabians? Toward Catholics, religion in general? Was it just disillusioned teenagers with a desire to watch something burn?

I didn't ask.

"There's nothing back there," David said, peering over the wall into the churchyard while he held me up. He looked at the windowsill. "You'd think someone would have cleared out the glass."

Maybe the town tidied the hedge so they could look down when they passed the church instead of up at another testament to violence. It was easier to pretend than to forget, easier to ignore than to fix. To fix the church would have meant acknowledging the fire and the darkness.

Almost fifty years before the church was razed, hundreds of Donauschwaben were lit like beacons in the river at night.

People watched them burn from the banks, watched the incandescent bodies tied to each other, wrapped around a pile of hay on a barge that carried bricks and mortar from Apatin's factories to Vienna and Pest. The bankside spectators heard the hay crackling because it was wet with tears and urine. They heard the crackling even through the screams, even through the popping of flesh and bone, until the Danube swallowed the sound.

As we walked from the church to the riverbank, I told David that the human torches were set alight as an example for the rest of the Swabian communities along the river.

He looked at me, then at the water. He said nothing. What was there to say? I left out the details: the orange and blue glow of conflagrant skin and hair and bone burned so bright you could see it for miles.

David waited by the road while I walked down to where the water met dry earth.

Beneath the surface, men slept, facing upward. They slept with bullets in their backs. They slept without eyes. Without eyes to close they slept restlessly, rolling in the current.

At least I didn't burn, they said. *At least I kept a body that can sleep. That can float. That can startle people into remembering I existed, when they look at the water and see me, if only for a fraction of a second, before I disappear back under and they wonder if they'd seen anything at all. At least I was there.*

I saw Opa in the river, fishing. He had wrinkles and age spots and veiny hands with long fingernails—especially on his left pinky. His skin was yellower than it had been the first time he stood up to his calves in the Danube. And his hair, instead of the full blond head of hair he'd had when he was a child, had the dark, wet, slicked-back widow's peak that used to remind me of a vampire.

There had always been a foreignness to him, something that made him separate. His tight polyester suits with overlarge lapels placed him out of time. There was his throaty accent, his long pinky fingernail. The way he used to drink every beverage—from Coca Cola to Miller High Life—at room temperature. And he was always so skinny.

He was an American citizen, though when asked what he was, he would rarely say that. He wouldn't say he was Swabian either. Or Yugoslavian. He would say, instead, that he was German.

Maybe it was easier. When Sid and I started dating, Opa said, "Did you know that Kohler is a German name?" He looked at me with a grin as big as the moon.

He smiled so wide for someone who knew so much destruction.

He knew, he lived it, but he never had to see the houses refilled with Serbs and Montenegrins after the Germans who built them were expelled.

He never had to see the starving people, the barbed wire fences, the pits in the earth where the bodies went. He didn't see what Oma had seen.

He never had to see the human fire.

I wondered what would be found mixed in with the rocks on the bed of the Danube if I swam to the icy bottom to find out. I didn't know how long it would take a body to decompose, if pieces of burned bodies could have gotten trapped in the river instead of gone out to sea, if burned bone dissolved. I pictured children standing at the river's edge, picking up pebble-sized slices of bone to skip over the water's surface instead of tiny rocks. The bones skipped higher into the air than stone, though they didn't fly as far. The bones skipped higher because they fought to escape the cycling current and the murky bottom of a bloody river. They tried to skip to Heaven.

"Marie," David said. Like Apatin's blue river and manicured hedges, the perfect mural in the broken church, I forced myself to look as if nothing was wrong. I didn't know what else to do. I smiled in spite of the ghost of fire on the river and in the sanctuary, in spite of feeling like I'd made a mess out of everything: out of this trip, Mislav, Gašinci, out of my marriage, out of the opportunity to ask my grandparents about what it meant to be who they were.

And David. His face was the same. He came down to the bank and brushed a stray hair out of my face. He smiled and held me, pretending he didn't know my mind was on the things I'd lost.

❖

Just over four years ago, I got the phone call: Opa was dying and I needed to come home. Oma's voice shook. "Hurry," she'd said. It was forty degrees. I stood outside my college apartment in a tank top. I leaned so hard against the brick wall that the rough face broke my skin. When I hung up, I packed a small bag and got into my car before Sid had time to leave his night class.

I drove in silence and watched the sky, stilling myself for speeding down I-95 toward whatever I would find when I arrived in Northeast Philadelphia. The sky was dark and full of pinprick November stars, and the waning crescent moon lay on its back in the darkness, grinning.

At 9:06, the dashboard went black.

With it, the radio stopped, the headlights dimmed, the heater shut off.

"Shit."

I pulled the Honda onto the shoulder and turned off the engine. My hands were earthquakes. I walked to the passenger side, grabbed the manual out of the glove compartment, and opened it to the fuse box diagram. Sharp flecks of gravel pressed into my knees as I knelt on the road and pried the plastic cover off the box beneath the dashboard. The wires in two of the fuses had split.

I found replacements in the emergency kit in the trunk, and when I looked up, the moon was smiling down.

Sid and I had both been home the week before, for Thanksgiving. Opa had sat on a stool in his kitchen and leaned his back against me so I could guide his hands to the feeding tube clipped inside his dress shirt. He'd been feeding himself through that tube since his stroke, but his fingers couldn't grip the can of liquid food anymore. I held it for him. His hands shook too much to keep the funnel steady, so I held it with him. Together we poured and watched it, thick as condensed milk, glide down the tube and into his belly. He tried to smile as I clipped the tube back onto his shirt and washed the funnel in the sink, as I rinsed the sick sweet smell down the drain. Instead he kissed my cheek and said, "Thank you, Puddin'."

I walked him from the stool in the kitchen to his recliner in the living room. I knelt beside him on the floor and held his hands, counted the age spots, so many more than I had counted at the toy warehouse two decades earlier.

He fell in and out of sleep in the middle of sentences. His sleep was fevered. He shouted in the middle of it, squeezed my hand tight, and said, "The people at the door, don't let them in."

I squeezed back. "It's okay, there's no one there."

"Can't you hear them knocking?"

It wasn't until after I'd found his books in my closet that I saw the strangers he'd heard on his stoop that night: uniformed men with rifles who spoke Serbo-Croatian and brutalized children in starvation camps. The mayor of Ansfelden and the Nazi soldier who came for my grandfather with a draft notice. Men covered in blood or Vojvodine earth, naked and waiting because they were all part of the same nightmare. One night soon, their knocking said, they'd come to take him home.

For three weeks in 1945, Opa woke up beside children in Nazi uniform. For three weeks, he wore the uniform, too.

Until he decided to fake a flat bicycle tire and flee.

"I've never peddled so fast in my life," he said.

It took him fourteen hours, but when he knocked on the barrack at Haid and his mother opened the door, he said it felt like he'd skipped forward in time. He said he didn't cry when he was kidnapped. That he didn't cry when he was handed his uniform the morning the Nazi soldier came. When he killed a chicken to eat it or when he was taught how to use an egg grenade.

But when his mother started crying, stroking his hair and kissing his forehead, when she fell to her knees and whispered, "Mein Sohn!" When even his father and his grandfather had tears in their eyes. Then, he cried. He told them everything. They told him to get out of his uniform and get into bed. To stay there until it was safe.

His mother burned the uniform over a fire in the cafeteria kitchen the next morning. Opa stayed in bed for two weeks, until news trickled down to the refugee camp that the war was over.

"I could have gotten official discharge papers after that," he said. "But because I was sent in with another boy's name, I never went."

I wondered if something sinister had happened to that other boy because Opa never filed his papers. If he, too, became one of the men waiting at the door.

Opa had a lucid moment as Sid and I said goodbye. He grabbed Sid's hand and said, "Take care of her."

"I will," Sid said.

I wasn't ready to leave.

I kissed Opa's hand. I pressed my cheek against it. It felt like marble. His eyes were already rolling in another dream. "I love you," I said, stroking the ridges of his thick, yellow fingernails. I brushed his fine black hair off his forehead and kissed his brow. It felt both hot and cold at once. And he was so thin. It looked as if he was receding into the cushions of his chair, disappearing.

When I pulled into the driveway on Anita Drive, he was already dead. "He went just after 9 o'clock," Oma said, sobbing at the kitchen table. "I didn't want to tell you while you were driving."

A desperate thought: the fuses in the Honda—was that him?

I wanted to believe it so much.

The men from the funeral home waited in the shadows of the living room. They left Opa lying in bed with his arms crossed over his chest and his eyes closed so I could see his body turned to wax before they took him. So I could kiss his marble hands again, count the age spots, brush the hair off his moon-white forehead.

So I could be the one to open the door to the men who knocked, though I didn't know it yet.

I would let them in.

MOLIN, SERBIA: 2012

MOLE PLODS SPECKLED THE DIRT along the side of the highway—big wet piles of earth. Vojvodine moles made mountains beside heaps of turnips and garbage: cans and plastic bags, paper and rotten food. They must have been fat moles because the soil was so rich it was black.

I wondered what the moles would see underground, if they could see more than shadows. I wondered what they would see beneath Molidorf, a village that no longer existed. The Serbian name, Molin, showed up on satellite images near a village called Aleksandrovo. But there was no town under the letters, not even a road—only measured rectangular fields in different shades of green. Just northwest of where the satellite placed Molin, something peculiar grew: a rectangle of trees and overgrown hedges. The hedges looked geometric, as if they'd grown around buildings. There were skinny fault lines between the green that looked as if they might have been streets.

"You've worried so much about risking our safety on this trip," I said, placing my hand over David's on the gear shift. "But this place seems the scariest to me."

Serbia had been demined since the Balkan Wars had ended. But on an unmarked road in a village overtaken by flora, how could you know they hadn't missed one?

"Really?" David asked, eyes narrowed on the road.

"What if we hit a landmine?"

"We won't," he said. "I've checked the region's demining status. They're all either west or south of here. It's not like the Croatian side of the border. But if you're nervous, we'll walk softly, brush the ground with our feet before we step. A lot of old

mines are duds, anyway. And stationary. Unlike the modern ones."
He squeezed my thumb.

"That's reassuring," I said, cracking the window. "I thought
our countries stopped making landmines."

"They did. Well, mine did." He shifted the car into a lower
gear. Keep your eyes out for dirt roads on the right."

I saw only fields and occasional skinny paths of squashed-
down grass where tractors had navigated through turnips and
wheat. I squinted. "It won't be a farm road, will it?"

"I don't know."

A trace of gravel appeared in the road between a field of tall
grass and a field of tilled earth. David checked the rearview and
downshifted again.

It looked like a driveway.

"Are you sure this is it?" I clenched the grab handle.

David turned up the dirt lane. I imagined one of the Spark's
saggy tires bouncing off an unexploded mine. I pictured the doors
blasting into shrapnel, mixed with skin and hair, rubber and torn
clothing. A colony of moles stippling the air like starlings. I wondered what it would feel like to hit a landmine: if it would be quick
like a popped balloon, if I would feel air rushing over the pieces
of myself.

I hoped, if we blew up, the investigators would dig up more
than just our bones.

"What do modern landmines do that old ones don't?"

"Jump," David said through his teeth, focusing on keeping the
Spark's tires within the old tracks on the road. "Three feet in the
air. And right before they explode, they emit a paralyzing gas."

"That's sick," I said.

"Maybe. But it also almost guarantees a quick death instead of
leaving someone to suffer in an empty field without their legs."

How do you know these things? I wanted to ask, but I didn't.
It was unnerving, after I'd seen the fearful side of David, how in
control he seemed, how suddenly sure. I read that the only way to
totally avoid landmines in this part of the world was to stay on
paved roads and worn paths. Not to wander into fields or drive on
disused lanes. So what were we doing here? Was this anxiety what

David had felt when he cancelled going to Croatia, when he wouldn't let Mislav in the car? When he stood leaning out of the train at the Hungarian border? Maybe I should have been more understanding. It wasn't his history he was here for. His gut wasn't hungry to swallow all the terrible pieces at any cost. Not like mine.

The track turned right.

A roofline appeared over wheat stalks.

As the Chevy trundled through an increasing amount of mud, more rooflines came into view: a cluster of buildings made of brick and plaster with few windows and no doors. The plaster was stained in the middle and chunks of it were missing from the bottom half of the walls.

"Was there a flood?" David asked, leaning over the steering wheel and squinting at the buildings. A bullseye had been spray painted on one of the farthest walls, at face height for an average-sized man.

Bullet holes riddled the plaster inside the rings.

"Yeah," I said. "Not long after the camp was shut down."

Mother Nature came to wash the death away.

David parked the car next to an outhouse.

"So, this is it, then?" David opened his door and stepped into the mud.

"I think so." I compared the picture in front of me to the photographs I'd seen, taken in the verdant height of summer. The buildings were a lot more visible in the starkness of January than when everything was green and overgrown. "It looks like the old yard."

Alter hof: where children were housed, stacked without blankets on top of each other, as they were kept in all the other camps. Only the other camps' records weren't as specific. They didn't tell you which building, which room, which stable had been filled with dying children. One of the buildings looked like a mechanic's shop. There was no garage door, but there was a hole in the concrete floor the size of a person. The shop still smelled like metal and motor oil.

Farther down the lot, another building erupted from the overgrowth. Litter scattered the dead grass by the entrance—litter and plastic tarpaulin and boar tracks. The door was missing.

David stepped inside first, brushing his toes over the ground.

The windows were too high to let sunlight in. Broken furniture obscured the floor: overturned chests of drawers, beer cans and empty rakija bottles, snack bags and half-pairs of gloves. Everything else was darkness—dark water stains on the interior plaster, dark wood beams on the pitched ceiling, dark, dusty cobwebs hanging from the corners and the boarded-up windows and the aged plaster walls. A hollow feeling. An owl pellet with tiny bird bones and half-digested feathers sat by my feet. Soggy cardboard. Empty plaster powder boxes. Sandbags.

Of the three thousand estimated killed at Molidorf, two thousand and twelve had been named. Jakob Armschlinger, Barbara Wagner, three Wilhelm Gemls. Josef Lesch—tied with rope and shot in the back while trying to escape. Elisabetha Schaus. Her husband's name wasn't on the roster. I found a photograph of the two, unsmiling, on their wedding day. She was thin and had cheekbones like my grandmother and a wedding headpiece that looked as delicate as tissue paper. He wore a felt hat and a vest that buttoned right under the knot in his tie. His boutonniere resembled a paper doll ballerina.

David and I walked from room to room, leaving footprints in the dust. All the rooms looked the same. We came to another doorway with no door and stepped into a field of rustling weeds. The daylight was blinding.

Something shot up from the grass at our feet.

My heart caught in my throat.

A pheasant—wings full of adrenaline—ripped through the air like shrapnel.

"I stepped on him." David said it as if it was impossible.

I forced a laugh. "So much for walking softly."

He put his hands on my cheeks and kissed me.

A stone building with no roof rose out of the grasses on the other side of the field. The tops of the walls looked like puzzle pieces. David walked ahead of me. Mud tried to suck the boots off my feet. When we got to the largest doorway, something flashed in the ruins.

Surrounded by colorless branches, weathered planks, beige-gray stone, a fox smoldered. He lingered, fiery and still, before he leapt over wood and scrap metal and burrowed himself into a tiny space in the wreckage.

"That was incredible," David said.

Molin was alive—not the way Prvi Depot and the sugar factory were alive. It wasn't continuing as if nothing had happened. It had new life, separate from human violence.

I remembered a gathering of my grandparents' friends from the United German-Hungarian Club: my Aunt Katharina—who I called Tante Ina even though she wasn't really my Aunt—her husband, Uncle Nikolaus, Mr. and Mrs. Albrecht, the Goldschmidts, my real Aunt Anja, and half a dozen grownups I didn't recognize. They were the only other people I'd met who spoke like Oma and Opa. And they smelled funny—a cocktail of Miller High Life, liquor, hairspray, and stale eau de parfum.

I made up a game where the dinner guests were animals in a zoo. I spotted a great crested bird with a bottle-platinum perm teased up to the ceiling. Slick, gelled amphibians with sweaty palms and too much aftershave. Flurries of fish with rainbow-sequined scales and red pouted lips. A stocky wild pig with dark stubble and hair up to his neck and knuckles who bared overlarge incisors when he smiled. My grandfather became a lizard in a burnt orange lounge suit with a wide-lapelled shirt underneath, unbuttoned one too many buttons. His gold "#1 Lover" necklace flashed from his skinny chest.

"Puddin'," he called out as I reached for a room temperature beer left unattended on the coffee table. "Don't drink that. You're not going to like the taste."

The next building David and I walked into looked like it had been a home. It had no essentials—no doors, appliances, or plumbing. There were white splotches on the kitchen walls where sinks and cabinets and countertops had been. The rest of the room was painted sea foam green. A shoe sat in the middle of the floor—a black sneaker with mud and laces.

Everything was missing part of itself.

The structure of the house felt comfortable: big sunny windows, high ceilings, a layout that flowed from one room to the next. There was something sinister in the comfort. A sunny doorway with no way to shut the night out. A hallway with pale pink walls and nail holes like tiny black eyes. Windows with hinges to open in the springtime, except half the panes were gone. Cracked tile floors with mud and discarded papers strewn across them. David picked up one of the papers. I did too. A bill from 1998.

"That explains the concrete posts where the lane widens," David said.

"What posts?"

"The ones that blend in with the wheat field," he said. "They were built to stop tanks."

I couldn't imagine Molin serving a purpose after three thousand dying breaths blew against the plaster, after it had flooded and stained and crumbled, but it had. And the sugar factory in Zrenjanin was still a sugar factory, even if it was asleep. Oma and Opa had built a home on Anita Drive to escape, but I'd returned to Vojvodina. The fox in the ruins was just that—an animal living in human wreckage. No history was separate from our violence. No history ended.

Wind pressed against the walls of the old house. I felt the pressure in my ear drums.

"This would've been a perfect hideout," David said.

We flipped through more of the papers on the floor, annotated in Serbo-Croatian. Maybe whoever hid in Molin in the 90's knew that it used to be a death camp. Or at least gave the abandoned village a new history: one of survival instead of loss.

A crunch fell outside the open windows like a footstep. David looked up.

"Did you hear that?" I asked. I heard it again.

"And the whispers?" David looked nervous. He dropped the paper in his hands.

Voices tangled in the overgrowth.

"David." I glanced at the doorway, the open one with no door to shut.

Oh God. Why had I thought it was a good idea to travel thousands of miles to visit a place that decimated my ancestors? It was naïve and arrogant of me to think I had the right to come here. That it was safe.

"Someone knows we're here," he said.

My mind flooded with images: an abandoned village, unmarked roads, strange men paid to keep Molin hidden. I felt the weight of steel links on the back of my neck.

David squeezed my hand as he tiptoed past me. Maybe the noises out the windows were just the wind. Or birds hiding in the rafters of the other buildings to keep out of the cold. I took one last glance at the papers on the floor—so white and crisp for being abandoned nearly fifteen years earlier.

I was reminded again: time moved differently in Serbia.

A horse chestnut tree stood sentry at the front door. Its shadow swallowed the doorway.

David hid behind the trunk while he looked out at the lane, while I stood surrounded by pale pink and cobwebs and watchful black nail holes.

"Looks clear," he said. "Maybe they made noise to warn us. Give us a chance to leave."

I stepped outside—in the sunshine everything felt different, lighter than it had in the house. My fear dissipated. A soft breeze rippled through my hair and my scarf without stinging my nose with cold. The air was quiet save the few quivering leaves still clinging to the horse chestnut. A single bird chirped from the direction of the outhouse.

The sounds we'd heard seemed impossible now.

But they'd been there, like shadows.

Like the footsteps of a guard whose soul had been dragged back to this place, who walked the same terrible circuit over and over while women cried under cupped hands and children breathed heavy from the weight of their bodies. While living people came to remind him that he was somewhere in between.

"Help, I'm here, can you see me? I can't stop walking. My legs are so tired. And this place is my nightmare, it never left me. All I wanted was for it to leave me. Please. I'm sorry. I only did what I was told. They told me these people weren't people at all. That they were something less. And I believed them. I was a monster, I

know it. It was so much easier to become one than I imagined it would be. But we were all monsters, then, weren't we? Have mercy."

"You heard the whispers," David said. It sounded more like a question.

"I did," I said.

But in the sunshine, in Molin, there was no sign of men.

HANNE BECKER:
BRISTOL, PENNSYLVANIA: 2012

MY FIRST MORNING IN AMERICA smelled like coal dust and subway vents. My second smelled like steaming grease and iron. When I stepped off the train the third morning, it smelled pastoral: wooden houses leaking honeycomb smoke, the sweet char of sappy logs in the damp predawn. I could smell frost on the marsh grasses and burnt coffee brewing in a waterside diner.

A thick layer of fog hung half a dozen feet above the river. Above the fog, the sky smoldered.

"The angels are baking kekse," my father used to say.

I knocked on doors along the riverfront. The few that opened revealed looks of disgust before shutting me out. The same looks awaited me everywhere. The left side of my face is disfigured: one eye wilted, lips swollen and pulled back so I can't close them. And my cheek—scars run across it like a dried up riverbed.

I'd knocked on doors long enough for the river to shake its sleepers, for the sun to burn away the fog, when I stepped up to a paint-chipped door with the surname Gray in brass letters beneath the knocker.

A woman answered.

"Housekeeping?" I asked. It was one of the few English words I could speak.

The woman opened the door and gestured for me to enter. I was seventeen and alone, and she made me breakfast: eggs and toast with a bitter mug of black coffee. I remember smelling bacon, but there must have only been enough for her husband because I don't recall indulging in the slick, crisp rashers I so ravenously sniffed from my seat at their kitchen table.

Mrs. Gray explained my duties, but I couldn't understand her words. She handed me a tray of food and beckoned me to follow her upstairs. I smelled her husband's sickness from the landing. When I crossed into his bedroom, he didn't look up. Instead, he focused on the thick green book in his hand. I placed the tray over his lap, careful not to tip coffee into his plate.

"Who are you?" he asked.

I stared at a knot in the floor.

"Are you deaf, child?"

When I looked up, his eyes softened. He pointed at himself and said, "Ernest."

Then he pointed at me.

"Hanne," I replied.

He nodded without smiling and returned his attention to the book. I looked past him at three large windows with heavy drapes pulled tight against the draft and the river.

"It's important to assimilate," Mrs. Gray said after an English lesson, squeezing my shoulder. "Don't worry, dear. It will come in time."

She also believed her husband's recovery would come in time. But Mr. Gray had been ill long enough that she'd arranged his bedroom into a museum of bedpans and bedside lamps—floor lamps, table lamps, a massive secondhand chandelier that cast prisms across the walls and ceilings. Except the room still seemed dark. Mrs. Gray only kept low watt bulbs in the sockets to keep the atmosphere calming.

It reminded me of Molidorf. The darkness, the sound of tired lungs, the smell of refuse.

"Darf ich?" I asked late one morning, pulling Mr. Gray's bed-sheets down to his ankles. His legs were pale and hairless up to the middle of his calves. Above his calves, the hair was dark and springy.

When he didn't respond, I corrected myself. "May I?"

He nodded and looked away. I cupped the backs of his ankles and pulled his feet out from under the covers, bent his knees so that his legs made two tall triangles. He wore cloth underwear pinned around his waist because he often lacked the strength to

get to the bathroom down the hall—or to shout for me to come
running with one of his bedpans.

A putrid stench rose from inside the cloth.

I pulled rubber gloves from my back pocket and slipped them
up to my elbows, thankful that nothing had run through the fabric
and onto the sheets.

The first time I saw what was underneath his cloth—when Mrs.
Gray showed me how to change him—I nearly got sick. It wasn't
just the sight and smell of refuse, the way it clung to loose skin.
Her husband's thighs were crumpled tissue paper with two fleshy
prunes between them.

Mr. Gray's whole body seemed shriveled, and he was easy to
lift when I slid the dirty fabric from under him, wiped his wrinkly
buttocks clean, and placed a fresh cloth where the filthy one had
been. He kept his eyes on the curtains with his arms at his sides,
pressing down into the mattress.

I wrapped the fresh cloth around him, pinned it at his waist,
and picked the dirty one up by the outermost edges, holding it with
the tips of my fingers as carefully as a stork would cradle a new-
born. I dropped it in the nearest bedpan and turned back to Mr.
Gray.

"Besser?" I asked.

He nodded.

Before I came to the United States, before the Partisans and
the Red Army swept through Yugoslavia, I'd been the daughter of
a baker.

As a child, I'd wake to the yeasty smell of warm bread, of
sweet rolls rising in the oven; of fruit-filled and savory strudels;
of the toasted almond, honey, and custard slathered between layers
of fresh bienenstich. Every morning, I'd awake to the aroma of
caramelizing sugar as my father's flour-coated hands lifted me
from bed and sat me on his tall stool in the kitchen. He'd say,
"Schatzi, my little taste-tester, yours is the most important job."

I'd pull apart a fresh roll and watch the heat escape in whorls
from the crumb. I'd eat the soft center and hand the crust back to
my father, smiling with my mouth full. And then I'd eat a pastry
of his choosing. Usually it was bienenstich. But at Fasching, Papa

would slide a plate of fresh krapfen in front of me and instruct me to pick one. I'd pluck an oil-hot, sugar-dusted doughnut from the plate and bite, hoping there wasn't a surprise inside. He used to fill a few with mustard and mix them in with the jam-filled ones. For good luck, he'd say.

Frau Müller would be waiting at the door when my father unlocked it at opening time. "Good morning, Therese," he'd say. "You've got the pick of the shop again." Others would soon follow. Father Werner always ordered plum küchen before his daily duties at the church and ruffled my hair on his way out the door. On Saturdays he sent the deacon and his wife to pick up eleven loaves of bread to bless for communion. Schoolboys would come in for strudel to eat on their walk to the schoolhouse. And nearly every housewife in Neuzerne came to fetch bread and rolls and sweets before their husbands returned from work—to present at the dinner table or squirrel away in their cupboards for later.

"Herr Becker," they would say, "what delicious treats have you made to bully our waistlines today?" And, "Little Hanne, so pretty you are—and spoiled with sweets!"

"Time for exercise," I said to Mr. Gray.

"Do we have to?" he grumbled, closing his green book and returning it to its place on the nightstand, behind the stack of books Mrs. Gray had placed there from his bookshelves.

"It's good for you." I smiled, holding his legs by the ankles and taking turns tucking them up to his chest and pulling them straight, pointing his toes.

He turned his gaze toward the curtains while I worked.

They were heavier than shadows.

"Sunlight heals," I said, pulling back the brocade just enough that a stream of sunlight burst between the panels and caught thousands of floating dust mites. Mr. Gray coughed at the particles.

I pretended not to hear him and went back downstairs to scrub the stains out of his underwear, which I'd left to soak in bleach. When I returned to the room an hour later, the drapes were closed.

"His eyes are not accustomed to the brightness," Mrs. Gray said while we prepared dinner in the kitchen that evening.

In the camp at Molidorf, sunlight would have been a blessing.

I didn't tell this to Mrs. Gray. I didn't want to add to her troubles. The pain she carried was visible on her slouched shoulders, in her thinning hair. It was visible in her mismatched clothing, her haphazard lipstick. It was there in the way she had me run errands for her, once she was satisfied with my ability to speak English—as if she was afraid of the questions she would receive if she ran into the local housewives at the supermarket.

"How is Mr. Gray doing?" they'd ask, peering over their skinny noses at the contents of my handbasket, looking for signs of disease: petroleum jelly, cod liver oil, ammonia. People are the same no matter where they're from.

"What did Mr. Gray do before he got sick?" I asked, stirring a pot of simmering noodles.

"He was a historian," she said.

She paused to adjust her apron.

"He was a good man."

All men seemed like good men. Until the day no one came to the bakery: not the deacon, not the housewives, not the schoolboys hungry for strudel. I didn't wake up to the aromas of my father's work. He didn't come with flour-covered hands to carry me to the kitchen and taste the day's menu.

I woke up late, well after the sun had risen.

The only other day I didn't wake to the smell of his baking was the day after my mother died. She'd had a heart attack in the street, walking home from the miller's. There were days long after her passing that my father still delighted in being a baker, in bringing simple, sweet pleasures to the villagers of Neuzerne. And then there were days when he'd remember that it was his cakes that weighed heavy on her bones. Her bad heart had come from his oven. On those days, the bakery suffered. He'd burn the edges of his delicate strudel, over-measure the yeast for his bienenstich. He'd mistake salt for sugar in his plum küchen, his streusel, his krapfen. I'd hear our customers mutter, as they clenched bags of ruined pastries in their fists:

"Poor man, the way his wife haunts that oven."

"I'd haunt it too if my husband made me lose my figure like that."

"She was so pretty when she was young."

"And thin."

"Can you imagine his guilt?"

"And that poor little girl."

I didn't feel unfortunate. Of course, I dreamed of my mother, of her plump lips against my cheek. In my dreams, her laugh was sugared glass. When it broke, it rang high and soft against her throat.

"Where are you from?" Mrs. Gray asked me once.

"Neuzerne," I replied.

"Is that somewhere in Germany?"

"It's in Eastern Europe," I said, hanging dripping sheets and stained cloths on the clothesline. "But my ancestors came from Baden-Württemberg, in Germany."

It was too complicated to tell her that after the First World War, my part of the empire was assimilated into Yugoslavia. I didn't tell her anything about myself. I imagined she'd scoff if I said there were German victims in World War II. It was bad enough trying to acquire Mr. Gray's smoked fish from the specialty grocer down the street.

"You," the owner said the first time I walked in and said hello in my heavy accent. "Nazi. You are not welcome in my shop."

"I am not a Nazi," I said.

"My family was killed by your people."

I stood at the fish counter and said nothing.

"God has cursed you for the sins of your father," the owner said. "For every soul that perished in the gas chambers, there should be a face like yours."

The pimpled boy by the scales didn't ask me what I wanted from the case. He stared at me the way everyone stares at me.

"You did not know my father," I said, and left without the fish.

When I returned to Mrs. Gray's stoop, there were tears running down the front of my coat.

"What's wrong, poor Hanne?" Mrs. Gray scooped me into her arms and out of the cold. She brushed the moisture off my scarred cheek with her housecoat.

If I told her, she would say that my people did bad things. That it's the kind of hurt that doesn't heal easily. And then she would continue: that's why it's so important to assimilate.

In the end, all I said was, "The boy behind the fish counter called me ugly."

In Neuzerne, there had been a fish monger. There had also been a postman, a doctor, and a town crier. Mostly there were farmers. When the war came, some of our men joined the German Army, some were drafted, some fought for Yugoslavia. My father continued baking.

Until the morning I woke up to a vacuum of smell.

I tiptoed around the shop, looking for him. The kitchen was cold, the oven was dark, and two men with guns were standing at the shop doors.

"Your sign says you open at six-thirty, little girl. But your door is still locked."

"We are soldiers, so you must open up."

"Nothing's been baked today," I shouted through the glass.

"Has the baker gone missing?" they asked. "We can help you find him if you let us in."

I had never seen soldiers before, but Papa sometimes gave the local police free streusel.

I walked up to the door and turned the latch. I opened it an inch and said, "We have yesterday's cakes in the back."

They stepped into the shop. Up close, they looked much larger than they had from the other side of the glass. Their boots came up to my knees.

"Aren't you a sweetheart," one of the soldiers said, stroking my cheek with his dirty hand.

I led them through the dark shop, down the hallway where the sun cast skinny streaks of light on the floor, into the cold pantry where my father kept the leftover pastries and breads. I pointed to the wrapped foods on the shelves. "Those are strudel, those are poppy seed, those are rye, and those are beer rolls."

They each grabbed a strudel and peeled back the wrapping.

They took such large bites that powdered sugar stuck to their lips and chin and snowed on their lapels. "Ugh," one of them said, spitting his mouthful on the floor. "Mustard." The other soldier did the same even though his was filled with cherries.

"Nazi filth," he said. In the Grays' house, my hands smelled constantly of bleach and ammonia. I could never fathom why Mrs. Gray collected so many bedpans. There were a few brass ones with carved wood handles that were strangely beautiful, a blue and white floral porcelain one, a handful of brightly colored Bakelite pans—even one that looked like a teapot.

I scrubbed the bedpans in the hallway, kneeling on a cushion just out of Mr. Gray's sight, but close enough that I could hear him if he called. Mr. Gray never looked at my face with revulsion, so I did my best not to lift my nose at the smell.

"Hanne," Mr. Gray called so softly I could barely hear him over the bleach water sloshing. I dropped my sponge into the pan and hung my gloves over the rim.

"Yes, Mr. Gray?" I asked, peering around the doorway.

"It's three o'clock," he said, nodding to the chair at the head of his bed. Every afternoon, Mrs. Gray insisted I read to her husband to improve my English.

"Would you like me to read the paper?" I pronounced *the* extra slowly, but it still came out *tuh*.

He shook his head.

"Me neither," I said, grinning as I rifled through the pile of books on his nightstand: antiquated volumes on war strategy, treaties, and religion. I passed over a couple of thick novels, which would have been a treat compared to the historical tomes. Instead, I pulled out the one he always seemed to be reading.

The green book had the texture of cheap linen. Embossed on the cover in gold: Dr. Ernest S. Gray. I opened to the title page and stared at his name typed in thick black ink. Below it, the name of the publishing house, some company out of Philadelphia. As I thumbed through, the smell of must and glue escaped the pages. The spine felt stiff, as if it had been neglected. Yet I'd seen him with it open so often, scribbling notes in the margins. Barely any paper showed through the ink. Some of the marginalia even crawled into the space between lines.

As I scanned down the page, his handwriting became less legible. His ink moved across the paper as if drawn by the tide toward a precipice. I wondered how many times he had pored over this book. It reminded me of my father on the days when he put salt in his pastries.

"It's a beautiful morning," said one of the soldiers.

"Let's have our breakfast outside."

"Won't you get the door for us, draga?"

The soldiers pulled the leftover baked goods from the pantry and stacked them in their arms. I held the door as they carried the whole inventory of breads and pastries into the back yard. They unwrapped them one at a time and threw them on the ground.

"Sweet child, what's the matter?"

My tears fell on mangled rolls.

"A little girl as pretty as you shouldn't cry."

"Papa." I wept, smearing my runny nose on my sleeve.

"Your father ran away," they said, stamping on the strudel until the cherries and plums and sweet syrups burst out the sides. The soldiers still had powdered sugar on their faces. "He is a coward."

I looked at them and shook my head, my lungs hiccupping with the force of my tears.

"You think we're liars?" One of the soldiers said, squatting down so his face was level with mine. There was cherry filling in the corners of his mouth. "Then where is he?"

I hiccupped and wiped my nose again.

"Is he here still?" they asked.

"Is he hiding?"

Before I could answer, I felt a boot collide with the side of my head. I heard a pop and felt burning before I hit the ground. The boot came down again.

I heard the soldiers' footsteps move back inside the house. The backdoor banged shut after them. Another noise: a wooden creak. I looked toward the fence. I couldn't see much, everything was blurred, but I saw the fuzzy silhouette of Frau Müller from next door.

"Hanne," she whispered. "Your papa didn't run away. All the men were taken. My husband and my son. There were gunshots in the night."

"Hanne?"

I could barely hear her voice. My right ear was ringing.

"Hanne, I'm so sorry. I wish I could help, but I'm afraid."

Darkness fell over my eyes, but I felt the sun on my face. I didn't have to see to know the neighbor had gone. Only the smell of grass and burst pastries remained, and the absence of the smell of a hot oven. I got sick listening to the soldiers in the house—table legs screeching on the floor, glass breaking, more footsteps and slammed doors.

I closed Mr. Gray's book, hoping I could slip it back onto the nightstand and grab another without him noticing the swap. He pretended to inspect the delicate curves and points of the curtains' brocade while I placed his book back on the nightstand behind the others. I picked up one of the novels, propped it open, and took a deep breath.

"That's enough for this afternoon," he said, his gaze still lost in the folds that blocked out the day.

I woke up with my face covered in blood and sick. My vision was fuzzy, but improved. I saw red vomit in the grass. The sounds of the soldiers in the kitchen had gone, so I pulled myself to my feet and went to my father's bedroom. His recipe book was open on the floor. The blankets had been torn off the bed, the pillows had been slashed, and the picture of my mother that he kept on his bedside table lay among shards of glass on the floor. The space on the wall where he hung his shotgun was empty. I picked a blanket up from the mess and climbed onto the bed.

I pulled the blanket over my face and settled into my makeshift darkness, breathing my own stale breath. My whole body ached. My head throbbed all the way down my spine. It throbbed in my teeth. I closed my eyes and tried to sleep, until I heard the front door open and shut.

I wanted to jump out of bed and run to the door in case it was Papa. But if it had been my father, he would have said, "Schatzi, where are you?" Or maybe he would have run first into my bedroom and then into his, looking for me. He wouldn't have taken the slow steps I heard move through the kitchen, down the hallway. His breathing wouldn't have been so quiet. He wouldn't have tiptoed over the threshold of his own bedroom and crept toward the bed. And when he tugged the blanket away from me, he wouldn't have smiled down at my swollen face and said, "You poor thing, let me make it better."

"I imagine it's difficult, being an immigrant," Mr. Gray said, turning to face me.

Yes, I wanted to say, but the word stuck in my throat.

He reached for his water glass, looked up at my face, and spilled the contents of his tea tray. I bent to pick up the plates and biscuits that had fallen, brushed the crumbs into a napkin, and put them back on the platter.

"Forgive me," Mr. Gray said, his hands shaking. "It's none of my business."

He looked back toward the curtains.

"I—" I started, following his gaze, imagining the wasted view of the river just beyond the fabric.

I considered telling Mr. Gray that it was difficult being an immigrant because of what the soldier did. Because of the town hall, where the soldier carried me. He put me in a pile of old men, women, and children. I looked for my father in the sea of faces, but I couldn't find him. Behind everything, I saw the empty space on the wall where he'd kept his shotgun.

I wasn't the only bleeding body. There were other girls with cherry red stains on their skirts and faces, mothers with bleeding mouths. They should have looked familiar, but they didn't.

We were lined up and marched eight kilometers to Molidorf. It shouldn't have taken as long as it did to walk such a small distance, but our bodies fought us. We couldn't control our bones enough to lift our feet.

I wasn't allowed to see a doctor about my face. It became infected. My skin started to rot. For years I watched death move around me in a windowless room, awed that my ruined face hadn't enticed death to take me, too.

The day the camp at Molidorf closed, I was as afraid as the day it was opened.

I followed the remnants of a family to Hungary. In a stranger's home, I saw my face in a mirror. Tears ran down ravines in my cheek, ravines shaped like boot treads. My swollen eye turned pink from the effort of making tiny saltwater rivers. I ran my fingers over the scars. There was a small relief in knowing I could never suffer loss again because I'd always be alone.

I wanted to tell this to Mr. Gray. I wanted to tell him that I missed my father. All but the smallest piece of me believed that he'd been killed the night before the soldiers came to the bakery. But there was a sliver of me that couldn't help but wonder, a splinter made of doubt and anger that poked at me sometimes. Its jagged edges reminded me of the soldiers' voices: *Your father ran away. He is a coward.*

It reminded me, too, of Frau Müller's words: *There were gunshots in the night.*

Had the soldiers taken his shotgun, or had he taken it himself?

"Hanne?"

Mr. Gray looked at me out of the corner of his eye.

"Don't apologize," I said in near perfect English. "But you're right, Mr. Gray. It's none of your business."

He fixed his eyes on the weft in the brocade. I picked the novel back up from beside the tray of spilt tea, settled back into the chair at the head of his bed, and read until Mrs. Gray rang the bell that meant it was time to fix supper.

We are supposed to continue like the steely river. My foundation is a fine mist of memory. Outwardly I have decayed into an American of indistinguishable origin. I haven't eaten bienenstich since I was a child, though I've passed beautiful squares of it in bakery windows, labeled as bee sting cake. If I succumb to temptation enough to step inside the shop, I'll order a slice of red velvet instead.

Mrs. Gray would be proud, though she's long dead. It took her husband three years to die of his sickness, and she passed not long after. They left me the house, so I continue life in Mr. Gray's dark bedroom. I have my own housekeeper—a Guatemalan girl who doesn't speak much English. She reads me the newspapers in the morning and brings me breakfast on a silver tray. I've told her

NOVI SAD, SERBIA: 2012

FOR THE FIRST TIME since arriving in Serbia, the Dinaric Alps were visible on the horizon. They appeared like a mirage over the dark fields as we drove.

I crossed my eyes and let the landscape bleed together until high tension wires became trees and tiny houses became potato heaps. Shirts and scarves and pants drying on clotheslines flew by in a muddled rainbow.

I rolled the window down and balanced my camera on the rubber seal. At high speed, my photographs looked like Alzheimer's recollections, out of focus and incomplete. Everything in Vojvodina screamed silently for what had been lost. Solitary shoes, naked branches, lonely shacks in empty fields. Faded graffiti. Rotting vegetables. Unmarked graves.

The small houses in rural Serbia with no mortar between the bricks, with laundry lines running from glassless windows to the trunks of plum trees, whose terracotta roofs were gnarled with time and from the hallowed mud slowly swallowing up the stone—I used to think my love for Sid was like that. Our windows were broken, the roof needed fixing, the kitchen sink leaked behind the cabinets. But I thought, even if fate buried us under a mudslide, our house would stand upright inside the earth. Each stone would have clung to the one beside it, miraculous in the way they held tight to each other.

Stone houses couldn't burn down. They couldn't succumb to termites or wood rot.

But they could still crumble.

We drove through a village called Zitiste, where, again, the streets were empty—aside from a statue of Rocky Balboa in the town square. I did a double take when I saw it, for all the times Sid and I watched tourists having their picture taken beside the Philadelphia Art Museum with this statue's twin. For the time we brought a blanket and thermos cocktails and spent hours giggling at middle-aged men flexing their arms in front of it and grand-mothers squeezing its bronze bicep. We finished that afternoon barefoot in the Logan Circle fountain and ended up part of a sum-mer romance montage on the 6 o'clock news: our jeans rolled up to our knees, feet kicking at the water as we sat on the edge of the marble, hunched toward each other, shoulders touching.

After we parked in Novi Sad's municipal lot, David and I didn't go back to the apartment on Njegoševa. Instead he took my hand and kissed my jaw and pulled me toward the main street. Cathedral bells tolled in the dusk, echoing the imprecision of time.

The windows in Novi Sad sat higher than they did in the cities I knew. They sat above my head, so that when David pressed his body against mine, pressed me against a wall, no one inside could see us. On the building opposite us, boarded up windows with graffiti spray-painted on the plywood read: *Intoxication is not the answer to our predicament.* I laughed and David buried his lips in the tender muscle between my neck and my shoulder.

"I've missed you," he whispered.

I wrapped my arms around his neck and my legs around his waist, lifting myself higher up the wall so the crown of my head almost crested the windowsill. A warmth came off David even when he should have been cold. It was twenty-three degrees out-side and the sun's meager glow no longer touched the streets. His hands were warm when they slid underneath my coat. His cheeks were warm when they pressed against my skin. His neck was a woodstove. His kisses tasted like promises.

We walked past The Name of Mary Church with its graffitied façade, past bars disguised as restaurants with cigarette smoke pouring out their open doors—doors open to the bitter January wind that pierced through layers of wool and seeped into my bones. Past the Hotel Novi Sad and Hotel Putnik. Past teenagers shooting firecrackers in Liberty Square and beautiful dark-haired women in coats too thin for the weather, whose cheeks weren't flushed from the cold.

"I'm almost getting used to sharing a mattress on the floor with you," he said.

The wind picked up, gusting strong enough to turn my face numb. The sound of distant house music thumped, invisible friends laughed and shouted. I could almost smell the beer and rakija in the air. Flags whipped the black sky, plastic bags blew like lazy balloons, footsteps echoed from a side street. A cat loped near The Name of Mary Church, rubbing its side against the plaster wall.

"I can't believe tomorrow's our last day in Serbia," I said. It felt like I'd been there forever. Yet, when I looked into David's face, it felt like no time had passed at all. Everything had been so similar and seemed so still, as if the whole trip was some awkward film someone paused. We'd been suspended in the same moment for days. I should have wanted the viewer to push play so my life could continue, but I wanted to stay frozen in that moment where there were no consequences.

"It's not enough."

One more night in Novi Sad. Another night in Vienna. Then home. It wasn't enough time to dig up the dead, to feel my grandparents' childhood in my bones, not enough time to find anything more hidden than neglected memorials and an abandoned village, a sugar factory that still had its death camp barbed wire fence, the silent, always-staring locals, peering from behind closed windows. Not enough of David.

Everything and nothing lay in the purple earth and the black sky and the air between our bodies.

A man stood alone at the bus stop on the corner, dressed in black. He stood in the road at the edge of the sidewalk with his arms at his sides and his legs close together. I couldn't see his face, but I could tell he was old by the droop of his shoulders, the loose fit of his trench coat, the slope of his dark brimmed hat.

He sang.

His song didn't have words. It was a simple tune of nonsense sounds. He stretched his arms toward the lamppost across the street as if its stillness rebuffed him.

"Moja ljubavi," he said. "Szerelmem. Meine liebe. My love."

When the lamppost didn't answer, the old man started singing again. He saw me looking at him and turned his head away.

A bus rattled down the street and coasted through two intersections. A cab honked. The bus driver, visible through the windscreen, bent over the wheel with a scowl on his face.

He drove too fast. When he approached the bus stop, he didn't slow for the old man standing in the street.

I wanted to throw my hands up and shout for the man to move, but it happened so quickly. The brim of his hat glowed in the bus headlights, and his black coat turned blacker. Bathed in halogen light, the man was a shadow. I watched him as he watched me, as the bus stopped inches from him and he kept staring as if he didn't notice. I looked at David, but he was looking the other direction, at a crowd of high-heeled women in short dresses wobbling on the other side of the street.

"They must be cold," he said, tugging his collar tight to his neck. Something about the tenderness in his voice made me imagine him warming them up. They were beautiful and dark-haired, with long noses and strong cheekbones. Naked knees. A pang of jealousy pricked my stomach.

The man in the street was old and I was young. He was from Vojvodina, I was from somewhere else. The scariest thing I knew was uncertainty. But he'd seen graveyards. Graveyards that weren't really graveyards at all. Pits filled with people harvested like rabbits.

I walked inside a butcher shop once and bought a rabbit for eighteen dollars. The butcher asked if I wanted it quartered. I said no. He wrapped it in parchment paper and tucked it inside a plastic bag. I was afraid it would get too warm and spoil before I got home. It was summer and the sun was hot enough that teenagers were outside trying to fry eggs on the asphalt.

I caught the bus. The bag swung like a pendulum between my calves as the bus rocked. I had to transfer to get back to East Falls, and once I got home to my windowless kitchen, I put the bag down on the countertop and slipped a cutting board out from under the sink. I tied an apron behind my neck and waist and grabbed the sharpest knife—an unused butcher knife that had sat in our wooden knife block since Sid and I opened our wedding gifts. I pulled the parchment packet out of the plastic bag. I unwrapped it like a present.

The paper didn't rip, but it was wet and pink, with red lines around the edges where the skinned rabbit had touched. I laid the rabbit on the cutting board, stretched its little anklebones to the corners. I noticed that it didn't have any ears, only holes where ears had been.

I felt an emptiness in the pit of my stomach as I cut the rabbit's head off, when I picked the palm-sized skull off the cutting board and stared at its eyes. But I felt something else when I palmed the back of the knife to release the forelegs from the torso, when I slid a thinner knife along the ribcage and pressed down against the thigh joints. I felt as if I was taking control, that I'd found something I could wrap my head and hands around. I used a smaller knife to cut the liver away from the other organs. I boiled the liver while the rest of the rabbit sat in my crockpot with vegetables and white wine. I creamed it with butter and added chopped mushrooms, salt, and pepper.

When Sid came home, a badly hacked rabbit thigh lay supine on his plate, with carrots and onions and potatoes next to it. A small plate of gritty pâté with crusty bread. The remainder of the bottle of wine split between our glasses. We ate in silence.

Months later, after reading about death and the mutilation of bodies, I pictured the rabbit's head with its beady eyes staring. I pictured Oma helping her mother butcher rabbits in their kitchen. Dead rabbits had no expressions on their faces. Were people the same? I wondered how I'd respond to a dead person. The only one I ever saw was Opa. He'd looked more asleep than dead before the men from the funeral home took his body away to fill it with the formaldehyde that all his veneer cabinets smelled like.

And that old man singing in the street, he welcomed death.

What did you have to survive to be able to make women out of lampposts? How many lifeless bodies or lost loved ones would it have taken for me to tempt bus drivers to run me over in the dark?

"Your face looks like ice," David whispered, rubbing my cheek with his hand. His hand was so warm it burned. "I can't wait to get you home so I can warm you up."

I smiled and intercepted a kiss as he reached to warm my cheek with his. His lips were soft and cold, but the breath that escaped them was hot and sweet. Home was almost five thousand miles away. Home was broken. It was a crockpot with a broken lid sitting unplugged and empty on the counter. It was a man somewhere in Washington DC, watching television alone. It was the man beside me, his lips, his breath, his hands. Home was Philadelphia. Home was my grandparents' house, their backyard, their dinner table. Home was the bottles of Vranac, the mattress on the floor, the black earth of Vojvodina. Home was a simple word, but it felt so heavy.

KNIČANIN, SERBIA: 2012

WAKING UP IN THE SEMI-DARKNESS, my belly felt hollow. I couldn't tell if it was from something I ate or if it was actually a feeling. The hollowness was so deep I felt empty everywhere else. I felt alone and unclean. I felt a sadness that could have swallowed me, a sadness like a hollow well I could have fallen into—as if the precipice of madness lay in the emptiness of my stomach.

I slid my iPod off the bedside table and switched on Opa's interview. I listened from the beginning. He started with his childhood home. As I listened to him describe the produce storeroom, I saw it. And the plaster. The dovecotes. The makeshift bridge over the drainage ditch. The yellowed lace curtains in the window. The shadow of a woman inside. I'd been there in real life. It didn't feel like real life.

His voice was wistful.

At camp we had a big dance hall, and every weekend we had a dance. My father was the cashier.

Other camps had dances too. The girls from our camp went to them. And other girls came to ours. Your Oma used to come. She met my father at the door. But I didn't know her then.

My family came to America by airplane on January 24th, 1950. Oma came on January 24th, 1950. By ship.

We were supposed to come by ship, too, the same as her. The same one. Can you imagine?

In America, I went to dance clubs. That's how I met your Oma. We used to walk 20 or 30 blocks because sometimes we didn't want to go to the trolley.

He said it with so much tenderness. *So we just walked.*

When he was nineteen, he was a refugee. When I was nineteen,

I was a child. I'd only just met Sid.

How had I forgotten the sound of Opa's voice that day when he spoke of my Oma. He spoke as if he'd never loved anyone else in his life but her. As if fate had brought them to America on the same day, introduced her to his father outside of Linz, and introduced the two of them—two strangers who weren't really strangers at all—at a dance club in Philadelphia.

I turned off the recording.

I don't know how long I lay awake beside David, with my eyes open and the church bells ringing haphazardly out the half-open window. David snored, more rhythmic than the bell-ringer. Birds chirped from the small balcony off the kitchen. As the sun began to rise, half a dozen pianos ran arpeggios across the street, notes occasionally jarring with other notes misplayed by inexperienced hands.

Footsteps echoed from the street, and voices: a man ordered a pastry at the corner, crumpled a paper bag.

I felt the hollowness of my stomach in my chest.

It didn't take long to pack our things since we hadn't really unpacked. We showered and dried off with Aleksander's musty towels, drank two small cups of Turkish coffee at the kitchen table, and hung the apartment key from the coat rack when we left. I almost forgot to shut the bedroom window, and when I ran to the back of the apartment in my coat and still-muddy boots, I paused to listen to the dissonance of dueling pianos, running chords instead of scales now that the sun had fully risen.

David gripped the steering wheel and glanced between a map and the road. I looked out the window. Why was the sky most beautiful in the morning and in the evening?

Everything was most beautiful at the beginning and the end.

The horizon whispered blue and peach. The blue came from the mountains. I didn't know if the mountains grew out of the earth farther south toward Bosnia, eastward toward Romania, or out west in Croatia. It seemed like they stood at a different cardinal point each time I saw them. Maybe the mountains shot upward on all sides, but the smoke and the clouds that settled over Vojvodina hid them from view. Maybe they didn't just grow from all sides, maybe they were closing in. Maybe they'd been watching all along.

Our last stop was Knićanin, formerly Rudolfsgnad. It didn't surprise me that the names were so divergent. For the most part, the German and Serbian towns had derivative names. Molin and Molidorf. Brestovac and Brestowatz. Jarak and Jarek. The only other one we'd been to that didn't relate was Zrenjanin, where the sugar factory slept. Of course the inhabitants didn't want to remember Gross-Betschkerek—just as the Knićanin Serbs didn't want to recall the days when their streets had German names.

Eleven thousand Swabians died in the camp at Rudolfsgnad between 1945 and 1948, mostly from typhus, malaria, and starvation. Others from diphtheria, gunfire, rape, and suicide.

The village was small, smaller than the rest we'd seen. It was astounding that a place so small could have been home to such a tremendous amount of death. The houses were smaller too—there were no homes with inner courtyards. Outside one tiny house, an old man balanced on the top rung of a twelve-foot ladder and leaned over his roof, replacing broken tiles. Farther down the road, a mother and her children pushed a wheelbarrow overfilled with wood. Only her youngest child wore a hat, too big and woolen and pulled over his ears. There were no cars parked in driveways or on the sides of streets in Knićanin. Everyone turned to look at us as we passed.

"I don't understand why they never smile," I said, embarrassed at the thought before the words left my mouth.

"Only Americans smile so much," David replied.

We drove slowly so we didn't kick up too much dust and cover the children with no hats carting firewood.

The memorial we sought was on the outskirts of the village, like so many others hidden among farm fields and best viewed from space. But it wasn't concealed in the back corner of a cemetery behind walnut trees and hedges like the one in Gakowa. It wasn't a tiny pile of mud like the one in Jarek. It wasn't flooded ruins like in Molidorf. It wasn't a factory, a canning facility, or a cold storage depot like in Gross-Betschkerek and Kikinda. It wasn't a renovated Catholic Church like in Brestowatz.

When David turned the car up the one-lane road we'd marked on the map, a cross thrust upward, visible over dried corn stalks. You had to know it was there to find it, but you didn't have to look hard once you arrived. The cross must have been twenty feet tall, and once it came into view, it didn't take long for four marble tablets to appear, followed by a center marble trifold and a platform made of concrete. The platform alone must have been fifty feet wide.

The memorial grew upward from a field of grass. Backing up to the grass: tilled fields of bruised soil and a cornfield where the ears had been left out to dry. David parked in the grass beside the concrete. Signs had been posted in German, one marking the dates the camp was open, another I couldn't understand. We stepped out of the car and onto the platform. Lethargic clouds moved overhead in clusters—dark gobs hovering below a thin cover of stratus.

The four tablets listed family names: Wohlfhart, Himmel, Köller. Every time we found a memorial, I looked for a name—Glas, Feiter, Konig—to make me feel closer to this place, to the blood in the earth that was also in me. When I caught my heart racing, I was repulsed that I could hope for more death.

The tablet also listed the names of places: Pancevo, Karlsdorf, Perles, St. Huberts, Gross-Betschkerek. And epitaphs:

To our dear grandmother. In awe and sorrow we remember the 184 deceased victims of Sigmundfeld (Lukicevo). Love, your children.

The marble centerfold was engraved with quotations written in both German and Serbo-Croatian. I took photographs so I could translate the words I didn't understand.

Aus einer wüsteward
ein blühend eden
aus sümpfen hob sich
eine neue welt.

Those words belonged to Adam Müller-Guttenbrunn. I recognized his name from the books I'd read. He was an Austrian writer who died two decades before the war, but wrote a poem called "The Swabian Song," lamenting the Swabians' status as perpetual foreigners—in Germany, Austria, Hungary, Romania, Yugoslavia.

From the desert came a flowering Eden, from the marshes rose a new world.

The words should have been filled with promise. Instead, they were filled with so much loss there wasn't room for anything else.

The usual memorial gifts lay strewn in a shallow puddle in front of Guttenbrunn's words: burned out prayer candles, a shriveled plant in a plastic pot, sun-bleached photographs. But there was something else—a concrete flowerbox had been poured into the floor. Two bouquets of silk roses poked out of wet, dark earth beside sleeping perennials: daisies, rosemary, chrysanthemums.

I wished I'd brought something to leave, that I'd left something at Jarek and Filipowa and Gakowa. In front of Opa's house in Brestowatz. Against the closed gates of the sugar factory, inside the abandoned buildings at Molidorf. Among the children's toys at the cold storage depot in Kikinda.

I crouched over the flowerbox and brushed my fingers across the dirt, willing Rudolfsgnad's victims to touch back. David put a hand on my shoulder. When I looked up at him, his other arm was outstretched, palm facing downwards, fingers wrapped around something in his fist.

"Something to leave behind," he said, pressing one of our Christmas walnuts into my hand the way Brno had done in the convenience store. David kept the other walnut for himself, kissed my forehead, and knelt. I knelt beside him and buried my fingers up to my knuckles in the raw mud. The soil packed upward into my fingernails, deep inside my fingerprints. The moisture worked into my pores. It smelled like iron.

I pressed the walnut into the hole and swept the earth back over it, tamped it with the heel of my palm. David's hands moved beside mine, burying his walnut cleanly.

The sky above us looked like the end of days—all shadow and gray, glowing with the weight of denouement.

"Do you think they used those buildings up there to imprison people?" David asked, looking at two skinny structures on a hill beyond the cornfield. They looked like the buildings behind barbed wire near the Jarek memorial—and the one with the collapsed roof in Molidorf.

"I don't know," I said. There was so much I didn't know. I couldn't trust my memory—it was distorted by what I wanted it to be. And as for the history, I only knew what a few small books had told me: incomplete stories passed down by survivors, shards of history and memory with pieces missing. There was so much between the stories. And there were so many hidden places. I should have spoken to strangers. To the women peeking through windowpanes. To the old men on the streets. To Mislav. I should have called my grandmother's sister until she gave up the stories she said she couldn't remember.

All she gave me was this:

"Hush now. It's done."

David turned his head toward the lane, listening to the sudden chugging of an engine. As the noise grew louder, David moved closer to me. A tractor came into view with tires as tall as my shoulders, kicking mud and rocks into the air. One man sat astride it, staring forward. Two men and a woman sat on a sofa in a wooden trailer hitched to the back. The sofa was mud-stained. So were the passengers.

The driver pretended not to notice us, but the three passengers looked our way, if only because the sofa faced us. I lifted a hand to wave. David sighed. One of the men shuffled his feet and nodded in my direction. The other man rubbed his moustache and looked down at his knees. The woman met my eyes. She curled one side of her mouth upward. Her face changed shape—something in her glance looked familiar. She leaned back against the sofa and crossed her legs. I saw a flash of Rosalinde leaning against my grandfather's desk. Of Oma smiling crooked. Of my own eyes staring back at me.

EMIL SCHEUSSLER:
NOVI SAD, YUGOSLAVIA: 1946

THE PRIEST HERE, Father Peter, wears a shirt with a cross-shaped stain on his back. The stain is pinkish from the comingling of blood and pus because the Partisan guards sliced a cross on his back, peeled the skin off.

They did more than that. I hear him groan when he urinates in the corner.

"Father Peter," I ask. "Who is your patron saint?"

"Saint Peter," the Father says. "Patron Saint of fishermen, bridge builders, butchers, and longevity."

Father Peter isn't the only Catholic priest in our camp. Each day more men come—priests and farmers and shopkeepers. I was a journalist, before all of this.

Our camp is crowded with two-thousand Swabians at night. In the day, we are pushed harder than oxen for our captors.

"Faster," the field guards say. "You Germans are so weak. We should shoot you all like dogs."

I haven't been here as long as some of the others. Father Peter has been here for a month. He is Hungarian, but he has a German name. Maybe it is better for him here. His brethren were taken to another place, where they'll pay for the sins of their soldiers, who marched civilians up the frozen Danube for the Reich until the ice collapsed around them. An eye for an eye. But a civilian eye, I've heard, is worth more than the eye of a soldier. Perhaps it is true we are all complicit.

I was brought in from Katsch. I wondered if I was taken because the Partisans were afraid I'd sell their atrocities to newspapers. But I am not so vital. I am able-bodied and Swabian, that is all.

"Longevity," I say to Father Peter. "How long do you think we have here?"

"I am a priest and a palmist," Father Peter replies. "I have always seen my lifeline. I will live a short life and die a violent death."

There's another man with whom I speak. His name is Wendel. He was the shoemaker in Katsch. He passed information about the expulsion to other Swabian families in time for them to escape camps like these.

This camp, a putrid pigsty in a swamp on the banks of the Danube, consists of two buildings—an actual pigsty and a bunker. We are lucky to live in the pigsty, though it reeks of swine and human feces. The bunker is saved for punishment. When it rains and the river rises, we are surrounded by swamp water, and the punishment bunker fills so those inside it are submerged up to their waists for days until they succumb to sickness. Typhus. Pneumonia.

So many nightmares.

I've heard that our women are housed above the floodplain. At dawn they are ordered into a roll call that lasts for hours and looks more like slave trade than inventory: the women are exhibited to a crowd of Serbs as their names are called. They are auctioned off for the bargain price of 80 dinars per day.

We suffer our own roll call here. It takes place in the evenings, when the Partisan guards with their heavy guns read off the names of men who won't be forced into labor, who instead will disappear into the bunker or who knows where. Men who are sick, men who are injured, who resist, men who are a threat to the regime.

The day I was brought to Neusatz, I marched with fifty other Swabian men to the sound of Communist patriotism. The men at the front of our march waved blue, white, and red flags with grand bloody stars at the center. The flag for the new Yugoslavia. A flag the colors of Capitalism, of all things—of Great Britain and the United States—so Tito can assert his likeness to grandiose nations.

The men marching us sang. They sang "A Song for Tito" to the tune of one enthusiastic bugle and a drummer. They sang about Marshall Tito, the heroic son, about Hell and clenched fists. It was hard to understand the Partisans' slurred words as they marched haphazard, stinking of brandy. And yet none of us captives ran, in spite of their inebriation, for fear of their guns and their fervor. They sang about enemies feeling their fists. About the misery and suffering the Partisans have undergone for Slavdom. As they marched, they punched the air with their guns.

A woman ran up to our parade with a basket of food. Before she reached us with her loaves of buttered *Landbrot*, a Partisan shot her in the neck. Vomit burned the back of my throat, but I held it in for fear of drawing attention. The older man marching beside me started crying. I looked at him and whispered, "I'm sorry. Was she your wife?"

And then I saw the husband collapse to his knees at the back of the column.

"Get up!" a Partisan shouted, shooting him before he had the chance to stand.

"She was always looking out the window when I walked home from the grocer's," the man beside me said. "She was young and beautiful and always framed like a picture in that window."

If my recollections seem impassive, it's because I'm only capable of feeling a fraction of what I felt watching that poor woman fall, staining her basket and her skirts red, her husband bleeding into the dirt. I don't know if the blame for my coldness lies in the overwhelming horror of this new kingdom or in my hunger. All they've fed us is hot water disguised as broth and small stale squares of bread.

There's a legend of a priest who collapsed on his ten-kilometer march to Neusatz after trooping in chains that restricted his lungs and made his chest and back bleed when he breathed. They say when he collapsed a glowing cross appeared above his figure and his body vanished into the divine light. Perhaps hunger is to blame for that vision, too. When I ask Father Peter about the legend, he tells me that miracles are possible but more often manifestations of human weakness. He says no such miracle is waiting for his soul.

"Do you know what is waiting for you, Father?"

"I know what Saint Peter and my palm have shown me."

"Can you tell me what is waiting for me?" I hold out my hand, but he doesn't take it.

"We all know what is coming for us, Emil."

I am surprised when both our names are shouted out at roll call. Along with Wendel the shoemaker and a handful of other men.

While the Partisans round us up in the yard, one soldier cranks a gramophone. A capella voices surge from the horn, but the Partisans don't raise their voices to sing along. Instead they sway, their drunken eyes turning from steel to mercury in the moonlight. The only sound in the crowd of men is the pure falsetto of a boys' choir—singing Tito's revenge. It's difficult to believe anything can make his ethnically pure, Communist nation sound handsome, but those delicate voices seize even the mechanism of my own heart.

A Partisan reads off our names for the second time, checking tick marks next to each as we're pushed forward into another march.

"Is this what you saw coming?" I ask Father Peter.

This is not what I saw coming. Why aren't they throwing us in the punishment bunker? And for what are we disappearing? Is it because I am a journalist after all? Or have I been moving too slowly in the fields? The camp is full and fresh men are faster.

Father Peter doesn't respond; instead he clasps his hands at his sternum, bows his head, and shuffles forward with the rest of us.

"Might I ask you a favor, Father?" Wendel asks from behind Father Peter and me.

"My son," Father Peter closes his eyes. "There is nothing to be done but pray."

"Could you pray for my son, and my wife and daughter?" Wendel persists.

The priest nods.

After a few moments, he lifts his head to look at me.

"Do you have anyone you would like me to pray for in these final moments?"

I leave nothing behind: words in rotting newspapers, a dead mother, a missing father, a sister who I haven't spoken with in months. I leave behind a house, small, untidy, and filled with unsent letters to a woman who fled for America because, she said, she could feel the blood gathering in the clouds.

Dorothea didn't leave an address when she left. She didn't even leave the name of a city.

Perhaps she never made her ship.

"May they find peace in this weary world," Father Peter says, not waiting for my response.

"And die quickly," Wendel mutters.

It's wrong that the night should be so beautiful, with stars glittering like flecks of crystal. There's a constellation of moles on my left thigh that Dorothea told me resembles Pisces. I think it looks more like a kite. But I think most constellations look like kites.

"Amen," I whisper.

Father Peter groans. At first I think he's pissed himself. His groan sounds so much like when he leans against the corner of the pigsty.

I follow his gaze to a heap of dirt: an arm protrudes with swollen fingers. It looks like a false arm, made of plaster or papier-mâché. The knuckles are impossible to discern, and the color is wrong. One Partisan laughs as he passes the dead hand and says sing-song, "Help! Oh, oh, help me!"

I do not know whose bodies are these in the mud. But when we are dead, we are the same. No one cares with whom we lie.

Tomorrow, the bodies on the surface will be the most familiar. These hands, these feet.

It's unkind for the moon to shine so luminous tonight. Even she can't allow the dead to rest with dignity. I almost hear my bones rattle with trembling as I march, picturing my left hand cast in plaster, reaching out of the earth as if it dug all the way up from the underworld only to reach the miserable banks of the Danube.

"They're going to drown us," Wendel suggests as we reach the riverbank.

The moon illuminates patches of color in the reeds.

"Strip," a Partisan says.

"They're going to mutilate us like they've done with Father Peter. Or worse. Rape us until our bodies float." Wendel kneels to untie his shoes. "What kind of men are these?"

I consider asking Wendel why that last question hadn't occurred to him before. These are the kind of men who march their neighbors to the banks of the Danube in the dark, have them cast off their clothing and throw their shirts and underthings into the reeds where the fabric piles up in a disturbing kaleidoscope. They are the kind of men our own men have been. The kind of men Father Peter's men have been. They are just men. And we will not only be robbed and ruined, the discarded clothing says. We will be forgotten.

"Leave your shoes and your belts. Toss the rest."

I look away as I throw my clothing, bunched up with my socks tucked inside my pant legs, in the direction the Partisan points. I line my shoes up beside each other so that if they were folded together like a book, they would become one shoe. My belt I lay across the toes so that no mud blemishes the buckle.

The Partisans shove around us like wolves pushing sheep, herding us naked into the river.

Father Peter's eyes are closed again. He prays in silence, miming the words with his lips. I wonder if he prays without sound out of despair for our souls or if he prays this way so the Partisans don't hear his pleas with God and flay his back again. Perhaps it's better for our souls if he prays. At least the angels will be with us when we die, so we don't die alone. Not that we would be alone, with all the men who passed before us.

The Danube sends splinters of cold into the soles of my feet. It rips into my calves like teeth. I feel the glacial river in my bones, suddenly as brittle and hollow as a discarded chicken carcass.

My feet go numb in minutes. I can't feel the rocks beneath me as we're herded into the shadow of a partially collapsed bridge. From the shadow of the concrete piers, there is no moonlight. The only light comes from Partisan flashlights.

I look around at my fellow men knee-deep in the river. Father Peter to my right looks more naked than Wendel to my left. Without the cassock and white collar, the priest's neck seems slight. The cross-shaped wound on his back blends into the darkness. And all around him, all around me, glittering stars float on the river, as if they've come down to guide us to heaven. It's only when Father Peter lifts his head from his constant prayer to look at me that I imagine the twinkling lights aren't stars at all, but eyes lit by Partisan torches.

That's when the gunfire comes.

So many stars perish without the burst of energy that super-novas have.

I feel pain in my shoulder and think I'm having a heart attack—until I feel pain in my side. It's too dark, when I press my hand against my side and pull it back to look, to see the blood already spilling. But I can feel its warmth as I fall. It feels heavier than the river water.

Father Peter lies in the water with his eyes open. Light still reflects in his irises. Wendel is gone. The night is dark. I register flashlight beams, but they move slowly until all light stands still.

The sky is the color of frostbite when I wake, but the night is warm and the earth is tender. My mouth tastes like aluminum, as if it's filled with dinars. I vomit. All that comes up is blood and dirt and river water.

I try to turn my neck, but my body is stiff. I shift my weight to my right shoulder and find a pain so deep it rips through my teeth. I slump and my arm slips out from under me. My cheek lands on the peach fuzz of a young man's backside.

I bite my lips until I bleed to stop myself from screaming.

My arm is cradled by a man's inner knee. I don't dare to look at what pillows the rest of me. So much naked, swollen flesh, warmer than the air but too cold. It feels like touching the skin of uncooked meat. Bile rises in the back of my throat again. I am in awe that there is any left.

There are more bodies than the number of us killed last night. More bodies than are taken from the Swabian camp to disappear, more than are pulled dead from the bunker. How many are trapped in a current below the river's surface? How many travel on, to Belgrade, to Bucharest, to the Black Sea? Can their spirits taste the sediment from where the river begins? In Ulm, in the Black Forest, where my ancestors buried their kin in cemeteries with tombstones and prayers and names to leave behind for the generations who would come after.

These men beneath me leave no names behind.

Nothing sounds in the grassy swamp besides my breath, the rippling of the Danube, the laughing song of a cormorant, the whistling release of gas from bloated organs. While I wait for the sounds of Partisans, I flex my toes, tense the muscles in my legs, clench my fists to ease the stiff aches in my bones. The cormorant jeers. He spews nervous laughter for the cruelty of men.

"Forgive me," I whisper to the lost men I press my knees and elbows into. Whatever their origins, they look the same now. Reddish-purple feet, waterlogged fingers, bloated stomachs, mouths leaking mud and water. Some faces without eyes, arms missing wrists, pelvises with absent genitalia. Am I the only soul who was turned away from St. Peter's gate? I drag myself slowly toward the grasses. Someone has dug a pit beside us, where the bodies will be discarded—like the grave from which the solitary dead arm reached. I almost fall into the hole, but instead I find myself amid the discarded clothing we left the night before. The shoes and buckles are gone.

I find a dry knit shirt and a sweater. I pull other men's trousers toward me and sniff them, one-by-one, until I find a pair that doesn't smell like piss. I pull them on—they're too tight and several inches too short.

It's difficult to avoid crunching grass beneath my toes in the dark. I've already cut the soles of my feet on the crisp stalks.

Something rustles in the middle distance. I crouch down as quietly as I can manage in the brittle November reeds. There are footsteps, and a shadow close to the ground.

A dog.

A stray, probably.

I wait a moment longer, in case the dog belongs to a man with a gun. I rock from side to side to keep my legs from getting stiff and prickly. The dog stops to sniff, lifts his leg.

It moves a few feet farther, toward the edge of the river, and stops again. It digs at the mud, kicking up wet clods. When it stops digging and lifts its head, there's something in its jaws.

"Let the beasts carry away their bones," I'd heard a Partisan guard say after eight Swabian men drowned in the punishment bunker.

It could just be a morsel of garbage that washed ashore, a shoe left behind. It's not hard to believe. After all, the Partisans who made us strip off our clothes and shoes had to carry guns and flashlights along with whatever small treasures they decided to bring home.

I walk away from the riverbank. The stray dog follows.

"Shoo!" I whisper, waving my arms at it. I'm waving to the entire population of Partisans in Neusatz: Sie da! I am here, come and get me! You missed one!

The dog wags its tail, stupid beast, and comes closer—with a human arm in its mouth. The swollen palm faces upward, cupped slightly, waiting to be filled with alms, with pity, with grace from an absent god. Perhaps the arm belonged to a man who believed to the very end, before his one-armed body was swallowed by the river, that God would spare him. Or perhaps the arm belonged to a man who was buried alive, as I so nearly was, and had enough energy left for one final gesture, one formidable extension of his arm that sent it bursting through the earth so someone would pull him from the mire. He could have held it there until rigor mortis held it for him, until the stray dog ripped his arm from his body as if it were a toy.

"Why don't you shoo?" I whisper, though part of me doesn't want the dog to leave. There is a comfort in it breathing beside me, in seeing water vapor crystallize and disintegrate in the hard night air.

A song moves through the reeds:

Of an ancient kindred we are,
But Goths we are not.
Part of ancient Slavdom are we.
Whoever says otherwise slanders and lies
and will feel our fist.

The reeds lean to and fro in the rhythm of Partisans marching more men to be drowned beneath the broken Prinz Tomislav Bridge.

I have two choices: I can hide in the reeds praying the dog doesn't give me away—or I can run. Either way, I might soon be with my mother and father, in all probability my sister and her children. My dearest Dorothea. If her silence means she hasn't forsaken me, that instead she's on the other side of the river Styx, I'll kneel at her feet, kiss her belly and know that the sins of this world don't reflect upon the next. She'll be as young as the day I met her, with eyes that burn like stars; her lips will be as sweet as Christmas marzipan.

The forearm still faces its palm skyward. Even after death it waits for Heaven to make its cup run over. There is no mercy to be found in this life. Father Peter was right to pray so fervently in the face of death—he no longer has to bear witness to the terror.

The Partisan song grows nearer. With the step of each military boot, my heart quakes. My blood ripples with the weight of their feet. I watch them gather at the riverbank in the moonlight, the Partisans and their prisoners, and I wonder—while these men peel off shirts moist with the icy sweat of fear, trousers soaked in urine—that so many of their bodies look familiar. That all bodies look so familiar. I think I heard one of the prisoners shout. It wasn't a sound made of words. It was human, animal.

I see the husband of the woman who was shot in the neck while coming to bear a basket of bread to our doomed platoon of captives. But he is dead. It's not possible for him to stand among the living, yet I recognize the despairing curve of his back while he stands at the riverbank. And there's Wendel, with his fear of rape and mutilation, clenching his buttocks so tight he could hold a pfennig upright between them.

I see the older crying man from my first march, when we marched from Katsch to Neusatz. His name was called the day before mine. How is it that he came to be here, on the riverbank? Perhaps he survived like me and was recaptured. His shoulders shine with tears. And there, unmistakably, is Father Peter. With the shape of the cross flayed on his back, visible even in the darkness. He kneels without his cassock.

"Get up!" a Partisan shouts, pointing his flashlight at Father Peter's back. The priest's head is bowed so low it looks as if he's just another dead body protruding from the mud—a body with no head, buried knee-deep in a swampy grave, hands clasped desperately in a final prayer.

"Father Peter!" I want to call. The bloody cross glows brighter as the Partisan moves closer to him. Surrounded by naked men, the soldier looks inhumanly large. "Why don't you stand?"

The dog's tail no longer wags. Its hackles are raised and the dead arm rests at its feet.

"Shh," I whisper, placing my hand on its head, afraid it will growl and give us away. Looking closer, the dog is cleaner than a stray should be. Its hair isn't patchy, its skin isn't rough with mange. And its demeanor, when I stroke its coat, softens like a household pet. Perhaps the dog, too, is displaced in Tito's new kingdom. Perhaps it followed its owner here. I look at the arm in its mouth.

Perhaps it found him.

It's terrible to imagine that the arm at this dog's feet belonged to its master. Terrible and foolish. And yet the dog guards it so carefully; the way it held that human morsel in its teeth was almost tender.

The Partisan's gun presses hard against Father Peter's neck.

God, have mercy. I am crouched like a frog in the swamp, forced to witness the deaths of these men twice over.

The gun goes off.

His body falls onto the muddy bank.

It's the only body still on land—the rest are beneath the piers.

"Hogy Úr ut këgyilméhel," Father Peter prays aloud.

The flashlight beams waver as more gunfire comes.

The mongrel barks.

The light grows brighter. Too bright. The reeds rustle.

A beautiful glimpse of perpetual light shines over the falling men.

It is the man from the legend.

There's no cross above his body as appears in the story. Just as there is no cross above Father Peter's corpse, lying chained and bloody while Wendel floats beside the husband without a wife and the old man whose tears have been washed away by the river. Just as there is no cross above the unfamiliar faces—so unfamiliar because there are too many of us to remember.

We have long forgotten our neighbors. And we've forgotten ourselves.

There is only the light of Partisan flashlights reflecting off wretched flesh and teeth and eyes until everything disappears into the glow.

I SAW SKELETONS on the drive back to Belgrade: skeletons of unfinished overpasses, concrete piers like rib bones, an unfinished shopping mall that no one had touched since the nineties because the parking garage was half blown up.

My eyes were drawn to the ruins, and perhaps that was unfair.

Colorful contemporary buildings sat back off the road, too—painted white and green, white and jonquil, built in geometric shapes radically different from the architecture the Danube Swabians brought with them in past centuries. Different enough to make everyone forget what used to be there. Different enough to cover the shame and the fear, cover it with floor to ceiling windows and wrap-around decks and thermoplastic roofs. I saw my grandfather in the contemporary apartment homes and offices along the road. They had the same aesthetic as the buildings he designed in Philadelphia.

Opa had designed Philadelphia's United German-Hungarian Club into an octagon with side-rolling door panels—walls that could shut off passages to a maze of hallways, creating a ballroom with unpredictable escape routes. It exhibited the midcentury minimalism that swallowed most of Germany and Eastern Europe while Opa studied architecture in America. He thought he'd left the Danube behind, but it followed him.

Across three European countries, it followed him—through the northern reaches of Yugoslavia, across Hungary, into Austria. He left the banks of the Danube behind as he traveled to France to catch an airplane to New York in 1950. He crossed an ocean, but the river lived in his blood. It followed him to Philadelphia. As it

followed the Albrechts and the Goldschmidts, Aunt Katharina and
Uncle Nikolaus. Aunt Anja. As it followed Rosalinde. As it followed my grandmother.

Everyone smiled on the Queen Elizabeth because they were
on the biggest ship in the world and they thought they were free.
But their smiles didn't reach their eyes. There was no such thing
as a new beginning—everyone carried their old beginnings with
them. Ships and planes might have brought Swabian refugees to
America, but chains would hold them to the streets lined with walnut trees and to the bodies left behind. It would find my
grandparents and bind them to each other. As it bound so many
thousands of Swabian souls buried in the Yugoslav soil. As it
bound them to the bodies laid to rest before them, and the ones
who came after.

As I would be followed and bound by my shadows.

I used to play hide and seek in the club, sliding the door panels
sideways so Oma and Opa wouldn't know which way I'd gone.
I'd hide in the bathroom down the third hallway to the left of the
bar. Or tuck myself between a door panel and the wall. Once I hid
so well they couldn't find me. It felt like hours had passed. Oma
called for me. I thought it was a trick, so I didn't come out. I stayed
hidden until my joints got stiff, and when finally I stepped into
the great octagon, Oma shouted, "You come when you're called!"
She pulled down my elastic shorts and spanked my backside. "You
could have been abducted!"

Airports were built like mazes too. An open, bustling hall at
the beginning that led to tiny hallways snaking off to gates and
arrivals and customs and secret corridors with signs that said *Ne
Ulazi.* Do not enter.

A billboard in departures at Belgrade International displayed
a man in a dark grey suit: *Invest in Serbia, we are business
friendly.* Behind the businessman and the English letters: fertile
corn fields. Corn and peas and carrots and green beans. The businessman's smile didn't hint at the history of their vegetable
storage. Another billboard—a blown up photograph of over-
whitened teeth. *Smile, you're in Serbia!* Except no one smiled in
Serbia besides tourists.

The PA crackled at the gate.

"We are now boarding flight 304 to Vienna. Thank you for flying JAT Airways."

JAT stood for Jugoslovenski Aerotransport, as if twenty years hadn't passed since Yugoslavia collapsed.

VIENNA, AUSTRIA: JANUARY 2012

IT WAS SNOWING in Vienna when we landed. David took me back to the apartment he'd rented when we first arrived. It felt as if we'd never left, as if the last two weeks hadn't happened. The sugar factory seemed impossible. Prvi Depot. So many quiet graves with too many people sleeping underneath. The whispers in the wind at Molidorf. The fox in the ruins. The burned church in Apatin. The locked one in Brestowatz. My Opa's house. The smell of the towels in Novi Sad. The women with bare knees in the January cold. The accordionists in the Dama Reka. The dog in the road.

We dropped our luggage off and walked to a café down the street. We ordered schnitzel and ate in silence. We didn't look at our plates. I looked at David's face in the dark. His soft, round eyebrows. Shadows in his crow's feet. He looked tired.

The walk back to the apartment was short.

I kicked off my shoes at the door. David put his hand on my waist and kissed my cheek.

"I'm going to run a bath," he said.

I touched my hand where I'd burnt it on the towel rail that first morning. The mark was gone.

David ran the tap until the water steamed, poured in soap until it frothed and the bathtub smelled like figs. He undressed. When he stepped into the water, the hairs on his legs stuck to his skin.

I slid in after him and leaned against his chest. Even in the bath he smelled like a forest. Even in the bath his body felt warm.

"I don't want you to leave," David said, his arms pinning mine. I rested my head on his shoulder and looked up. Thick pine beams stretched across the ceiling at perfect angles.

"I don't want to go," I replied, kissing his stubbled, soapy jaw.

Perhaps that was the best time. If I was ready, there'd be nothing left to want.

A cell phone rang. David jumped.

Bathwater sloshed over the edge.

"Is that mine?" I asked.

It was ringing from my pile of clothes.

I stepped out of the bath and wrapped a towel around myself, picked up the phone.

"Hello?" I said.

"Mrs. Kohler?" The voice on the other end spoke slowly.

"Who is this?

"My name is Kathy. I'm calling from Bayside Nursing Home."

I don't know how much or how little time had passed, or how I'd ended up on the floor, but when I looked up, David stood sopping above me.

"Oma died," I said.

Died. The nurse didn't say 'passed away.'

Death was such a small word.

David knelt on the floor in front of me and put his palms against my cheeks, pulled my face to his chest.

"Oh, my love," he said.

There were the men carved into the bedpost. Men carrying firewood on bicycles, disappearing old men lugging water jugs. The guard who called the police in Zrenjanin. The drunk man at the bus stop. There was Aleksander, waiting to show his movie to Westerners. Mislav sitting at his sister's place in Sombor. There was Opa. David. Uncountable men buried inside the earth. The men who put them there. I'd even imagined ghosts in the Spark and all three of them were men.

What about the women? The ones who'd lost everything and didn't have voices. The ones who were left behind when their men had died or were fighting or had gone into hiding. The ones who ended up in death camps made of empty villages, sugar factories, milk halls. The ones who died. The ones who survived. The ones who watched.

And what about me? I might as well have been a ghost. I didn't speak to anyone.

The woman in the tractor yesterday. She was silent and full of knowing. The women peering from behind curtains: in Linz, in Brestowatz. In Kikinda. I didn't even see their faces. Rosalinde. All I really knew of her was what my grandfather kept in that box.

And Oma.

Where was she?

I had a nightmare when I was small. I woke up crying and she held me close. In the dream, she'd shrunk and shrunk until she could fit inside my palm, and then she disappeared. I was afraid I'd dropped her, so I searched the floor. I looked between the thick pile in the carpet. Under Opa's big cabinet and under the sofa and even under the treads of her garden shoes.

But she was gone.

The day before I flew to Vienna to meet David, I sat at the edge of the Great Egg Harbor Bay. Oma sat beside me in her wheelchair, bundled in a winter hat the nurse brought from her bedroom. Her cheeks were pink from the salt breeze, and the hat didn't belong to her. It belonged to a woman whose name was a small black smudge on the tag.

"I'm going to Yugoslavia," I said.

Fish schooled beneath our reflections.

"They're hungry," she replied, looking first at the water and then at the back of her hand. She rubbed at the wrinkles as if she could wipe them away.

It was a habit I thought had come with the Alzheimer's. Picking loose bits of string from her clothes until the hems unraveled, brushing her palm over her Ultrasuede sofa until the fibers laid smooth and flat, turning my wedding ring when she held my hand so that the diamonds faced out just so.

But she'd been doing it for years: fixing, scrubbing, straightening. She'd done it with the seashells I'd brought her at the shore. The ones with holes eaten away in the centers, corners missing, ridges sliced out. I'd never noticed they were broken, that pieces were missing, that each shell was only half. But Oma scrubbed and scrubbed at the ruined clams until the insides glistened. Until they shone so brightly of opal we forgot they were bones.

But there were things she couldn't make clean.

At the beginning of her Alzheimer's, all she talked about was the war. While she folded laundry. While she rifled through kitchen drawers. While she sorted jars of plastic buttons.

Her story was disjointed. Her words were simple. But the pain in her retelling was complete.

Our house was a little house. Beautiful. Our village was not too big, not too small.

A lot of Partisans came with fires and guns, big ones. And many times they shot people who didn't, you know... [she trailed off]. And that was at night. And Father told us, make sure at night you are dressed. You always have to be watching.

It was three years like that. And what can you do? Many people got killed, women and children.

She shook her head as if a memory would fall out. *Where did I go?*

To the city. There were a lot of people, a lot of carts, all waiting to go to Hungary. A man said, "We cannot send you all at once."

We waited a week to leave. It was sick and rain. It was the beginning of September.

She skipped ahead to Austria.

When the bombs started, they came like fire. People were in pieces. Austrians too. A leg here. An arm there. Some of them didn't have hands or heads. There was nothing but big holes. We couldn't get home there were so many. When I think of that, it was not, you don't even know the way you should talk. But we were okay.

She kept saying, *Then the Americans came.* They appeared in her story when she was still a twelve-year-old girl in Gašinci. They appeared in the city she waited in to join the exodus. They were in the road on the way to Hungary. *Then the Americans came.*

She didn't see Americans until she arrived in Austria. But they became ghosts that walked through her memories as if there were no walls between them.

They also became home.

We carry our beginnings with us.

We carry our endings with us too.

Mine were in the sound of my phone ringing on the floor. Sid's name on the screen. In the way the phone crawled across the hardwood when I didn't pick up. When I thought, God, all I needed in the world was to hear Sid's voice telling me it was going to be okay. That she was with Opa, my mother. That my grandparents weren't gone because it was real, Opa visiting our bedroom in Philadelphia. That he'd felt it. That I should come home. That there was still a home waiting, in Washington or Philadelphia or wherever I wanted it to be.

They were in my hands when I didn't pick up. When the phone rang again and again and I still didn't answer.

They were in David's face when I dripped tears into his naked lap.

They were in his arms, in his lips pressed to my forehead.

They were in his eyes, following Sid's name on my phone as it buzzed beside his knee. They were in his silence. In the steady beat of his heart, the unsteady beat of mine. They were in the empty space between us that existed because we were too new to quiet grief.

They'd be on the airplane the next morning, in my skin.

Were the things Oma carried in my skin too? And Opa?

Flying felt like time traveling backward. If we kept traveling backward, how far would we go? Past the smell of hope chests and familiar sweat, past stone fruit lips and the science of raindrop vortexes. Somewhere before all of this, where I'd be waltzing on Opa's feet knee-deep in the ocean while Oma laughed from the shore. And I'd come running from the sea, feet too big to fit on his feet anymore, hoping for a mug of mint chocolate chip ice cream and the smell of citronella candles burning in the cold night air.

But instead I'd find myself in Oma's arms in the middle of the night, half out of the covers and face wet with tears, holding tight to her nightgown so she couldn't disappear.

"Oh, my little angel," she'd say, stroking my sleep-mussed hair. "*Keine Angst*. Don't be frightened. I'm here."

But under everything, she'd know: even angels are made of bones.

END

ACKNOWLEDGEMENTS

My heart belongs to my grandparents—my Oma and Opa—for sharing their stories with me, for being such incredible nourishers of my spirit. This book is for them, though they are gone.

A massive thank you to Mick Felton, Amy Wack, and everyone at Seren for bringing this book to life, and with so much care. To Nemonie Craven, my sublime and thoughtful editor. To my rock star agent, Jennifer Lyons, for believing in this project and never giving up on it, or me. To Stephen O'Connor, for his wisdom, kindness, and x-ray vision into the souls of stories. To Mary Morris, for knowing what this book was about before I did. Thanks to Nelly Reifler and David Hollander. The Sarah Lawrence Graduate Writing Program. To my killer workshop group, without whom there would be more wine in New York, but so much less brilliance: Dennis E Norris II, Leah Schnelbach, Kelly Devine, and Kate Schmier. To what feels like an ocean of unendingly supportive, inspiring, and talented writers, readers, and friends: Sara Thomason, Capricorn sister and fire lighter; N Michelle Aubuchon, queen of blue and heart; Kate Brittain—to wandering until we are lost and finding ourselves again. T Kira Madden. Ursula Villareal Moura. Tiffany Trent. Thanks to Sara Nović and Blunderbuss Magazine for being the first to publish a piece of this book. To Matt, for having the generosity and patience of a saint. To Vikki Ford, Rick Ford, and Jenny—for being my foundation. To those I haven't named who have supported me, encouraged me, shared with me, who read this book or parts of it in its myriad forms. You know who you are.

To the people I reached out to while I researched, who were kind enough to share resources and give advice. To the Donauschwaben who left their stories behind. To everyone who leaves behind stories that seem unspeakable, because they show us the world and teach us who we are.

To those of you who are holding this book in your hands, thank you for reading. And immeasurable thanks to Byron, my husband and partner—for his boundless love and support and for making me a better human. I owe so much of who I am and What Remains to you.